Carlos Martínez Moreno

EL INFIERNO

translated by Ann Wright

Introduction by John King

readers international

The title of this book in Spanish is *El color que el infierno me escondiera*, first published in 1981 by Editorial Nueva Imagen, S.A., Mexico, D.F.

© 1981 Carlos Martínez Moreno

First published in English by Readers International Inc. and Readers International, London. Editorial inquiries to London office at 8 Strathray Gardens, London NW3 4NY England. US/Canadian inquiries to Subscriber Service Department, P.O. Box 959, Columbia LA 71418-0959 USA.

English translation © 1988 Readers International Inc.

Cover art entitled "Constructive Art" (1946) by the Uruguayan painter Joaquín Torres García (1874-1949)
Cover design by Jan Brychta
Typesetting by Grassroots Typeset, London N3
Printed and bound in Great Britain by Richard Clay Ltd., Bungay, Suffolk

Library of Congress Catalog Card Number: 87-63467

British Library Cataloguing in Publication Data
Martínez Moreno, Carlos
    El infierno.
    I. Title II. El color que el infierno
    me escondiera. *English*
    863

ISBN 0-930523-47-4 hardcover
ISBN 0-930523-48-2 paperback

El Infierno

Contents

Introduction

The social context. Uruguay for the first half of the twentieth century had a stable democratic system and was known as the 'Switzerland of Latin America'. From the 1950s, however, rapid inflation, low economic growth and a stagnant export economy (which had previously generated the wealth of the country) put great pressure on this, the first welfare state in Latin America. These contradictions, which the traditional Blanco and Colorado political parties struggled to contain, led to the emergence of an urban guerrilla organisation, the MLN, National Liberation Front, also known as the Tupamaros, after the eighteenth-century Andean Indian leader Túpac Amaru, who led a major rebellion against Imperial Spain. Among those who joined the ranks of the Tupamaros were students, professionals and state employees, predominantly the young and middle class. They began to harrass the government with 'offensives' that included bombings, bank robberies, and kidnapping of high-ranking citizens and foreign residents.

The civilian government, unable to combat adequately the Tupamaros, called in the military. Many innocent citizens were casualties of the ensuing successful military operation that crushed the Tupamaros and led to the coup of 1973, heralding one of the least publicised and most severe military dictatorships in the history of Latin

i

America. The country became, in the Uruguayan writer Eduardo Galeano's phrase, 'a vast torture chamber'. In the following years, some 300,000 people (20% of the population) were forced into exile, including Carlos Martínez Moreno.

This novel, written in exile and first published in Mexico in 1981, bears witness to the Tupamaro movement and the growth of state repression. It is only in recent years, with Uruguay's return to democracy, albeit a tentative one, that the exiles have been able to go back and political prisoners have been released. *El Infierno* has now been published in Uruguay, winning the 1987 Ministry of Culture award under the new democracy. But its author died in exile in 1986.

The literary context. The literature of Uruguay has always tended to be eclipsed by that of its big River Plate neighbour, Argentina. It is Argentine writers such as Borges, Cortázar and Puig who have established international reputations. The work of Uruguayan writers has not been as widely translated, which means that there is almost complete ignorance of one of the finest literatures in Latin America, and here not only Martínez Moreno but also Mario Benedetti and the great Juan Carlos Onetti spring to mind as major novelists deserving wider attention.

Carlos Martínez Moreno was a well-respected writer of Uruguay's 'generation of '45'. He published nine important books of short stories and novels between 1960 and 1974. Of these his early novel *El Paredón* (*The Wall*, 1962) is most often cited in literary histories as a key work showing the influence of the (then new) Cuban revolution on intellectuals in Latin America. In addition to being a successful writer in Uruguay, Martínez Moreno was a practising lawyer who defended a number of political detainees from the early 1970s until he himself was threatened with arrest and forced to leave the country. Once Martínez Moreno found himself in exile, this direct experience of testimonies, affidavits, accounts of torture, kidnappings and reprisals—what he called 'this echo chamber of voices within'—produced *El Infierno,* his last and most accomplished work.

The issues raised by *El Infierno* are significant both to Latin America and the wider world. Firstly, exile, internal and external, enforced or voluntary, has been a constant condition of Latin American experience. Martínez Moreno's examination of the responsibility of the writer in exile is nuanced and profound, and here the model of Dante, both in the structure of the work and in the narrative voice, is paramount. Secondly, Martínez Moreno bravely confronts a theme which urgently requires historical revision: the nature of guerrilla movements in Latin America.

In the recent past, the *guerrilla* was a subject either of hagiography, for example Julio Cortázar's *A Manual for Manuel*, a panegyric to Argentina's armed left-wing groups in the early 70s, or some parts of Costa Gavras' film *State of Siege* (which focuses on the same kidnapping of a U.S. adviser as *El Infierno*), or demonology, a version which allowed the Armed Forces in the Southern Cone of Latin America to commit mass murder in a 'crusade' against what they termed Communist terrorism and subversion. Now a more balanced historical account is emerging, but to my knowledge this is the first fictional account reflecting this process. And of course a novelist can explore the human nuances of an experience left out of sociological or historical treatises.

Martínez Moreno is uncompromising in his attack on

North American torture advisers, on the brutality of military repression, but he does not create a pantheon of heroes in opposition to them. The idealism, the heroism, but also the human weaknesses, and the questionable strategies of the Tupamaros are discussed. This is a real achievement.

Finally a clear picture is given of the nature of military dictatorship. Once again there exist a number of testimonial accounts of repression, especially from Argentina (*Nunca Más*, etc.), but this novel complements and adds to this recreation of a popular memory stifled by the dictatorial regimes of the Southern Cone.

Now is the time for memory in these societies which are gradually healing the scars of dictatorship. And a critical account of the recent past, rather than a nostalgia for a heroic age, is what is required. *El Infierno* is very important to this process of recovery. These lessons are also important to learn in the English-speaking world and this book can help our knowledge of, and hopefully increase our support for, the fragile democracies of the River Plate.

John King
Lecturer in Cultural History (Latin America)
University of Warwick

...And at his touch the colour they had worn
Ere Hell had overcast it, they regained.
Dante, *Purgatory,* Canto I

The Adviser and His Beggars' Opera

E io, che di mirare stava inteso,
vidi genti fangose in quel pantano,
ignude tutte, con sembiante offeso.

And I, staring about with eyes intent,
Saw mud-stained figures in the mire beneath,
Naked, with looks of savage discontent. *

Dante, *Inferno*, Canto VII

As the Cuban tells it, the adviser detests swearing, crude jokes, or even too great a show of friendship. In his chair at the center of the basement, which is both his workshop and his stage, he is unfailing in his courtesy. He is more like a professor than a policeman. Even his clothing is always scrupulously correct, without the slightest hint of informality. However hot those sessions became, nobody could remember seeing him in shirtsleeves or with loosened tie. Grey suit, with a white shirt, always; his ties usually one solid, somber colour (maroon or navy blue, almost never black); only rarely does he let North American vulgarity creep in (palm trees outlined against a tropical sunset, chains of melted watches à la Dali), but never naked ladies, champagne bottles or glasses, or lists of airports, lucky numbers, baggage tickets, hearts, or psychedelic motifs. His picturesque ties are his only concession to a

---

* All translations from Dante are based on Dorothy L. Sayers' English version, *The Comedy of Dante Alighieri* (London: Penguin Books, 1949).

timid sense of fantasy, to frivolity, to innocent, irresponsible decoration, to pure whim. The adviser is fat, and is well aware of it. He's probably known it ever since those distant days back home in Richmond, Indiana. He never wears check or shiny jackets: they are a uniform slate grey, at most highlighted by a single thread of white or light blue. His trousers are always so sharply creased they could have been drawn with a plumbline. Gold studs rather than buttons for his shirts. Though almost invariably white, the pocket handkerchief is the only other detail of his dress to echo the extravagant note of his ties. Perhaps this is a faint recollection of his time as a police captain working to preserve democracy in Brazil during the 1964 *coup*.

The adviser is an expert from AID, the Agency for International Development. *Aid* means, according to the dictionary, 'to provide with what is useful or necessary; to give assistance; help; assistance, protection.' All that is part of the adviser's task in Uruguay: he helps, provides useful advice, assists, instructs, demonstrates. He is here, on his platform in the basement, for officers from the police and the armed forces to learn how to interrogate, how to discover, whatever the cost, 'all that the country may find useful and necessary in its fight against subversion and chaos.' At least, this is what was being written in the papers and broadcast on the radio, though not as yet with reference to him. That was why nobody had welcomed him publicly on his arrival. Their praise came only once his virtues of caution and discretion had been stripped of all value, after he had been kidnapped, after what was to happen had happened, and when the country was flying its flags at half-mast in his honour.

For the moment though here he is, presiding over his classes in the basement—grey jacket, white shirt, maroon tie. As yet he is not newsworthy.

One night I got a glimpse of him, close up, without knowing who he was. Though it was only that once, his face, his discreet charm and well-concealed portliness made such an impression on me that the day his photograph appeared in *El Día* I recognised him immediately. That winter in 1970, an Italian company was putting on *The Kibbutz* by Indro Montanelli in the Solis, and there were fears there might be an anti-Israeli demonstration inside the theater itself. A few months earlier, in September 1969, I had met Cemi Boscovoyne in Viña del Mar and Valparaíso, in Chile. She was always showing off her Uruguayan Cultural Foundation card, claiming to represent that organisation in Chile. She gave lunches and dinners in restaurants, always with the same smiling falsehood: 'The Foundation will take care of the bill.' She accused all of us writers of being spineless cowards: to her mind, we should have been attacking Frei and Valdes. She dressed ridiculously for someone no longer young. She wore tailored outfits full of flounces and frills like a bird's plumage, and topped them off with triangular hats that looked for all the world like birds' beaks. She was like something out of the Commedia dell'Arte under the harsh light of 1969. A rumour went the rounds that she was with the CIA, but she appeared untouched by it. (Can it still be true that to look absurd is the best disguise for spies?) All of us were of two minds. I now find it ridiculous that the CIA should use anyone with such a poor memory for faces.

3

The play had already begun when Cemi arrived to take her seat at the Solis immediately in front of me. She looked at me without remembering who I was. On this occasion, her birdsuit was complemented by a mink stole. She was looking for someone, and the person turned out to be a man with greying hair who was apparently using the interval to study the program and learn all about *The Kibbutz*, which had not held his attention on stage. I've often wondered since, whether despite his name, he was unable to understand Italian. He had allowed his half-moon spectacles to slip down his nose, so that the tortoiseshell arms stood out clearly above his ears, where they opened two slender furrows in his well-groomed silvery hair. Cemi went up to him and said something as he sat next to the red-carpeted aisle. It must have made an immediate impact, for the man left off scouring his program to peer at her over his glasses. She said a few more words, at which the plump stranger stood up courteously and quickly raised the hand she was profering to his lips, without actually kissing it. She laughed, and the stole slipped off her shoulder; he helped her re-adjust it. I was no more than a few yards from him. She had not recognised me, and in those days I had no idea who he was. They went together out into the foyer. He offered her a cigarette and lit it. She was beaming, and he was making an effort to be friendly and overcome his ingrained habit of never smiling.

Barely a few days later, on August 1st, I saw his photograph in the newspaper, and the memory of that meeting flooded back into my mind quite vividly (the photograph showed exactly the same side view as I had got): Cemi in her mink stole, the adviser with his glasses slanting down his nose. He had been abducted the day before, on Friday, July 31st, and only now did they publish his picture and details of his career: his stay in Brazil, the story of his numerous family back in Indiana, what he had been doing in our country.

It was the Cuban who told me what went on in the basement. The adviser was a perfectionist, he reckoned. He rented a house in Malvin, on Rivera Avenue. The garages have direct access into the main building, no sounds escape from the basement, the neighbours are a good distance away, insulation and sandbags make sure nothing is heard. Yet this is not a clandestine prison. Its purpose is purely educational. The adviser never lets anyone else check the final details: he must test everything himself. He goes painstakingly round all the electrical equipment, the seals on doors and windows, making absolutely sure. The palm trees, which make only a rare appearance on his ties, are very much present in his musical preferences. From childhood he has loved Hawaiian music, and though in Indiana it played only softly in the background, it is blaring out now at full volume in the basement.

He then begins a lengthy, stately inspection of all the rooms in the house. He pauses to listen, gauge, then continues on his rounds. He is trying to discover how far Hawaii reaches, the extent of its beaches, palm trees, its musical moon. He sets up the loudspeakers that will be used for his audience of colonels and police captains, and verifies all the padding, cushions, plastic strips, and bits of cotton wool used to seal doors and windows. He goes up to the ground floor to make sure that nothing can be heard beyond the bend in the stairs, in the center of the

5

living room or over in a window alcove. His job is always to explore the far reaches of death. No sign of emotion: neither Hawaii nor silence produce a flicker on his face. He rarely looks at anyone else; seems to use his eyes solely to stop them looking at him. Is he imagining real tortures, or simply going through possible pedagogical problems? He pulls out a Magnum, gets them to fire it downstairs, after warning him via a system of bells: no sound from the report reaches him in the living room. He then stands in a corner of the basement itself, and has the gun fired at the opposite end of the room. He notes with satisfaction the way the dull crack dies without an echo. 'And so on, endlessly,' the Cuban writes. Silent and unsmiling despite his success, the adviser moves on to the next item. Time does not matter; only perfection and patience count.

There were twelve places in the course, split between the army and the police. Many more had tried to get accepted: perhaps the adviser was influential at Fort Gluck, or would hand out invitations to Fort Leavenworth? While everybody was desperately trying to find out, the idea of opening the course to more participants was rejected. The adviser said it would be impossible to teach any larger number of students because he could not guarantee a proper atmosphere with more than a dozen present. Among those he had selected were colonels, lower ranking army officers, and some police captains. To be methodical, they were to start on a Monday. Once they were all settled in their chairs in the basement, the adviser opened with these words of warning:

'Gentlemen: everything we are going to do here is absolutely necessary.' (His pale, expressionless eyes are

6

fixed somewhere above his audience's heads—the army men in uniform, the police officers in smart suits as though they were attending an official function.) 'If you don't agree, there's no room for you here. I allowed you a few moments to settle down before we got started, but let me say straight out that I am not here to amuse you. This is a lecture: you are here to learn. It is part of a complete course.' The smiles on their faces contract to more respectful, neutral expressions which reveal neither anticipation nor tension. The adviser speaks good Spanish, though with an American accent: 'I didn't come to this country to waste my time, and I'm sure you don't want to waste your afternoon listening to jokes from me, do you?' (The question is a purely rhetorical one, marking a pause. A cadet takes the opportunity to pour mineral water from a bottle into the glass in front of the adviser, who ignores him.)

'This is a serious matter,' he goes on, in a gentle voice that belies his words. 'It is serious from the start, and will become more so as we deal with the various topics...and as you try things for yourselves.'

His assistants hang several charts behind him, and he raises a pointer in his right hand. One of the charts is a diagram of the human anatomy.

'Functioning of the nervous system,' he explains.

The colonels look blankly at one another. The police captains stare at their feet. Can it really have been for this that they came here? Here, where this schoolteacher who, after getting them to present themselves as briefly as possible and greeting them with a complete lack of warmth, has now launched into his lesson without the slightest concern for any exchange of ideas with them.

7

At no point during that first class does he hint that these nerve centers and sinews will later be used to guide the electrical prod: he goes over everything as though this were a medical faculty lecture room, employing only the most aseptic, neutral, scientific terminology.

For the Wednesday lecture there are not even any charts. They are already sitting waiting when he comes into the room. He nods perfunctorily in their general direction. 'Today we will look at the mentality of fugitives and prisoners.'

There is nothing particularly perceptive in what he has to say, but then they were not expecting there to be. He ends by inviting comments or questions, but as yet nobody has had the courage to make any. This time the adviser looks at them rather than above them, with a gaze that is neither stern nor indulgent, as if simply wanting to measure their reactions in order to discover more about them. The police captains suddenly busy themselves taking notes. One of the colonels asks if he may smoke, but when there is no reply, does not insist. 'Thank you, gentlemen,' are the adviser's closing words. 'Our next class will be on Friday, at the same time. I trust you are all as aware as I am of the need to be punctual. Then we will begin to examine our case studies.'

'Our case studies' turn out to be four, three men and a woman. A police officer who has not been prominent in the previous sessions now boasts of being the one who arrested them, though this was hardly a great feat since they lived out in the open, sheltering in makeshift hovels or abandoned wharves in the port, huddling at night in the corners of crumbling buildings. To protect themselves from the cold they would make fires that blackened the roofless walls with soot. They would eat their scraps, take a swig from their bottles, then curl up to sleep on sheets of newspaper or beneath sacks, in the rags they wore all day long: jackets out at the elbow, battered felt hats, or frayed knitted hats, and soleless shoes over bare feet. The proud captain has hauled them in from these refuges to stand before his colleagues and the adviser in the basement. What he has to say is probably nothing new to the colonels or his fellow policemen: they are all Uruguayan and need no explanations. But the adviser is a different matter, he is a foreigner: 'We call their booze ''birdseed'', sir, because they make it from meths and a few grains of millet—the stuff you give birds. This swells and ferments, and gives the bluish alcohol a taste you or I would find disgusting, but that these people enjoy. Anyway, it keeps them warm.'

The adviser is visibly irritated. 'Okay, there's no need to go into all the details of how these people live. This is not a sociology lecture.'

But the talkative captain will not be so easily put off: 'Yes, sir, I'll make it brief. They're not even what you'd call beggars, sir. They never beg for anything. Sometimes they're given a bowl of soup at convent gates. Then they all line up like they are now (he points at them) with their tin can. They never actually beg. We call them *bichicomes*, sir...'

'It's how we say the English word in Spanish,' butts in the emboldened colonel who two days earlier had asked for permission to smoke.

9

'An English word?' the adviser repeats, momentarily interested.

'That's right, sir. It's *beachcombers*, like the ones on Miami Beach...in Spanish that becomes *bichicomes*...they're not beggars, they are hobos who live in the sewage outlets on the estuary.'

The adviser raises his hand to prevent any further digression. It is true, the three men and the woman are lined up just as if they were about to hand in their tins to receive a lukewarm broth from divine charity, with its blobs of grease and a few floating noodles. But this time there will be no handout. They do not seem in the least concerned, nor even to have heard what has been said about them. They have been talked about to their faces as though they did not so much as exist, as if they were dogs, horses, or, more accurately, mere flies.

So there they stand, as though about to undergo a police check or a photograph. But the police already know exactly who they are, and are not the slightest bit interested in checking them or putting them on file. The first man on the left stands facing the audience in peeling shoes that have lost their laces. He stares out oblivious, with an expression of profound disdain on his face, like that of an Old Testament prophet, and typical of *bichicomes* when after years of neglect their bushy beards invade gaunt features. This man's is grey, voluminous and hopelessly tangled—not the pretentiously bohemian growth, but the true rambling mass of a beggar and tramp, and crawling with fleas. The two next to him are younger, and clean shaven, with weak chins and straggly rat-tails of hair that barely reach their shoulders. The woman in the group, though possibly even older than the bearded tramp, is also the least typical: she is wearing a pair of black, ankle-high shoes, a pair of stockings either filthy white or pink, a short skirt that reveals her bandy legs, and a bristling crown of hair midway between blonde and grey standing up spikily as if she had been surprised at her dressing table by the police. She is well known in the first district police station for her impertinence and long history of arrests. Her real name is Berta, but the nickname Doñita has stuck. For years now, that's how she's been known, and a whole generation of police are unaware that there was a time when she was Berta. 'Call me Doña Berta, if you don't mind; after all, I call you inspector when you're only a sergeant,' she is credited with having said once. 'Donã Ber-ta, please,' she insisted, stressing each syllable. 'I'm not a young woman any more, you know.' 'All right, Doña, don't go upsetting yourself,' the sergeant had replied, laughing. From then on, the nickname stuck.

It was still rumoured that, in her prime, she had been a high-class whore in Porto Alegre, Brazil, and it was there or from some frontier town later on in life that she got her Brazilian accent plus a rare wealth of flowery language in both Spanish and Portuguese. Whether true or not, it did seem her profession had left her with a lady-like air of pity towards her fellow inhabitants of the dockside slums. Those far-off days of her youth could be no more than conjecture. What was indisputable was her persisting love of cats. At night she wandered around the old town in search of empty windowsills in old houses where she could deposit scraps of food to feed the stray cats. Windowsills and titbits to feed the whole world's cats—

11

such were the horizons and dreams a beggar could cherish. Absorbed in her task, she patiently sought out the best spots to sprinkle the contents of her greasy paper. A little more here, a bit less over there. Best of all were the windowsills behind iron railings, which provided a secure place for her to deposit this earthly sustenance. And above all, she liked those on which the shutters had closed forever—ruins in the making, houses long since abandoned—since there is nothing those phantasmagoric cats, all of them grey in the night, adore so much as the smell of dust and decay given off by cracked and crumbling marble floors and the accumulated stench of other cats in the corners, especially if accompanied by a darkness alive with fleas, and high above them niches dug in the walls overlooking the silence or the clatter of the streets.

For a while, a man was seen doing her rounds with her. Nobody ever suspected any sexual relation between the two. He was a pasty-faced, plump character who gave the impression of having been castrated in his youth, which made him pity all the cats who had not suffered a similar fate and were thus condemned to howl with hunger and desire from their early morning vantage points. Be fat! Be chaste! Eat! Stay calm! he would tell them as he scattered the bits of food, and Berta smiled infatuated, nodding her agreement.

Smiled her agreement until the day her companion vanished. Alone once more, Doñita returned to her night patrols, on the lookout for cats in the darkness just waiting to pounce on the scraps as soon as she turned away. Her lips never again came to life in her face, were never seen to open again for even a moment's smile. Among true lonely spirits, infatuation does not necessarily mean happiness.

He raises a hand, and though nobody can be certain they actually heard him, orders the prisoners to be led away. Absent even when there, they disappear completely in only a few seconds. They do not so much as look round or fix their gaze on anyone. Their audience, however, is more perturbed, and for several minutes is full of questions. Had they all been given a bath, as someone (perhaps the officer who brought them in) suggested? Why do that if afterwards they had to be crammed back into their same filthy clothes? Why? What would happen next? Would they now get a second bath before they re-appeared, naked this time?

Showing not the slightest notice of any concern among his audience, the adviser begins to speak again.

'The art of interrogation is a complex one,' he says (as the Cuban tells it). 'It has several stages. The first, as you are all well aware, is that of softening up. What we are aiming for here is that a person should feel alone and defenceless, completely cut off from reality, face-to-face with infinite fear. To achieve results at this stage there should be no interrogation as such, no dialogue about anything whatsoever with the prisoner. No questions: nothing but blows and insults. The experts will assure you that, in however distorted a fashion, questions always lead to some relationship being created between the interrogator and the interrogated. However harsh they may be, words are bound to produce familiarity between the people involved. Whenever two people talk, they cease to be completely alien to each other. And what is required to make the softening up process as effective as possible is that the prisoner should feel utterly alone, lacking all support, defenceless, with only himself to rely on, in the grip of an anonymous system that has him at its mercy. Ideally, the interrogator should not know anything about the prisoner during this phase. The aim is to provoke panic, a solitude that is so desperate we can later offer to alleviate it in return for whatever we are interested in obtaining. The deepest despair—but not a total surrender of hope, nor a wish only to die.'

'Blows and insults, before we give any explanation of what we want to discover, before we reveal how much we know or think we know: that is what can produce this feeling of intense loneliness, of a fear of going mad, that boundless, unreasoning fear of madness that is one of the furthest extremes the mind can imagine...' Then he goes on, without the slightest sign of any emotion: 'If you'd care to describe it in this way (and it would be an accurate description), you could say that this situation sets in motion a process of self-destruction. What we're trying to do is to break down an individual's resistance. We can achieve this all the more easily if he is kept in the dark about what is wanted from him, what secret we are trying to prise from him, how much we know of what he has done, how far he is still anonymous to us, a merely physical presence exposed to the violence we are threatening him with, and which we may or may not unleash on him. Some of this I mentioned the other day, when I was discussing the mentality of the prisoner, the captive. Once he is back in his cell, and is waiting there to be called out again for interrogation and he is not called...then he can't help but think,

14

on and on until he's exhausted…what will he be asked, and how is he going to reply? He builds up a structure of possible replies, takes it apart, tries not to construct any scheme at all, but finds he is busy confusing questions he is certain to be asked with ones no one will ever put to him. This terror that has no definite limits is the worst kind. An infinite terror…' he muses, clearly engrossed in his words, with a sort of abstract concentration as he weighs their meaning.

'That is why the best cells are those that leave the individual completely on his own, and deprive him of any reference point in space or time. That way he has nothing around him to fix on to, he has no idea when he will be called or when he will be able to talk to someone—with anyone, no matter who, even the interrogator who presents himself during the final stages of this destructive solitude. The prisoner has been isolated by the hood. He has no watch to help him measure his wait. Then when at last he sees someone face-to-face, that person hits and degrades him: nothing but blows and insults, not a single word that might help him relate to another human being. And this gets worse and worse, threatening still more horrors, without anyone saying so directly or any indication of how far this ''treatment'' will go. That is the first phase, the softening-up phase. The name speaks for itself. Have you all understood clearly what I've been saying?'

Nobody has ever spoken to them like this before. It is all very clear, but at the same time they are stunned. Torture, in the hands of the police officers, had always been a confused affair of kicks, punches, angry swearing, insults that led to more violence, flying fists and a brawl in which none of them knew for certain where it all might end. They flung themselves into it blindly, passionately and even when the desired result was achieved, it left everyone exhausted, covered in blood. Sometimes, in the brutality of the attack, the prisoner died on them, so thwarting the whole object as he took with him the knowledge they wanted. They had always gone about it in this chaotic, disorganised manner until now; but here is the AID adviser to help improve their techniques and their mental preparation. The adviser offers them a different perspective, and different methods, a way not to waste their efforts. They used to get angry—that is something that should never happen, since signs of anger in the police or army personnel offer the enemy an incalculable advantage, opening chinks in the system he might be able to exploit. They lost control—that is something they should never allow to happen. No hatred, no display of emotion. No fear, no arrogance. Method and more method.

The Cuban, who is no writer and was not there at the time with that in mind, still cannot help mentioning the look in the adviser's eyes: 'They were like plastic, showing no spark of life.' And he tells how caught up he felt in the unreality with which the adviser was describing the most horrific acts with cold, calculating efficiency. Though unable to describe the scene in quite this way, he does suggest an air of science fiction, of unearthly objectivity surrounding the adviser and all his gestures, his tone of voice, his judgements. Also the clinical aura he imparts: 'his vocation as a teacher, his attention to the smallest detail, the precision of his movements, the surgical cleanliness he demands from everyone, as though they were in the operating theater of a modern hospital.'

Some of his audience are taken aback by his approach; others give in, fascinated as though gripped by a mysterious power. They have neither the imagination, the candour, nor sufficient faith to know whether they have ever come across the devil, but they dimly realise that were they to do so, he would appear to them in similar guise. Something in the atmosphere in the basement suggests that this might lead them into a perversity they would never have dared approach alone.

One of the colonels finally plucks up the courage to express his doubts: 'Yes, sir, that is all very clear. But how much of what you have been saying applies to the four people we just saw?'

'That's a good question...a good question,' the adviser repeats, but the emphasis implied by the repetition hangs emptily in the air. 'I was expecting someone to ask me that. Shall I explain it to you?'

Everybody nods.

'With these people, things are completely different. To begin with, they aren't subversives, they are...what did you call them?'

'*Bichicomes*.'

'That's right—hobos.' (He is apparently unwilling, due to the proprieties of his profession, to use such a common word as *bichicomes*.)

'Yes, but don't forget that I called them our "case studies". In other words, they are simply a test, an exercise. If it weren't such an ambiguous term, we could call this a "simulation". An exercise carried out in laboratory conditions. An "experiment", if you prefer to call it that…'

He bends over the glass of water, and takes a long drink.

'This creates a very different situation. First, we will never reach the stage of questions. What do we want to know from them? Nothing, absolutely nothing. They are our guinea-pigs, nothing more. What possible answers could a guinea-pig give? Nothing, nothing at all. Here are the pros and cons', he announces, as though drawing up two lists on a board. 'Disadvantages: we will have no way of verifying the effectiveness of the softening-up process, insofar as this is shown at the stage when the prisoner is finally made to talk, in terms of how long this takes us, how much pressure we have to put on him, and so on. These people are after all immune to psychological pressure or anything of that nature. Due to the lives they lead, they have neither the imagination nor the awareness to react to it. They are not going to feel any mental anguish beyond purely physical suffering. They are incapable of feeling disturbance and disorientation which create that kind of despair in political delinquents—who by definition are people with imagination. Nor do tramps have any sense of guilt—far from it. We have to rule that out. Simply, and perhaps even this will be to a much lesser degree than in normal people, our test cases will feel the physical pain of being punished…but beyond that, they have nothing to tell us, there is nothing more to find out, only the resistance their bodies offer to what we do to them. This implies a distortion, or rather, let's call it a frustration, since we are not going to be able to test the ratio of pressure to information obtained, which is of course fundamental in those instances where we are working for real.'

He punctuates his speech with another short sip of water.

'Advantages. One: we will learn how to do it, on a purely technical level. As we will not be worried about what we hope to get out of our work, since we know beforehand that we are not trying to achieve anything, we are all the more likely to be effective. We can observe clearly any physical reaction, and the effects of each application on the part of the body we are dealing with. It's a good way for you to train for when you have to do it for real. Two: these tramps have no one to raise a fuss about them. If things turn out badly, nobody is going to demand an explanation, we won't have to account for ourselves to anyone, there is no risk of a scandal—none of which means that a mistake, from the professional point of view, is any the less regrettable.'

As they all digest what he has said, the adviser concludes: 'It is most important to know from the start if we can allow ourselves the luxury of having the person die on us...'

Again the room is silent. The adviser raises his hand to make sure the quiet will not be broken, then motions for the first *bichicome* to be brought in.

Stripped of his clothes, the tramp with the prophet's face seems less tall, though his beard looks even more prominent, more tangled, even more like a wasp's nest, jutting out towards the audience like a ship's figure-head. He doesn't say a word, blinking as though the light is too bright for him, though it hasn't changed from earlier, when he had seemed half asleep.

The assistants have brought in a stretcher, which is simply a long board with four extensions at the corners.

They lay the bearded tramp down on it, pass straps round his forearms, his thighs, and his ankles to secure him. Flat on his back, he seems, except for his head, to cease to exist—even his bony knees and the lines of his ribs. First they sprinkle water all over his body, then a man in shirt-sleeves begins to probe at him with a cattle prod he has just plugged in. He presses it to his penis, his scrotum, very precisely, almost delicately, as surgically as the adviser has been recommending. Despite the straps, the tramp begins to writhe on the board; he screams. It's a brief, hoarse yelp that lacks either power or intensity, the scream of someone unaccustomed to it, who is suddenly horrified to find he cannot avoid doing so. At the second application, the scream grows louder, as though a rent has been torn in the tramp's throat. His third sobbing cry seems to excite the colonel who earlier had asked if he could smoke. He is a tall paunchy man in battle fatigues, and leaps out of his seat to come and stand next to the policeman as he is about to apply the prod again, as though he wanted to inspect from as close as possible this new technique. At the fourth shock, the tramp desperately arches his back as if trying to rid himself of the dispropor-tionate weight of his huge head, dangling on such narrow shoulders. Suddenly the colonel, who is bright pink from so much concentration, bursts out laughing. By now the prod is moving over the tramp for a fifth time, and it's as though the whole of his body were electrified, while a moaning gurgle and a frothy liquid like lava or soap come out of the slit of a mouth in the midst of his beard.

'Look at the way his balls are shaking, dammit!' the colonel splutters. 'No...they're not his balls anymore,

20

they're just bits of dangling flesh!'

He appears to have set himself the task of conveying to the others everything he is seeing from close up. The assistant lifts the prod and looks over inquiringly at the adviser. Should he go on, or stop there? The adviser signals for him to wait.

'Colonel,' he says, 'it would be better if you used the correct terms for the different parts of the body. I would also ask you to remember your military discipline. And please, could you not speak unless spoken to.'

Slumping back into his chair, his scarlet cheeks sunk into the collar of his shirt, the colonel's one remaining desire seems to be to fade away. If anyone from his own country had spoken to him like that...but the adviser is different.

'A precise pain in a well-defined spot,' the adviser continues, to deflect the colonel's anger and bring the tramp's respite to an end. 'Everything in the correct dose, the exact amount needed for the purpose.'

Like a monstrous chicken with its head lolling over the side of a basket, the *bichicome* seems to know that this pause is at an end. For many years, his eyes have been incapable of expressing terror; now, in brief flashes, they simply reveal his total incomprehension.

The prod returns, moving from penis to anus. As he contorts violently, the whole board is lifted in the air. His screams have by now become entirely indistinct, and finally he falls silent. At another signal from the adviser, the two assistants and their colleague untie the tramp. One unrecognizable arm, mottled and ashen, flops over the side of the board, while the other claws its way up to the tufts

21

of hair on the man's chest and remains there, paralysed. His unconscious head rocks from side to side for a moment, until it lies lifeless on his left shoulder.

'These people are trash,' the short, stout police captain calls out, as though this were a measured observation. 'Completely decrepit, useless...it's due to the way they live.'

Instead of checking the captain for this interruption, the adviser seems wearily to give in to it. They have no notion of how they ought to be feeling, thinking, reacting. He presses the silvery grey hair at his temples, as though his own head were too tired to follow his instructions. The tramp has been carried out, inert on the board. Music blares out briefly from the record player, only to be quickly silenced as the adviser, for the first time with an edge of anger to his voice, calls for them to quieten down.

Doñita has contrived to underscore her importance by keeping them waiting. Later they were told it was because she had tried to stop the assistants undressing her, and had struggled so fiercely that they had had to force her to the floor to remove her rags. Her skirt got caught in her wildly scissoring legs as she pedalled like a desperate cyclist flat on her back to prevent them stripping her naked. But now she stands there facing the colonels and the captains, naked, wrinkled, shrivelled up like an Egyptian mummy, with two enormous coffee-coloured medallions where her nipples had once been, a few straggling pubic hairs, a ring of scum round her ankles showing how high her shoes had reached. Her wretchedness must be less offensive, or more profound, than the prophet's, because no one laughs.

'Why have you brought me here?' she demands, taking advantage of what she senses is meant to be a sacred silence. 'What do you want from me? What are you after?' Then again: 'What can I possibly tell you, what do I know that could interest you? Leave me be, you sons of bitches!'

'She's the one with the most life in her,' the captain blurts out again, encouraged by the fact that the adviser had not pulled him up after his earlier intervention. 'It would be a woman, wouldn't it?'

'I'll thank you all to keep your observations to yourselves,' the adviser cuts in, smoothing down the first signs of crumpling in his tie. 'This is a work session, not a circus. If you can't understand that, we won't get anywhere...'

'And me? What use am I to you? Why did you bring me here, take all my clothes off, and put me on show like this?' Berta wails.

'She's right, from her point of view. She doesn't have anything to tell us. She doesn't know anything, and we have nothing to ask her. But that is precisely what makes all this fantasy, and that is where one can best learn to...'

'Eh? What are you saying?' She cannot follow the adviser's reasoning, and nobody is willing to listen to hers. 'Sons of bitches,' she repeats.

As explanation, they fling her down again, this time to fasten her to the board for the session with the cattle prod. They fasten her more securely than the prophet, wary of her fighting back. As soon as the prod begins to explore her vagina, her writhing is so fierce, her screams so piercing, that the audience now apparently wishes only for it all to be over as quickly as possible, though the effect

23

on the technicians seems to be the opposite, as though her screams are their favourite music to work to. The stretcher leaps from the floor with Doñita on it in a grotesque parody of a surfboard. Can the assistants really enjoy this more if they are having insults heaped on them?

But her screams of abuse have stopped altogether by the time one of the men sits her up on the side of the board, as if hinged on her coccyx, while the prod operator, barely modifying his position, forces open her apparently moribund lips. Easily overcoming her faint resistance, he forces her to swallow two or three gulps of a liquid brought to him in a cup. For a second, Doñita's head slumps forward again. Then all at once the emetic surges up through her body, making her shudder with a violence that is dredged up from the deepest realms of unconsciousness or death. She opens her mouth gaping wide, like a mythological fish that has the vague shape of a woman, and then Berta the fearful mermaid begins to retch up all her empty insides. She has no breath left for anything but a slimy yelping sound that emerges from her lips between successive waves of vomit. She brings up all her long years of hunger together with the final stubborn vestiges of her will to live.

The short captain must always have imagined he was very tough, but it takes only a few seconds for him to realise he was wrong. Perhaps it's the smell of the emetic; perhaps it's a smell foretelling death in a body still alive, a chalice aimed at his lips as unavoidably as the cup was thrust into those of the old woman: there is scarcely time for the colour to drain from his face, or for him to stand up to leave. He just manages to turn his head to one side and, with a humiliated cough, begins to vomit. He isn't 'trash', but in this case his strength only adds to his ignominy. Even Doñita greets the gushing flow as an unexpected homage. She half opens her gluey eyes above the foaming gap of her lips and, as far as the mist in which she is dying will allow her to do so, she stares at him.

The others leap out of their chairs to give him as wide a berth as possible, as though a tidal wave of vomit were pouring from him and they had to scramble to safety. There is no way he can pretend this is the first time he has witnessed torture, at his age and with his experience. Yet he is overhwelmed by an irresistible force. He is to be exposed at the very moment when he would get the chance to practise the skills he has acquired. He will be discredited, to have the adviser's opinion of him destroyed, see his career prospects crumble, any chance of reaching the United States disappear. This is what the adviser, on his feet now for the first time in the whole session, is telling him in so many words:

'You let yourself be affected, captain. As you can see, there's no point being a loudmouth, or laughing at someone else's misfortune too soon. Please leave the room, they'll look after you in the dispensary. There are very few moments which are crucial in our lives: but you have just failed in one of yours.'

The captain staggers out, swaying, whey-faced and sweaty. He knows the sessions are finished for him, that he has no chance of returning. He won't even see what happens to the two other beggars. But when the next day he hears that, unfortunately, the four case studies ended in death, he will still feel he is as guilty as the others. And

25

he has now exchanged his tough-guy image for that of a coward, for the rest of his life.

'One must never let them lose all hope,' the adviser had told him once (perhaps in his office the day he chose him to come on the course). 'One should always leave them with a last ounce of hope and fear...(he had smiled, unusually, as though in anticipation of the end of his sentence)...You see, you might not believe it, but when all's said and done, I am a teacher of hope.'

A city is a honeycomb. Each layer is unaware of what is going on underneath. In this system of tunnels, the *bichicomes* live at the lowest level. They are oblivious to what is going on above their heads. There is never anything to ask them. Though their lives are at stake, they don't know what to reply. If one or four of them die, it's all the same. A *bichicome* is not an adviser. There are no flags at half-mast for a *bichicome's* death, no expressions of remorse, no threat of national disgrace, no burial mounds, no pleas for them to be spared, nothing. A *bichicome* dies when he cannot withstand any more torture, not because someone refuses to bargain for his life. If one or four of them die from the prod or drowning in their own vomit, it is not because their executioner wants any secrets from them. Nobody wants to ask the *bichicomes* anything, nobody is anxious for their answers. It's simply a question of testing the limits of their resistance, how long their ribs, testicles, arms, or lungs can hold out. This is torture at its most gratuitous, a pure form of torture as experiment.

Wouldn't it be better to feel sorry for the poor fat police captain, with his homespun cruelty, his disorganised tortures, a loudmouthed cop who has just seen an attack of nausea utterly destroy his career?

Is it not unjust to segregate him, ban him, discard him forever, pension him off? If he had been a colonel rather than a police captain, would they surely not have found him a cushy sinecure, an aide-de-camp's job, or a diplomatic posting, a well-lined supply position? The adviser cannot even ask himself such questions as he sits in his chair at the end of the day and listens to his favourite Hawaiian music. What he knows is that someone like the captain is no use to him...no use at all. It's perfectly clear: it is something he has learned in Panama, put to the test in Brazil, had drummed into him back in the USA.

Il Dottore Gaetano

Se tu pur mo in questo mondo cieco
caduto se'di quella dolce terra

If thou into this blind realm of the dead
Art fall'n but now from those sweet Latian shores

Dante, *Inferno*, Canto XXVII

I am recording this tape of my own free will a week after being released from captivity, on the eve of my departure for Italy. The ambassador is not present on this occasion but I have to say that I have benefitted from his advice, cooperation and protection in everything. I must also thank my friends for their support, solidarity, and help throughout. They acted as go-betweens in my release, negotiated the terms, and facilitated communication with my wife which, in turn, was such a decisive factor in keeping my spirits up for more than two months. I have learned many things since my release, things I did not know at the time and which I have now incorporated into my reflections about what happened to me and around me, reflections which still have not brought me to any definitive conclusions.

I want to begin with two provisos. The first is that the Uruguayan authorities have assured me that they will not prejudice the cases of my above-mentioned friends by distorting events and circumstances so as to make them appear guilty by association or of aiding and abetting a crime. They have already told the police quite truthfully of the part they played in the events and the sentiments which motivated them. I wish to thank them very much.

The second proviso is to do with the fact that this will be my sole and last word on the matter. I am in no position to accuse anyone, nor will I do so. The people who performed their functions in my presence did so with hoods on. I would not be able recognize a single face, nor identify a single voice. Apart from details of the initial physical conditions in which I was detained, which I will talk about in a moment, I have no grievances other than the obvious ones connected with the unsolicited deprivation of my liberty. I was never mistreated, either physically or mentally. I have children in this country which I am now leaving, whether permanently or temporarily I do not know. I do not wish my family to be harrassed. My wife has already availed police officers of the letters I wrote to her, as well as those of her letters to me which I was allowed to bring with me from captivity. They are the only things we have. We do not think they will be of any use to the investigation. The police have photocopies of all these letters, the originals are in a safe in the name of the bank's lawyer.

Some days ago a police officer came to see me. He brought a photo and urged me to identify it, naturally I could not. He said it was Indalecio Olivera, an ex-priest and member of the MLN, the National Liberation Movement, who had been killed in a gun battle during my last week in captivity, and in which an agent of the security forces had also been killed. He asked me if I could identify the ex-priest as one of my guards. I said no. None of them took off their masks in my presence. I hope that in my remaining twenty-four hours in Uruguay no one asks me that kind of question again: it is important that I

29

recognize no one, no one at all.

Having said that, I will continue with the facts. My personal details are given at the beginning of this tape, but in any case you had them long ago. I am one of the owner-directors of the bank, and I also manage it. It was founded by my father. Since the bank also bought the Montevideo evening newspaper, I am part owner of that too and the corresponding morning issue. I manage both of them. I am a lawyer by profession, a graduate of an Italian law school, but I am more of a businessman and industrialist now.

I suppose there must have been many more important bankers than myself, but they were usually political leaders too and surrounded by bodyguards. I did not have security men following me. In this sense I was very easy prey, so they made do with me. Even kidnappers have to be realistic.

Last September 9, a Friday I think, I drew up at the doors to the newspaper's garage, in Bartolomé Mitre Street between Reconquista and Sarandí. It was about nine in the morning on an almost spring-like day. I was intending to spend a couple of hours sorting out a few administrative matters, then go home, have lunch, and come back to the bank for the afternoon, because things are always complicated at the end of the week.

I drove up in my four-door Peugeot saloon, model 404, colour blue. Just as I was about to ask for the garage door in the basement of the building to be opened, four men approached me. One of them pointed a gun at me and forced me into the middle of the front seat while he sat at the wheel. Another one, slipping an arm through the half-open window, opened the right-hand door and sat down on that side. The other two got in behind. The one at the wheel seemed unnecessarily nervous. Before starting the car, he shouted 'Take this, Eyetie!' and slammed the butt of his gun against my forehead, and a lump came up. The car was blocking the entrance to the garage, straddling the walkway. The man who had hit me reversed the car and drove off abruptly. At that moment Devoto, the telephonist, came out of his cabin and appeared at the top of the three steps. He must have been the one who raised the alarm because I could see from the expression on his face that he realized what was happening. As the car drew away, the man to my right handed me some glasses and told me to put them on. They were lined with black cardboard and impeded my vision. It was useless to shout, or attract attention. The corner of Solís Street, across from Bacacay Street, was deserted at that time of the morning. We went along Buenos Aires Street, and I imagine we turned down Liniers Street to get onto the coast road. My head ached from the blow, and I stopped wanting to look…I couldn't from behind the blinkered glasses anyway.

The men did not speak, nor did I. The one at the wheel carried on insulting me for a while, very excitedly. They must have signalled to him to be quiet because he suddenly stopped.

From the very beginning the one thing I did not want to do was lose my sense of time and place. I have to admit that my struggle with time was over within days but, on the other hand, I made as precise mental notes as possible of all the material references to do with place. When they transferred me to a van, for instance, and made me lie on the floor with a hood on, I noticed that the floor was corrugated iron or metal like in a goods vehicle. I limp slightly from a war wound in my foot and I used it to explore the nature of the floor. We continued for a good while, I could not say how long exactly, but I guessed about half an hour. The van left a properly paved road and took another, full of potholes. My body bumped around on the floor, and my hand felt the sandy consistency of the dust filtering through the gaps in the somewhat creaking bodywork. I imagined we were going somewhere with sand dunes. When we arrived, two of the men tied my hands and helped me down so that my crippled foot again probed the ground and found it soft and muddy but, I might add, there were no pine needles. They half carried me so that I didn't fall. I guessed there was foliage, because I sensed its smell and movement, a kind of rustle, in the gusts of wind. There was a freshness in the dank air, an overall vegetable freshness but no really definite fragrances. I tried very hard to detect sea smells—or rather effluvia—but I am not sure there really were any. Afterwards, when they transferred me to a simple hut which smelled of damp and dry rot, and I walked a few yards down a hallway of uneven flagstones, I was sure I was somewhere in the country, far from any main road where cars passed. If they discover the place some day when I am back in Italy, I will have photos taken and sent to me. It is an amazing experience imagining a place without being able to see it and feeling the nervous tingle of gradual reconstruction. If I were blind, I would prefer for my own peace of mind to have been born blind.

Inside the hut, I heard cocks crow and now and again the odd plane; the cocks seemed almost to touch me and the planes were flying very low. It must be that area of small farms near the airport, I told myself then. But now I am not sure. The noise of cars was intermittent and very distant and, except for a few very remote furtive bursts from a radio (in the two long months), the noise from neighbours was practically nil. But I heard it only very late at night. For a time I wasn't sure if it was a radio or a tape recorder because I never heard an announcer's voice. As the days passed, however, I became convinced that it was a radio and that someone turned down the volume when the music stopped. Once the beginning of a well-known program slipped through, but it was strangled straightaway. So I learned to identify silence with midnight. It acted as my watch, in the absence of any other. Did they do it so that without voices, with none of the patter that ends each program, time for me became shapeless and immobile...frozen? I do not know, it could very well have been; I had suspected something similar when I was a wounded soldier in the sanatorium. I am a banker, I know nothing of possible time-vacuum therapies. I was thankful for the music, it was a great consolation to me. Never had listening to music been so important.

What I did find horrible, totally inhuman, was the place I was put in. I said just now that I could not get rid of the idea that I was not the original choice for the kidnapping. But I had not expected the next terrible shock. They kept me in a place that was not even properly ready; they had not made the slightest attempt to make it bearable.

33

It could not have been the place prepared for Peirano. I imagine that when they switched people, they could not be bothered to finish it, because I cannot believe that the kidnapping was so urgent it had to be done that very day regardless of the state of their preparations.

Anyway, they made me go down into a narrow pit, lowering me so that I reached the bottom without knocking myself about too much. Yes, it was an apparently freshly dug pit, impregnated with damp and crawling with worms. It oozed water, there were cracks which trapped my feet, and dark spongy patches not properly absorbed by the uneven bits of sacking which, replaced by the guards every now and again, penetrated my shoulders and back. The little tomb was so narrow there was no room to move, and my subsequent immobility made the damp penetrate deeper and deeper. My situation was atrocious. The puddle in the bottom grew under the weight of my body and became more and more muddy, unhealthy and unbearable. I shouted, protested, asked if they were trying to kill me. One of the guards answered, rudely, that they were not. 'Rich people are too used to comfort,' he said, 'they never think of the others who go without. It will only be for a day or two, while the other room is being finished. This won't kill you.'

The first day I chose not to eat, rather than eat in a pit. The second day I accepted a few spoonfuls of hot soup which I think a masked woman, in total silence, put to my lips. The hot liquid brought me momentary respite from the horrors of the ditch. I asked them to take my clothes off, because being soaked they aggravated the terrible effects the place was having on my body. So they left me in my underpants, but the woman still went on feeding me quite naturally. Once again I had the neutral, innocent sex of a sick man I had had in that hospital bed in Salo.

Even more absurd was the fact that while I was in the pit they questioned me about some of the bank's transactions. They tended to think of all bank or stock exchange negotiations which they did not understand as illicit, crooked and fraudulent. I tried to explain the mechanism of each operation, like someone explaining the big bad wolf to frightened children. One of the young guys had previously worked in a bank, I could tell. He did not know, however, that certain restrictions had been lifted and when I explained them to him, he put it down to the manouevrings of Pacheco and Peirano to placate the oligarchy. There was a certain left-wing manicheism in these judgements.

I do not know if the days spent in the ditch were meant to be punitive. I will never know if the punishment had actually been planned for someone else and was merely passed on to me by the circumstances and finances of the moment, something to which we ourselves are so sensitive. The costs had already been incurred, so a ransom and a rationale had to be found.

After three days (or four or five) they moved me to another place. My curiosity was rekindled when I saw that my new lodging did not seem to have been specially prepared for me either. Had another occupant been recently released ? It consisted of a bunk which filled the corner of a closed room. If there had been other openings, they were now hidden behind partitions which lined the corner and were obviously fastened from the outside by bolts.

35

The room formed by these partitions was continually lit by an electric lightbulb. The wallpaper was a collage of newspapers, as was the carpeting on the floor. This is where I stayed, day in day out, until my release. They were discreet, they allowed me to do my necessaries without a guard present, although they may have watched me through some secret spyhole. Day and night, always the same.

When I finished reading the walls and the floor, press cuttings about two months old, someone offered me the *Diary of Che in Bolivia*. They must have been surprised by the eagerness with which I accepted; apparently they had expected resistance. It was almost certainly some time before October 8. I heard nothing while in my prison, I cannot even claim to have noticed any particular commotion during the Pando operation, which must have been very important for them since it cost three lives and several prisoners. Once they tested my sense of humour by quoting Berthold Brecht's phrase about which was a worse crime, robbing a bank or founding one. 'It depends on the bank,' I replied. 'What about yours ?' 'Well, you may well be doing something to close it right now.' They laughed. They were amazed that a banker had heard of Brecht. They liked the story about the German who remained indifferent when they came for the Communists because he was not one, and when they came for the Jews because he was not one, and saw it was too late when the Nazis came for him. We are often astonished by what others, incredibly, know. They by me, and I by them. One day, I gave one of my guards a letter for my wife. It was open. I always handed them in open so they could be sure I was not providing the outside world with guesses, signals or clues as to my whereabouts. The letter was addressed to 'Dear Laura'. I had just finished writing it. I did not have my hood on. My guard, on the other hand, did. 'Laura,' he said behind his mask, 'like Petrarch's lady.' I must confess I was surprised, undoubtedly because I was prejudiced against the place and the people. I was tactless. 'So, a man of action can know who Petrarch was too?' 'Even one who is not Italian,' he said. He was obviously disgusted, and never did guard duty again. He took it as a personal insult when it was merely foolish generic astonishment; I had just learned that guerrillas read as well...

I can still hear the tone of the man's voice *'Even one who is not Italian'*. Of everything that was said to me in the whole of the sixty days, it is probably the only voice I could recognize. I would deny it, however, even though I had just heard it and was sure I identified it.

Like almost everyone who reads Che's Diary, I was especially impressed by his final words when, under a thin September moon, totally defeated, he sets out for Nacahuazu and certain death. I said so. I was talking to the young man guarding me (this one must have been very young) and he had asked what I thought of the book. All persecution is distressing, I said. But persecution can have greatness too if the man being persecuted is great or the circumstances lend themselves greatness. I got carried away by my own enthusiasm and by the vision evoked of my own youth. I conjured up an old man of almost seventy who had ruled the world, now a fugitive roaming the highways and byways of Italy with a magnificent young mistress at his side, until a partisan finally sticks them against a wall together and shoots them…Chiaretta crying, he impassive.

'Mussolini was never great,' replied the young man. 'Fascists can't be great.' 'It happened thirty-six years ago,' I replied, 'I was as young then as you are now. I'm no longer a Fascist, but I would never dare deny his potential greatness as you do. Heroes are not, as we would like them to be, all on the same side of the fence.' The boy went out. They probably called me the Fascist from then on, and even avoided talking to me. That was the first night of my captivity to have rain, a real downpour. A torrential spring rain beat down on the roofs, and I discovered as the rain drummed on it that what lay above the ceiling was made of zinc.

Negotiations for my release began a few days later. They made me set out the terms in a letter to Laura. But only now, now that I am free, do I know exactly what they were finally. I asked Laura to notify the newspaper's editor (or the bank's lawyer, it was the same person). The lawyer received phone calls calling him 'friend' and asking him to go to a hollow tree in Villa Biarritz for details of the deal. He was frightened but he went. He got out of his Polara at midnight, and walked with his cocker spaniel to the darkness of the huge splintered tree to collect a letter containing demands and replace it with another containing counter-proposals. They paid fifteen million pesos to a rural school and a relief fund for workers at a meat-freezing plant. All this will soon be history. The lawyer for the workers in the freezing plant proposed, as an additional condition, that our newspaper publish a letter about the sentence passed on one of his sons who was in clandestinity. The money was delivered, the interminable letter was published. The lawyer had been up all night writing it. His wife drew the curtains at dusk, so they said, and pulled them back at dawn. He wrote in the name of his fugitive son, signed on his behalf, and invented generous but unintelligible phrases. How I was freed is of no interest to anyone, exactly where, the place by the sea, how frightened I was. Now I can embrace my wife, I want to go away with her and my children, I want to leave here. Do not ask me to understand what I have still not absorbed. I sometimes think I would need more time in a pit to fulfill within myself the myth of man's destiny, one like Plato's Cave which I touched on in my adolescent reading in secondary school. I do not want to think about those days, and even less about the bank in Misiones Street. No. As I stood there that night, next to the Cabaret de la Muerte, when I was afraid I would be shot by people who were not my enemies but might covet me as a propaganda prize, a trap, or a reprisal, and I prayed for the lives of those who did not think as I did (I can see that noble, aquiline face in the calm night behind the cemetery on November 20), I swore I needed time, oblivion, time to reflect on my passion, my greed, my hate, time, more time, time in another place, perhaps... When will that time come? I ask you gentlemen, you who will take away this tape and in return, on this bed of so many dead leaves, will allow me to leave tomorrow. I am asking you, if you know that is, with an almost disillusioned smile.

The Beggars' Opera (II)

O cacciati del ciel, gente dispetta...

Outcasts of Heaven, despicable crew...

Dante, *Inferno*, Canto IX

What did they do with the bodies of the four beggars; the prophet, Doñita, the two little ones?

Sometimes, they say, when someone dies from a slight miscalculation in torture, they are buried at night in the drainage pipes of the Northern Cemetery. Some claim to have seen a bundle, others a cheap wood coffin, unloaded from an army jeep. The jeep stops at the mouth of the pipes where they open onto the earth, the often wet earth, churned up by heavy duty boots and the furrows of caterpillar tires. They carry no spades or hoes, there is no grave to dig. They prise open a cylindrical cement lid, in the light of the jeep's headlamps. They put the coffin (or the waterproofed bundle of tarred cloth) in the pipe and push it in a few yards. Sometimes one of the thinner soldiers crawls in, crouching over, he shouts from inside the tube, shines a lamp over the ridged interior, scrapes with a trowel as if to scare the worms and bats away, he pats the wall, his veins swelling with the foul water, and gives an order. From outside, in turn, comes banging and sometimes shouting. Are they answering? Strangled shouts, muffled by the humidity and silence, in the dampest, latest and emptiest hours of the night. The thin soldier comes out again, they replace the cylindrical lid, laugh a little, light a cigarette, have a pee, get back into the jeep and disappear. They leave behind the heaviest footprints, and the track of the thin soldier's gumboots.

40

There are no numbers to give out, no relatives to inform, no rites, no memories.

Watching all this from behind a darkened tomb could cost you your life. If they find you, you had better pretend to be body-snatcher. You will get off lighter that way. But there is a list of body-snatchers just as there is a file on subversives. And if your name is on the latter, you've had it. Because you have information that someone, there, that night, was buried secretly. It is bad luck knowing that, even if you don't know who the corpse is. So, investigating is a sport only for important cases, United Nations cases. No point bothering about something so soon forgotten, something that leaves so little trace in this world, as the tomb of four *bichicomes*. No, no one will bother burying *them* in the drainage pipes of the Northern Cemetery; that is reserved for important people, for wiping from the face of the earth people who might leave their mark on it. No one will bother burying the *bichicomes* there or even taking them out to sea at night, tying cement blocks to them, and throwing them in. When the *bichicomes* leave the morgue, they are nobody, they can be buried in broad daylight. Or, better still, they can be used as exhibits for anatomy lessons at the universities. Who could identify the prophet if they were given his jawbone to dissect? Who would ask who those breasts of dark lacerated fiber had belonged to if they held Berta's thorax in their hands? There is even more anonymity there than in the night, in the pipes. There are no potential spies or phoney body-snatchers. Why waste a space which is getting smaller every day if, as they say, the universities always need more corpses? A *bichicome's* tomb fits into a bottle; a bottle

41

without a label, without the inscription which will, in all likelihood, adorn the adviser's tomb in Richmond, Indiana.

Ulysses' Monologue

Le sue parole e 'l modo della pena
m'avean di costui gia letto il nome;
pero fu la risposta cosi plena

The words he used, together with his mode
Of torment, were sufficient to betray
His name, as thus my pointed answer showed

Dante, *Inferno*, Canto X

Listen, Marenales, do you understand (as fast as I understood that morning) why I asked for this identification to be done one person at a time? Well, when you came in and held your arms out for your handcuffs to be taken off, my secretary told me that *you* weren't the policeman. He'd been wounded in the chest (what am I telling you for, you were the one who shot him) and thought he was going to bleed to death on the back seat of the car. This gave him a rather special view of things, a sense of anger at having to leave this life, I can't explain it properly but I felt it at the time. He's a brave young man, that's obvious, and he was still conscious, but he was very upset, very upset. When you came in just now, he whispered to me, it wasn't him, that policeman had bulging eyes and his eyebrows were bushier. So I thought it best to suggest what I did, that he and the chauffeur should leave and we do the identification one by one. D'you see why? Because I'm their boss and I don't want to influence them. If he sees I'm so sure, my secretary might have second thoughts, he might change his mind, and I don't want that. This way there will be no problem. I'll say yes and my secretary

43

will say no. And the chauffeur? Ah, that's another story, it's rather comic. The chauffeur will say no without looking, no matter who they put in front of him. He told me so on our way to court. He has orders from his wife. Our son's at secondary school so you'll do nothing to provoke them, she said. So, no matter who they bring in, you don't recognize him, OK? He won't recognize you, he won't recognize anyone; he's protecting his son, from your people. It's one way of looking at things. So don't worry, I'll say yes, they'll say no and that will be that... And why will I say yes? Well, because I wasn't wounded, I wasn't pushed around much, and I wasn't even insulted. I was very cool, calm and collected, watching what was happening as if it were happening to someone else, like an observer, but an observer who has to remember afterwards, and I think that was mostly due to you, Marenales. Identifying you has nothing to do with hatred or vengeance, believe me, I'm not getting my own back, it is merely my duty to the court as a witness. I get no particular pleasure from it, but as soon as you put your arms out to have your handcuffs taken off (or even before that, as soon as you came into the room), I recognized you. Don't think I was influenced by the photos in the papers, I was in Germany for a few days when you were arrested and I can assure you I hardly saw any photos. No, it's not that, it has nothing to do with suggestion. Look, if I were a camera, I could record everything that happened that morning without a single distortion, a single blemish, or a single detail left out. And when you came in just now I said to myself, this is the one, and when you said a few words to the judge I knew, this is the one, and now you're

44

standing in front of me, I have to say it again, this is the one. Yes, go on, shake your head and smile, of course, I know you have to deny it. You have your game to play. But let me tell you once again, believe me, I'm not playing any game. I could just say it was your people who kidnapped me, one of you, any one of you, that you're all in it together as far as I'm concerned, and what does it matter if the phoney policeman in charge of the kidnapping, the one who gave all the orders, was you or any other of your comrades in jail or underground, who cares? And I'd feel I'd discharged my duty by saying it was your organization, or anybody, or nobody. But that's not the point, in fact it's just the opposite. I recognize your hands when you hold them out, your not very large but sinewy hands, pale, with veins like laces, a sculptor's hands or a stonemason's, as they say you say you are. I recognize your voice when you speak because although you didn't talk much during the kidnapping, you were in charge and you had to speak now and again to give orders, and you also spoke to me as you pushed me and afterwards, when my secretary tried to resist and you fired the only shot, a shot which grazed his chest but could have killed him. You'd left the chauffeur down on the coast road by then but still had not got rid of my secretary, and we were driving off when you (well, you say it wasn't you but the calm voice in which you deny it makes me certain it was), when you asked me if I knew what this was and I said a kidnapping and you repeated it because that wasn't the reply you wanted, so you asked me if I understood why you were doing this and I said for publicity I suppose and you said I see you've caught on straightaway, we can understand each other without too much discussion. And you said it in a voice which, how can I put it, in a voice which reassured me, a voice that made me feel that nothing would happen to me if I didn't bring it upon myself. And I think you actually said that, and you added that my secretary was stupid for interfering because you weren't even after him, and that was obvious when you left him on the pavement. So if I'm truthful (strange isn't it because you were the one who used your machine gun on my secretary), I have to admit it was *you* who made me feel calm, *you* who made me understand, in a few words, that nothing would happen to me if I didn't complicate things, if I took the situation in my stride. Not an easy thing to do under the circumstances, because just think, I leave my flat one day to get into my car and drive to a board meeting, and you all appear, and a couple of you grab the chauffeur and a couple of others immobilize my secretary, and you push me, not brutally but forcefully, and say something like come on, get in quick, and I had to absorb the whole picture in a flash; that you were dressed like police yet weren't my regular police bodyguard but (excuse the word, because it conflicts with the way you treated me) terrorists and that I wasn't going to the office but to God knows where, a kidnapping, an abduction, whatever... But this in itself made me feel that while you were in charge, nothing irreparably awful would happen to me, if I didn't ask for it, or course. You gave me that confidence, I don't know how, with a few words, with none at all, and thinking back I should be grateful to you... That's why I say that this is a judicial identification, not vengeance. It wouldn't make sense otherwise! You treated me well and

I knew that if I stayed calm nothing would happen. Believe me, Marenales, I am merely fulfilling a duty, a legal duty, not against you or anyone in particular. I am a witness, understand, that is my position. I am a witness and they've brought you here for me to say if I recognize you, if I think I might recognize you, and I have to say what I am absolutely sure of. A witness! It seems incredible that after everything that happened, I am reduced to a mere witness, reduced to saying whether you were the policeman or if it was someone else. Well, witness or victim, or 'passive subject' as lawyers put it, none of these words alter the situation. They asked me to come and if I hadn't wanted to, they'd have forced me to anyway, they asked me to come here and brought you from your cell and stood us face to face, and believed me, although you smile with a certain disdain and stand quietly in front of me, your lawyer and everyone else without saying a word, and although the operation was violent and unexpected and there was a wounded man bleeding down his unbuttoned shirt lying between us and you called him stupid and he was my secretary, in spite of that, in spite of *all* that, I must confess that I find this situation more violent (yes, don't deny it with your smile). Violent because you don't understand me, because you bestow on me evil intentions I don't have, because I seem to be breaking a gentleman's agreement which though not open was tacit from the moment you said that reaching an understanding with me was easy and there was no need for much discussion. After that came all the other things, but they were nothing to do with you, and that's another thing I'm sure of, you were never present again, although as you know very well the

47

people who looked after me in the room and brought me food and fetched the washbasin or gave me Plato's 'Republic' to read were all hooded and I couldn't tell them apart, but I'm certain you weren't among them...well, you know all that because you know how your organization works. Anyway, no one was ever rude or brutal and I've no particular grudge against any of them, but very clear duties arise out of the situation all the same, duties which become extremely unpleasant when now, on top of all those months, I have to face you and say, It Was You. You were the phoney policeman, you were in charge, you had the machine gun, you were the only one to speak to me, to face me calmly, to ask me a question, and when I answered didn't think it necessary to ask another... Well, you know all that as well... Look, I'll say it again, I don't think you were there while I was a prisoner because, although they had hoods on, they didn't disguise their voices and I'm certain I didn't hear your voice again. Yes, of course, you shake your head, you even move it in a certain way I recognize from the car journey. Of course I'd say no too if I was in your shoes, of course I understand...look, I was in the middle of the back seat, leaning a bit backwards with my chin up because my secretary's drooping head was slumped on my chest so that, with a little help from your shoulder, I was sort of propping him up until (as soon as it was clear nobody was following us) they drew in to the curb and slid my secretary out, leaving him there, sitting or rather hunched over. Then they drove off again, and it was then, then, that you spoke to me again and warned me you were going to give me an injection, just to send me to sleep, again you made me feel calm, again

48

you assured me nothing would happen. Look, Marenales, just turn your profile a minute, yes, like that...listen, now I'll tell you something else. I remember your sideburns, the hair at the bottom where they start growing, the first threads of hair turning grey, grey strands running inwards, towards the ear...I saw those hairs slightly flattened with sweat as the car drove off and you took your cap off and passed your left hand over your head, to cool yourself down or calm yourself, you who made others feel so calm. And then my secretary insulted you, said something nasty like he'd come looking for you and kill you, and now he's the one who in a minute will tell you to your face that you weren't the one, that that policeman had bulging eyes and bushier eyebrows, people's memories are like that, the memory of hate which some think so blindly infallible, so obvious, so unimpeachable, you know, all that stuff...but you took no notice, I think both you and I knew that he wasn't going to die if a few minutes after he'd been shot he was still talking, even though his voice was different, at least I knew the guy wasn't going to die, because of the sense of calm you transmitted. I thought it good that you didn't answer his insults. Then, across the boy's head, I looked over at you and saw your face silhouetted against the window pane to my right, and I saw the curve of your forehead and the outline of your nose, not so I'd remember it, not so I could talk about it now, I just looked that's all, to check that you wouldn't shoot the boy again, because I don't think you had the machine gun in your right hand any more but down by your side, between you and the door, yes, yes, that's it because you picked it up again after you opened the door to let my secretary slide out onto the pavement. I looked at your face, there was no shadow over it now that your cap was on your knees and the hand that had stroked your hair had dropped, and I could study you at close range and you didn't care. You didn't care then and you wouldn't have cared before. I saw the sweat from the cap on your temples and saw your forehead and your flattened hair and I'm absolutely certain that you weren't wearing make-up or any disguise, you were just like you are now, as I see you now, except that perhaps I was closer to you, the details were more finely etched or, perhaps because of me, because of the extraordinary circumstances, I saw them more intensely, more intensely in a visual not a nervous sense because you know I was emotionally calm and was taking everything in. I think it's all very clear. You shake your head again and smile with amiable disdain, if I can call it that, because you have to play your part, as I do mine, but deep down your heart's not really in it. Why do I say this? If you didn't conceal your features or hide your face with your cap, it's because there are no half measures in your life, you play to win or lose, no excuses made...that's why you didn't even make me look the other way, when you realized I was studying you. Either you took part in operations quite openly, cocking a snook at the police, your traditional caution lying only in not looking too much like your old photo with the big moustache (you'd shaved it off), or you got caught and then nothing mattered. Being in charge of my kidnapping or not would not alter your fate when the chips were down...and so, in your heart, you think that everything happening now is ridiculous and maybe you're right, and that's why you smile and look round at your lawyer and the judge, as if the whole situation (I can't explain it very well, but I feel it) as if, well, as if the whole situation made you feel sad, sad and sorry and even ashamed. I feel it too, the shame of senseless situations. Yes, but you feel pity for the situation as a whole and for all of us in this room, not only for me and you, ah, no, least of all for yourself, because you're the master of the situation again, master of your silence, master of your sardonic smile. Yes, your role is the easiest, once again it is easier than mine, you do it by shaking your head in a no, and when I ask you to show me your profile you do it mockingly, yes, yes, mockingly behind your polite exterior, as if you're responding indulgently to the whims of a child, as if it were all a ceremony, a ritual act which didn't concern you but which, how shall I put it, you have to go along with and placate me for a while, as if it were the price for reneging on an agreement, the agreement we made with so little discussion. Look, you hadn't given me the injection by then, you hadn't thrown my secretary out, none of that had happened yet when I looked across and saw your profile against the window, your features at rest, just as they are now, but without the slight smirk on your lips and eyes, although that makes no difference, in fact I'd almost say it reinforces the impression that they are the same lips, the same eyes, just as it is the same forehead, the same sideburns, the same grey hairs and the same hands...and looking at you now I could almost imagine the wounded man's words...I'll come looking for you, I swear I'll kill you, you bastard, he was saying, and you decided to ignore him although you knew they weren't the insults of a dying man but of someone who was going to be OK, of someone who will come into this room in a minute and say... So there's a moral in this story, a moral that goes something like this, it's better to wound a man than reassure him, because he'll come and say no, he'll choose another photo in the police files (that guy Amodio I think) rather than your face of that morning here in front of him. Yes, and I also remember your only moment of anger, when the driver of the car (I only saw the back of his neck) went the wrong way and a truck followed us for a while and you lost your temper and said stupid idiot, didn't I tell you where to turn off? Well, I don't know, you say you would never call a comrade an idiot and that may be true, but your anger got the better of you momentarily then and you said it, yes you did, I remember your words even more clearly than my secretary's. You said it but you calmed down afterwards because a Volkswagen, probably one of yours, drew up almost alongside and then slotted in behind us blocking the truck, and we lost sight of it, and that's when you took your cap off and wiped away any traces of irritation, of anger. Oh yes, I'm absolutely certain, I saw your face so close up, your left sideburn, the eye on this side, the curve of your forehead, the outline of your nose, your hairline, no doubt about it, it was you. I wish you no harm, prison lies between you and me now, and I've no reason for pushing you any further towards the abyss than you already are, not even with just the right amount of force for you to feel the urgency, just as you pushed me into the car that day, no, not even that. You'll say, what urgency do I have? Because you made me believe nothing would happen to me and you repeated it when you told me I was getting an injec-

tion, just to make me sleep, and that's all... And I think
your voice encouraged the easy, speedy agreement you
predicted, I didn't even have time to reply before the man
on my left made me slip my arm out of my jacket, roll
up my sleeve, and with the care one would receive in a
hospital, no more no less, began rubbing my arm with
a little piece of cotton wool soaked in alcohol as he produced the needle. I refused to look at my arm, at my nurse,
I thought I'd go to sleep straightaway, you had said I
would, and I preferred to keep looking at you, to look at
you looking straight ahead. So let me tell you this, I do
not, I could not, even if I wanted to, have any doubt at
all, and I don't even know, Marenales, if I would want
to have any doubt. I once read that love is a long patient
affair, well, I can tell you now that recognizing a man,
after what you and I experienced in that car that morning, is a long detailed affair, a long detailed act of
remembering, a detailed act of remembrance...an act of
remembrance, not of *trying* to remember, because I have
no trouble remembering you, you still float in front of me
like a transparent profile which never merges with any
of my other memories of those days (my captivity as the
papers called it). Those memories are more conflictive,
muddled, if I think about what I ate, what I read, what
I said, if I want to concentrate on any one of the various
hoods that took turns round by bed, or the chair where
they sometimes let me sit, yes all that can be painful and
confusing and I think, I'm sure, that you weren't there.
Your people divide things up, that's what they say anyway,
you share out the tasks and I think yours was finished and
you didn't appear again. But the memory of that morn-

53

ing, until the injection left me unconscious, is of a total and, I'd even say radiant, clarity. It doesn't matter, the other two will say no, you weren't there, it was somebody else, it was nobody. And it's better that way, that's why I made them leave before I started talking, so that I wouldn't influence them. It's better that way, *I* fulfill my duty and *you* can't accuse me of wanting revenge, so long afterwards, or wanting to hurt you, or pushing you back further into your cell. That's not the point, it's not that at all. I have to say what I remember, I can't deny a part of my life, such an important part! And that's why I say without a shadow of doubt, not because we're facing the judge here but because we face a kind of Supreme Judge we may think or believe exists or does not exist, I say without hate, animosity, bitterness or satisfaction, I know you, Marenales, believe me, I know you...

The Adviser (II)

...purgando la caligine del mondo

...purging away the tarnish of the world

Dante, *Purgatory*, Canto XI

Pilcomayo Street runs parallel to the coast road. Where it crosses Ytu Street two blocks to the east, it looks suddenly out over a vista of the river. From up on that cornice on calm clear days, the sea-like river seems to rock the glittering white horses, especially at eight in the morning when the sun crowns the hump of Punta Gorda. From there too the treacherous east wind blows when a storm is brewing. But from the intersection of Pilcomayo Street and Gallinal, the sea in the distance seems less agitated and the turmoil is all in the vortex on the rocks below. From this vantage point, the road descends abruptly to the beach at Playa Honda. It dives two hundred yards and the sea rises to meet it at a tangent, reaching up with wild gasping breath, the horizon folding like a screen against the bare windswept seafront with its solitary threadbare palm trees, housefronts corroded by the relentless brine, ruined window latches, and blinds in tatters. Winds torn from grey skies, large clouds deformed by blizzards, descend and threaten with their brown or leaden reflection on the waves.

Orinoco, Aconcagua, Pilcomayo, streets like terraces on a steep mountainside. America is present only in the names, not in mountains, tropics, jungle or snow. From his cornice on that flight of terraces, the adviser may feel protected by the gale which is laundering the horizon, purging away the tarnish of the world. Yes, but there in his little garden, is he not himself the canker?

His hygienic operations on wounded bodies, the professional precision of his joyless language, his rule of doing only the absolutely necessary, all this tallies with the smooth unencumbered drive from Gallinal and Pilcomayo down behind the gasoline station, to Playa Honda in Malvin, to the breakwaters and the sea. Yes, but if he were the tarnish of the world, others could be watching him, waiting for him. They could ambush him, overpower him, transfer him from his embassy car to a stolen station wagon. They could kidnap him. And at eight o'clock on a winter's morning, on that freezing corner with not a bus in sight, it would be unlikely that there would be any passersby to act as witnesses, unlikely that anyone would be lying in the sun like lizards at that hour of the day and season of the year.

The deed is quicker than the telling of it. In the deserted early hours the adviser's car is intercepted, he is made to switch cars, with just a little force but no superfluous words. At Pilcomayo and Gallinal, no one runs out in their shirtsleeves to help because they heard a couple of shouts at eight in the morning, a mere month and a few days away from the longest night of the year. They push him across to the station wagon and throw him on the floor, he offers token resistance so that he will not reproach himself afterwards for being passive, until he is convinced that things will take their course whether he struggles or not. He opts for dignity. He falls to the floor, someone's shoe on his neck holds him where he falls. Someone insults him and another hothead—a kidnapper without the aplomb of the kidnapped—fires a shot which scrapes the nape of his neck.

56

The others shout rebukes for the firing. They give him some crude first aid, they will see he gets proper medical care later on and his assailant will be punished. It is morning, July 31, 1970. When the adviser feels the blood burning on his neck—the actual blood rather than the burning—he thinks, he must have thought, that this is his last morning and, two blocks from the sea, his very last moment. The dignity he opted for has one tiny flaw; he mumbles an oath in English, in the tone of voice used for an oath but careful not to let the others know it is an oath rather than a dark sob, entrusting himself to God in a language they hate. The station wagon speeds away, there is hardly a vehicle in sight. The fat man is on the floor, bleeding through his torn shirt, suddenly unencumbered by his tie (an arm goes down to take it off—is it humane relief or room for another bullet?).

At the adviser's house, no one looks out or sees him disappear, no one immediately alerts the police. They know that today he is going to Centenario Avenue, not very close by. Down on the station wagon's metal floor, the fat man begins to realize that while he might have died from that one senseless shot, there is no danger of another one. It makes no sense to kill him before he talks, before they bargain and put a price on his head. He is worth something, he may be worth a lot.

They put a hood over his head, and then cover his body with a sack. Fifteen minutes go by. He can guess the time without looking at his left wrist. The slight noise of a latch, the station wagon stopping, then slowly starting again, tells him they have gone through a door and into an enclosed space. They heave him out of the car and help him climb a flight of stairs. They make him sit down, with his hood still on. Several minutes go by, then a man wearing a mask rips the fat man's shirt collar a bit more, not violently though, takes his hood off and observes him. The fat man looks at him, they look at each other.

'I'm a doctor,' says the man with the mask. 'The bullet only grazed you. You're in no danger.' He asks if his anti-tetanus injection is still valid but gives him another dose just in case. He dresses the wound. The adviser lets him do it without a word. In his work he is used to accepting authority unquestioningly. The doctor is that authority now, so he feels at ease with him and relaxes. He examines him carefully and checks his blood pressure. They give him a white shirt to replace the one he was wearing and a grey sweater instead of his jacket. There is no trace of blood on his body, nor his clothes. He is given a sedative which he apparently does not need but swallows anyway. They tell him he has an hour to rest and will then be inter-rogated. He listens, nods, but asks no questions. He has long since understood whose hands he is in. There is no need to add anything.

'We'll be putting out a communiqué about your cap-ture in an hour.'

He inclines his head in a ceremonious, almost courtly, gesture. He is a serious man, he makes no concessions, so he does not seem to expect any. Before he lies down to rest on a bunk not nearly so narrow as the one in his office, he realizes that they are going to put a hood on him again; he does not object.

'Do you know why we've kidnapped you?'

'I suppose it must be connected with my work as an

adviser for the Agency for International Development.'

'What work is that?'

'We operate under the terms of an aid and assistance agreement between the United States government and your government. AID has five divisions and I belong to the Public Security section.'

'Name the other four.'

'Education, Agriculture, Finance, and Planning. The Public Security division, to which I belong, is the most recent...'

'In terms of penetration, are your department's objectives military?'

'No, not specifically military. The mission is technical assistance. I wouldn't associate it with any kind of penetration. In fact, the AID fifth division has taken on board criticism provoked by the activities of our military missions. It's something quite different.'

'How is it different?'

'It specializes in advising on the newest techniques...'

'Which techniques?'

'Techniques and systems for the police.'

'Where have you taught them previously?'

'First in the United States. People come there for training, Iranians, Africans, that sort of people...'

'Do they learn much?'

'They can't learn everything, because every society is different. The important thing is that they learn the newest and best ways of doing things...'

'What things? Things you learned in Vietnam?'

(He does not reply.)

'You used to be a chief of police. Where was that?'

'In Indiana.'

'Is Indiana a big place?'

'It has four million inhabitants. But I was a police chief in Richmond, a city with only fifty thousand inhabitants.'

'Was the work difficult?'

'It was a job like any other, like being a teacher or a street sweeper. Cities need lots of jobs done and somebody has to do them. Some people work in factories, others do outdoor jobs. Police work is a bit different, quite a lot different sometimes. In a city like Richmond it wasn't too bad.'

'When did you stop doing it?'

'In 1960, ten years ago.'

'And now...is your work different?'

'Yes, completely different, now I work *for* the police.'

'And in Brazil? What did you do in Brazil?'

'I was an adviser...I advised the Military Police.'

'After 1964?'

'Yes, afterwards, later on. I worked in the interior of Brazil, training the Brazilian police force. We try to find the quietest way of doing things, the best way. For them, and for everyone else. So that their work is more in tune with ours. Better use of equipment, more careful methods.'

'All this...was it done in the jungle?'

'No, it wasn't that kind of work.'

'All right, what can you tell us about the CIA?'

'Well, you won't believe me, but that doesn't bother me...how can I convince you that I have nothing, absolutely nothing, to do with the CIA? Nothing at all.'

'And with the FBI?'

'Ah yes, I know a lot about the FBI. I graduated from

the FBI Academy. I know everything, well, not everything but I *do* know a lot about the FBI.'

'What is the connection between the FBI and other divisions?'

'Well, I know all I do about the FBI because it's a very open organization. It has information divisions and investigation divisions and agents in every state of the United States who work closely with the police departments. But the FBI can only act in certain cases. For instance, if a thief steals two or three thousand dollars (it has to be above a certain sum) and escapes to another state, he comes under federal jurisdiction. It has nothing to do with protecting people or the secret service.'

'How can you say you know nothing about the CIA? You must know something...'

'Well, all I know is that the CIA is the same as similar organizations all countries have. How the CIA operates internally I don't know. I'm very sorry, but I don't know anything. I'm being quite truthful...though I don't suppose you'll believe me.'

'You must know something.'

'Well, I'll tell you about my division. I know nothing about anything else.'

'And if there *is* something else?'

'I swear I know nothing.'

'Look, you know we have our own CIA, and it's quite good.'

'Yes, I'm sure it is.'

'We both know, we're both intelligent enough to know that each has his own intelligence gathering system.'

'Yes, I know, but I'm not a part of ours. I'm not sure

you believe me...'

'Come off it... What about when you worked with the Military Police in Brazil? What connection did you have with the DOPS, the Department of Public and Social Order?'

'With the DOPS? Ah, well, I didn't know much about the DOPS in those days. That's the political police, isn't it? I think one of the problems with the DOPS is that they are policemen appointed because of their politics. The Military Police's training is military. I didn't have much to do with the DOPS.'

'But I believe the Military Police are trained in anti-guerrilla tactics. Isn't that their speciality?'

'We didn't do that in those days. The problem wasn't with the guerrillas. We trained them to control strikes, labour unrest and even demonstrations. We taught them humane methods, how not to hurt people if it could possibly be avoided...but also how to be tough if need be. We read them manuals on interrogation and special techniques. It's all very interesting.'

'Yes, life's cheaper in Brazil than in Uruguay. But they torture here too. Didn't you know that? Fleury, the head of the Brazilian Death Squad, was here doing some training four or five months ago.'

'Really?'

'What opinion have you formed of the Uruguayan government since you've been here?'

'I don't know the President. I haven't met many people really. Just the ones I deal with in my job advising the police, no one else.'

'And the Minister of the Interior?'

'Yes, I've met the General.'

'And what did you think of him?'

'I don't think he's very able.'

'We're sending our terms to the government for them to consider. We're demanding that all our *compañeros* in prison be released and put on a plane to Peru or Algiers. What's your opinion?'

'Nothing. I have no opinion.'

'I mean, how d'you think the government will react?'

'About me?'

'Yes, you and the other prisoners we took this morning.'

'I don't know them.'

'One is the Brazilian Consul.'

'Yes, I've heard someone you call Consul, but I haven't seen him. He seems to shout more than I do, and he complains more...' (He laughs.)

'What do you think they'll do?'

'I don't know. I hope they'll bargain with you.'

'And your government? What will it do?'

'I can't answer that either, but I trust they'll talk to the Uruguayan government and ask them to intercede. But I don't know what they can do.'

'Is there any agreement? What is it?'

'I've no idea.'

'Do you think they'll put pressure on?'

'I hope so, and I think they will. They've done so in other countries.'

'Yes, that's true.'

'How long will it take?' The adviser asks a question for the first time. 'Do you know?'

'That's not up to us. Everything has been prepared to

keep you here for months, but we hope it won't take that long.'

'That will be best for everyone. I hope so.'

'Tell me, how many children do you have?'

'Nine, four boys and five girls.'

'Any of them here?'

'Four are here. So is my wife.'

'If everything goes well and you are freed, will you retire?'

'If I see my family again, I'll go back to the U.S. as soon as possible.'

Meadows, local kids
playing baseball, manicured
green lawns of a faraway
summer in Richmond.
Will the fat man fit in?
Or will a retired expert in horror
bring discord to the scene?

The Adviser (III)

Lo fei giubetto a me delle mie case

I made my own house my scaffold

Dante, *Inferno*, Canto XII

When the house in Malvin Nuevo where members of the guerrilla high command were meeting was captured at noon on Saturday the 8th, many people thought that the government had won the battle of its own intransigence. It had repeatedly stated in the newspapers that it would not negotiate with terrorists. Meanwhile the hours ticked by and patrols, armed to the teeth, searched the University Hospital convinced that it was the source of all evil and that the prisoners were being kept there. In the ideology of repression, the University and the 'Orga' were one and the same thing. But the prisoners were not in the hospital, neither were they in the churches which were often searched, even during religious services. The hours ticked by. They kept on ticking by, until Saturday the 8th when the 'forces of order' surrounded the villa in Almería and arrested the group meeting there: Sendic, Bidegain Greissing, Candán Grajales, Luis Martínez Platero, and others. Some people thought this surprise attack would end the business of the three kidnap victims—the adviser, Dias Gomide the Consul, and Fly the agronomist. Did the adviser in his secret hideout (if he knew, that is) agree with them?

It is Saturday, the 8th. Sendic is taken to Police Headquarters and, invoking the Geneva Convention, declares himself a prisoner of war. He denies knowing the whereabouts of the prisoners and adds, 'The lives of these

65

hostages no longer depend on me.' It is almost certain the adviser never knew this, he never even had the chance to guess. The recorded tapes, left in the toilets of certain cafés, are by now common knowledge all over Montevideo. Could he have done anything, could he have advised them even if he had known? Surely not. He advises on interrogation techniques, not on problems of state. The government declares, categorically, that it will not negotiate with common criminals. Now that it has its hands on some of them, it can put pressure on. But unfortunately there is so little time and somebody, somebody with a lot of imagination, suddenly suggests drug serums. The life of the adviser, he reckons, may depend on injecting one of the prisoners and making him talk. The deadline runs out at noon on Sunday, the 9th. Too much time has passed, it is already the 8th. The adviser is a problem of international relations, of possible government-to-government pressure. There is no special hour-glass for him and if there were, there would be very little sand left in it. And if arrogance enlightens, the adviser could be in even more danger now; a new high command has taken over, it faces a new challenge. Should it go ahead with a pending operation now that the original decision-makers have been arrested? This kidnap deadline will be the first to run out, the one which will set the precedent for all future operations. They could always say, of course, that the 'Orga' has a life of its own, that it does not matter how many prisoners are taken or how many new people take over the leadership. Everything goes on as before, with an ultimatum pending, as if nothing new had happened after the deadline was set. But that would be untrue, pure fiction; the decisions of a guerrilla organization have to be flexible, while there is a chance to change them, rework them, correct them, confirm or refute them, there is no last word on the subject. That is how guerrilla organizations are...swift and sinuous.

'For land, with Sendic.' Had the adviser heard this slogan? Did it take on a more powerful meaning for him after Sendic was taken to jail? From his cell, Sendic says he does not know where the adviser is and denies responsibility for him. From his place of detention, the adviser does not know of Sendic's whereabouts. This symmetry imposes its own reality, its own routine; nothing moves, except the hands of the clock. Station CX6 plays classical music, but has still not taken the decision to broadcast communiqués as the situation changes throughout the day. That is why they let the adviser lie on his bunk listening to Brahms. CX6 booms out in a world of frozen programs, in which neither he nor they are news; time with music, but no substance.

In the early hours of Sunday the 9th, the adviser learned that they had decided to dye his hair, they wanted to change it from grey to blonde.

'What for?' he asked.

'In case we have to take you somewhere,' came the reply.

'Take me where?'

'Just in case we have to take you somewhere,' the guard repeated curtly.

He imagined this had something to do with his freedom, his eventual ransom. But no one said anything as they cut his hair in a straight line across the back of his neck, like people condemned to the guillotine awaiting execution. At least they won't behead me, he must have thought. The guillotine did not figure in the repertoire of possible deaths for him, he could be sure of that. Take him where? Nobody told him. The two hooded barbers began to dye his hair; he wouldn't see it when it was finished, there were none of the hand or wall mirrors you get in hairdresser's. The cutting, the dyeing, were part of a mystery, a mystery that might include a journey, a disguise, elaborate ceremonial forms of his own life. A prisoner, without news, he had no reasonable alternative but to let them have their way. He could get no information out of any of them, his usual refined methods of doing it were no use to him here. He felt the freshness of the lotion, and the professional patience of hands that combed sideburns cut off at the earlobes and stripped his neck with a razor as they would a cock. If the denouement of the mystery was his freedom, Indiana would see him with his hat down around his ears.

But Indiana did not see him. The journalists, with their proverbial dog-like instinct for smelling death, began getting excited from Sunday morning onwards. At three in the afternoon the football match would start and, even though Peñarol and Nacional were not playing, the radios would be droning on with other subjects, leaving news of the adviser alone for three or four hours.

On Sunday the 9th, Dr. Payssé Reyes sent the following letter to *El País*. It was published on Monday the 10th, the very day the adviser's body was found in a street in the Puerto Rico district:

Payssé Reyes: 'My life and my liberty for their freedom.'

Dr. Payssé Reyes, it said, offered his person, his freedom and his life, in exchange for the foreigners kidnapped by subversive elements. Yesterday he sent the media a signed communiqué containing the following words: 'The kidnapping of foreign citizens compromises our most sacred national interests and could affect our sovereignty. No Uruguayan has the right to do that.

'National divisions, no matter how deep, must be solved internally, without encouraging or provoking foreign interference.

'For this reason, and moved only by a profound sense of nationalism and a desire to preserve our friendship with the peoples of Brazil and the United States, I offer my person, my freedom and my life, in exchange for the freedom of the three prisoners. Those who adhere to an ideology which is alien to me and see violence as the solution to our national conflicts could subsequently negotiate my fate with whomsoever they consider appropriate, in accordance with their own consciences. Each one will shoulder his own responsibility.

'I put my honour at stake and hereby declare that I will go to any place of their choosing and hand myself over, advising no other party of anything.'

(signed) Hector Payssé Reyes'

Strange things happen. Years ago, a Uruguayan senator was mugged in Harlem, the black area of New York. His gold watch was stolen and he was beaten up. Now, moved by a profound nationalism, and a desire to preserve our friendship with the people of the USA, Dr. Payssé Reyes announces that he is prepared to go to wherever the kidnappers indicate, offer his person, his freedom, and his life, and in so doing put his honour at stake. Did he wait by the phone (9-64-76) all afternoon and night for his offer to be accepted? The message, however, was not published in time and no one negotiates dead bodies over the phone.

At noon on Sunday a radio announcer began interviewing people in the street. How could we save the adviser's life? One woman suggested a referendum because that was how we always resolve important matters in our democratic system. This radio flash was not broadcast on station CX6, however, so the adviser was not aware that a referendum had been suggested, a vote for his life or death.

Sunday the 9th, one in the afternoon. A pompous gentleman arrives at his residence in Suárez Avenue, looks at the people gathered there and, addressing himself to one in particular, says: 'Tito brought me some black last night' (and he didn't mean rum but Johnny Walker Black Label). 'Shall we open it?'

The Minister of Defence, General César Borba, had pre-empted him, albeit with a lesser known brand, and was drinking scotch as if it were beer. At the second glass, he began to have ideas, most of them dreadful. There were two hours to go before the match started. Under the circumstances, would it be all right for a member of the government to go to the stadium? Nobody wanted to advance an opinion.

There is a film which would have us believe that at that very moment votes were being collected in cafés, on street corners, while asking for a light, everyday encounters in crowded weekend streets, random meetings on the back seats of buses, or in cinema entrances. It looks very picturesque in the film, but it is not the truth. At noon on

Sunday the 9th, the deadline is up. All that remains is to give the order and carry it out. There is no time to rush round the city collecting votes. Contrary to what the woman in the street might think, there is no point having a referendum on the adviser's future, not for the people, not for the 'Orga'.

During Sunday night, his captors told him to get ready to leave. They were leaving, that's all they said. They handed him a grey plastic raincoat, under which he wore only a T-shirt and a pair of trousers. They helped him dress. Then they put his arms behind his back and tied his wrists with home-made handcuffs. Where were they going? Nobody answered. They were changing hideouts, that was the easiest thing to believe . Perhaps that hideout had become suspect and they needed to change it. Had something happened that afternoon? He was standing, with his raincoat collar turned up, his wrists tied. He no longer spoke, convinced as he was now of the futility of questions. No longer a mouth, only two large eyes in a face. A long car, an old model, painted grey or light blue with metallic glints, filled the small garage (the weak light from a single bulb meant he could not see it properly); men who no longer hid their faces (a slight twitching of the advisor's lip showed he did not like that) surrounded him and minutes later made him get in the car. It was established afterwards that the car in question was a 1948 Buick convertible, number plate 241-692, stolen the night before. It was also established later that the *nom de guerre* of the driver was Francisco (a couple of years later a prisoner would see his corpse tied to a chair with leather thongs in a small workshop of an army barracks). Seated to Francisco's right was Alejandro. In the back seat (the convertible wasn't very roomy) sat the adviser and a small quiet man whose eyes never left his face, as if he was afraid that the slightest distraction might allow the prisoner to escape. As the four men settled themselves in the car, nobody spoke. It transpired later on that unbeknown to the prisoner, Octavio had handed Carlos ('the Galician'), the smaller man seated to the adviser's right, a .38 revolver. This the Galician concealed in his clothing. Octavio and Marcos, seeing them off with their faces also uncovered now, were obviously in charge of the trip. The other three in their seats, and Francisco at the wheel, were only following orders given by people who, as the car drove off, were very far away.

There in the car, arms tied behind his back and gagged with a long knitted bandage, the adviser seems totally surrendered to his fate. When will he have realized, deep down inside, that he has been left totally alone? When will he admit to himself that he is abandoned and dead, dead more than alive? Perhaps he already knows but he does not let it show, that is the last rule: do not let the enemy know. They might notice it but *he* will not tell them. If he did, they could not really be surprised, although they might pretend they were. Not to let the enemy know for reasons of elementary logic. Better still, if they have doubts, let them keep them. He can no longer doubt, but he gains nothing by showing his hand. It would only give them grounds for triumph, for seeking absolution, and he would never grant that. If he said, 'They have abandoned me, you have no choice but to kill me,' that would be like committing suicide. He doesn't want that. If he said, 'My people have abandoned me now,' he would dispell the air of desperate nobility from this final moment. Nothing is his own any more, his life, his work condemn him. Christ, abandoned on the cross, could appeal to God. *He* can appeal only to Reasons of State, somewhat less attractive. Even less so if, when you go into details, those Reasons of State could have dirty implications, or not very elegant, at least. So in the end he remains silent, to die alone, one of the loneliest in the history of mankind. Even in ritual ceremonies, when people go to their death, they are thanked for services rendered. The fat man dies, yet who would mention the cause for which he is dying? Its ugliness is reflected in his payment. Be glad that at the moment of truth, the moment of pity, that ugliness is turned to silence. It cannot do more than that. He might spare a thought for the ones who will never abandon him, his wife, his children, because his job is nothing to do with their love for him. But unfortunately they do not count right now, they do not decide his fate. The ones who decide, the main protagonists, are the ones who have decided to turn the page. Finis. The garage door opens slowly behind the Buick whose engine has been running for some time. It backs out carefully into the depths of the night.

What time is it? There, in that place, time has no meaning. And space leaves no mark behind the dirty scratched windows. The adviser is not wearing a watch. Anyway he will never look at his wrist again. It is impossible to know if anyone is following their route (as later it turned out), moving from Centenario Avenue to the deep hollows of Puerto Rico, along the notorious bank of the Union, an area of muggers and destitutes, not the usual intinerary for a foreigner. For that particular gagged foreigner there is nothing but darkness and the back of Francisco's head which never turns round but concentrates on driving through those godforsaken parts. Towards another prison perhaps? One which only Francisco knows. The Buick slips through the impenetrable streets, and the silence. The adviser looks at his smaller guard, impassive at his side, but the Galician is no longer so attentive. No chance of escape now.

A few minutes more and the Buick which was never going very fast, slowed down even further. Have they arrived? It was then that Alejandro seated alongside the driver said, 'Time for a smoke.' It was the password, the order, but the adviser did not even have time to realize it. A shot exploded at his right temple, and he fell against the door. Another shot, this time near his ear. Like stone on stone, a third shot pierced his back. When the Galician finally leaned over to examine him in his slumped position and shot him for the fourth time in the chest, the adviser was no more.

The Buick came to a complete stop and the three men got out. The adviser's face sank to the floor in the gap between the two rows of seats as if he had finally succumbed to the weight of his dyed blond head. His legs were doubled up under his body but he did not disappear into the gap between the seat altogether because he was fat and the gap narrow. It was dawn. No doubt about that. They knew it as soon as they got out of the car and the cold of the early August morning hit them. A motor cycle and another old car drove up. There was no one else around. Just themselves and their 'logistic support' (in the jargon of the war), one on the motorcycle, two in the escort car. They got in. As it stopped for a moment to cover the car's retreat, the man riding pillion on the motorbike glanced up at the name of the street written on a mutilated sign hanging from a lamp-post on the corner: Lucas Moreno Street.

A book published in Spain around 1966 had this to say about Lucas Moreno Street: '...but this name is more likely to appear in the crime section of the newspapers than on the social pages. The hero of the Independence War has ended up in a slum which every so often provides crimes, hideouts, secret cemeteries, for a Montevideo which prefers to ignore it.'

On the morning of Monday, August 10th, 1970, a patrol car discovers the adviser's corpse there in that street, inside an abandoned car. The name Puerto Rico, neighbourhood of soldiers and tramps, was cabled to the whole world because of the death of an AID officer. The radiophotos showed the stolen mournful old 1948 Buick, number plate 241-692, a dark puddle of water under the radiator from water seeping out at night and from old age, and another dark puddle beside the left-hand rear door from the adviser's blood leaking through the floor. Other photos concentrated on the dyed blonde head, the gag round the lips to the back of the neck, and the hands handcuffed behind the back of the body, tucked up inside the car in a foetal position. And in the background, shots of the neighbourhood, eucalyptus trees, shots of wood and corrugated iron, and the local inhabitants enjoying the fleeting glory of their notoriety.

Radio interviewer—And you, madam, didn't you notice that big car parked over there all night?

Woman—Yes, I get up very early and I saw it, but I said to myself 'some couple...'

Radio interviewer—'What about you, Sir? Has anything like this ever happened before?

Man—Well, not exactly the same. But this is Avellaneda, it's a very tough neighbourhood, you wouldn't believe the things that happen here...

Bystander—Avellaneda? This is Puerto Rico. It's famous!

Other radio stations prefer the theme 'Terrorism and Democracy'... Senator Cigliutti, a secondary school history teacher, is indignant, 'Even in the Middle Ages, people weren't shot like this!'

On January 21st, 1969, a municipal worker, Arturo Recalde, was shot in the back by Colonel Cándido Rodríguez during a union demonstration. The Colonel said it was self-defence, but a photo published by the newspaper *Epoca* showed the worker walking away with his back to the camera at the very second he was shot and the Colonel taking aim, his arm outstretched, just by the gates of the Foreign Office. The Colonel turned the tables and accused the court that was trying him of being Communist. He was free at the beginning of August, 1970, in time to declare on the radio, 'This is a shameful murder...'

Press, television, speeches. That same afternoon, Monday the 10th, television viewers form long lines in the drizzle of a maritime winter to mount the steps of the Embassy where the adviser will lie in state. Wreaths, albums

76

(another line to sign at a stated time), flowers, collective grief. Yes, grief and shame. A radio announcer sobs, assumes the country's shame, and mournfully addressing the dead man, exclaims several times, 'Forgive us, forgive us, forgive us!'

Will Dr. Payssé sign the album, will his memory register the exact moment on his second gold watch? The government offers a million pesos for information leading to the murderers and promises total discretion. Someone suggests naming a street after the dead man. (Will General Lucas Moreno, soldier in Oribe's army and minister in the Cerrito government be erased from the mutilated street sign?) Someone else suggests printing stamps with the adviser's profile. A third suggestion wants him declared a 'Martyr of America'. A fourth wants to reinstate the death penalty, retroactively ('Yes, but the Constitution forbids the death penalty.' 'Bah, it can be changed.') A day later, an enormous USAF plane (Pantheon) arrives to take the body back to the USA, an unknown corpse in the Richmond fields. Once again, television, funereal music, the coffin wrapped in 13 stripes and 48 stars (or 49 by now, or 50). When the coffin is carried to the plane on the shoulders of the marines, soldiers salute, women cry at the airport railings, a widow in exaggerated mourning clothes, the pale face of an orphaned child, Senator Echegoyen with his hat in hand, reverent ministers, almost prostrate deputies, flags at half-mast, the promise that our little ambassador will be in Washington to receive the coffin, the inadmissable backwardness of a country unable to film it, record it, and cry it in technicolour: underdevelopment. This is a small country, gentlemen, but it has always been an honest one.

The majestic bug revs up, takes off, once airborne swallows the landing carriage, and disappears out of sight over the military salutes, the tears, and the funereal clarion call of a bugle. 'I made my own house my scaffold.' Yes, he did. Then he climbed it. We all did.

Candelabra

Oscura e profonda era e nebulosa
tanto che perfica lo viso a fondo
io non vi dercernea alcuna cosa.

Deep, dense, and by no faintest glimmer lit
It lay, and though I strained my sight to find
Bottom, not one thing could I see in it

Dante, *Inferno*, Canto IV

Seated on the mattress, the writing pad on her knees, she writes. She is alone. They have suffered in different places. In different parts of the prison and the body. She is alone. She writes. There is nothing to tell, this evening they will collect the letters. He does not write to her, nor she to him. Would they reproach each other, argue about who was to blame (they both would say they were), say they loved each other? So they do not write. They write to different relatives. Each one to their own. She begs them not to bring photos of him, tortured letters from him, phrases, fragments memorized (distorted?) from his letters to his relatives. No, no please, don't. She prefers to remember him as he was, happy, forthright, witty, not the bearded wreck she said goodbye to in the military courtroom, whom she saw for a moment in the prison yard and passed as she might have passed a perfect stranger in the metro or in the street. No, not like that. She doesn't want his letters, his anecdotes, or his photograph. She could not bear it. Yesterday was their wedding anniversary. Sitting on the mattress, writing pad on her knees, she writes.

Nothing, nothing happens. They do not let anything happen. No books, no handicrafts, no uncensored letters. Nothing. Sometimes, to break the emptiness, she invents a chair, and furnishes that emptiness with it, a visitor sits there, and they talk. A childhood friend, lost many years ago. Her mother. They talk. No one interrupts the conversation, between those bare walls. They don't even interrupt this letter. It is noon, is it noon? No one interrupts, time does not stop, it flows by itself, there is only one time. Seated on the mattress, writing pad on her knees, she prefers not to say nothing is happening. The days are horribly the same. The hours are eternal. She prefers not to say it, something inside her knows it is better not to say. The people who wait for her letters already know, they know the days are the same, inside and out. The same when they are not worse. They always think, they always say, the worst is over. She could not bear it, she talked. Now she is destroyed, she was badly beaten, she is at peace. She was badly beaten, she is empty, she is mad. Mad or not, nothing happens. The days are all the same, nothing ever happens. Morning, noon, and night. Three big holes, a single hole. Nothing happens. The same, empty, the dim light filters through the sealed skylight. What time is it? Everything is the same—the dim light, the stifling air, watches are not allowed. She writes.

Yesterday was our anniversary and Walter was here. I set the table for two and we had dinner together. Walter was the same as always, clean shaven face, chubby cheeks, those brilliant black eyes you know so well. Do you remember? We shared a bottle of wine, but he drank most of it. We said so many things, we laughed so much! I served the cold chicken you sent me, mama. Walter tore it in two, he used his hands, he devoured it, swallowed it down with large gulps of wine, drinking from the bottle. We began to laugh, to talk in loud voices. I went to the sealed peephole and tried to listen. No one seemed to notice. We hugged each other and he kissed me, he was like he used to be, no shadow over his face, his wide toothy laugh. He went away. When will he come back? When? Tell me when?

The Commandant fingers the piece of paper lying on his desk, his hands seem to have twisted it after he read it, he raises his eyes as she comes in. He tells her to sit down, and asks her if she wrote this letter. Yes, she wrote it, yes, that is her handwriting, she recognizes it. You know what censorship means, we have to read every letter. Yes, she knows. When was this? he asks in an expressionless voice, poking the paper with his forefinger, as if everything is fortuitous, the letter, the dinner, the interrogation. When did it happen? The letter is dated yesterday, you can see it. It is dated yesterday, and it says yesterday. It was the day before yesterday. The day before yesterday? The Commandant hesitates, takes off his glasses and puts them on the letter she admits having written. The day before yesterday at what time? At ten at night, she says. Ten at night? How did he get in? Who? She was about to ask who, her mind has wandered but she pulls herself together. The Commandant paid no special attention to the pause. I don't know, he pushed the door open, that's all. How did he get in? he insists. Get in where? she asks in turn. I see, he seems to be saying, his eyes do not blink. I see. Here, in your cell, where else? I don't know, *that* way I suppose.

81

Behind his back is the window which gives on to a paved alleyway. At the end of the alley is the gate. She points to the gate, the fugitive's goal is measured in paving stones. That gate I suppose. She points, raising the arm of her grey, numbered, prison garb, an arm that cannot pierce the window pane, the man's stout presence, the thick air of that room smelling of leather which has flags, trophies, cockades, pennants, diplomas, but not a single book. He opens the desk drawer, and fingers his lists. The guard duty rota? The night before last? he asks, he repeats it absentmindedly rather than questioning. The day before yesterday was the 28th, he said, pointing. He slides the letter over his desk, taking his glasses with it, and leaves it in a slanting position as if it weighs less heavily on him further away. And you had dinner with him? Who is he? Her mind wanders again looking at his square hands. Oh, yes, yes, Señor, I had dinner with him. Let's see, your cell is in Block No. 2, Hallway 3, he reads rather than asks. Yes, Señor. What number? Thirty-six right. 36R, he writes. What is your number? Two eight six. 286, he writes it down again. He raises his head, looks into her eyes. This is all very serious, you realize that, very...se...rious. She nods her head, because he is looking at her. This is all very serious. Very serious, very serious indeed, he repeats mechanically, as he checks the notes. Very...se...rious.

He is well past forty, greenish shirt, wide sideburns of a fair man turning grey, brown eyes. Very serious. A serious face, she thinks. A noble face. Trust faces! Very serious. He looks at her, but probably does not see her. Is he thinking of his responsibilities, discipline, arrests, punishment, whatever? She doesn't know. She looks at him and tries to guess; she begins to doubt, begins to be afraid. Does he really mean it, or is he just playing games? Is he as sadistic as they say? He still seems distracted, a vertical line cuts the space between his eyebrows, he is absorbed with the problem of ordering arrests and writing an explanatory letter to his superior officer. And how did he get in? Him? Yes, him, who else? She shrugs her shoulders without answering. That doesn't concern her. Why not ask him, she could have replied, but she doesn't. Ask him. How could he have? We have to telephone at once, put out an alert, is that what he's thinking. Who the hell could he have persuaded, who the hell could he have bribed? How could he?

He looks at her again, he looks at her as if seeing her for the first time. His eyes begin to gleam. What time did you say it was? Ten, ten at night, she replies. Think carefully about what you are saying, do not lie to me. Ten at night...lights go out before that, you would not have had any light then. But, now, *his* room is flooded with light, and there is a glint of light in his brown eyes, a certain cunning. How did you manage? Does he mean how did they see each other's faces, how did they pick the chicken clean, gulp down the wine? Are there more accomplices, he may be thinking. Someone provided them with light, and that is even more serious. And she, in turn, feels that the tangled web of his story, arrested guards, accomplices, go-betweens, will end up involving her...involve her in explanations, inventions, confrontations with others, sanctions, letters, dossiers, curtailment of visits, punishment cells... Mother would not have believed her but this man does, mother would not get her letter now or understand why her Sunday visit is cancelled, but this man knows and will cancel it. Her imagination wanders, alone, to the brink of the abyss, it will fall in. How did you get the light? I have two candelabra, she says. I put them on the floor, I lit them. Does she know why she is saying this? Does she know or does she imagine? Did you light them? Yes, Señor, Walter had matches, he smokes. Did you light the candelabra? The brown eyes gleam with the light of understanding, a light that comes not from the candelabra but from inside...

Excuse me, Commandant. The officer comes in and stands to attention. Nothing to report, everything in order, Sir. At a wave from the green-shirted arm, the officer disappears. Nothing to report, everything in order. He has searched the cell from top to bottom, he would have found the candelabra if they were there. So... The Commandant puts his glasses back on, the lenses magnify his eyes, making them huge and catlike. The huge, catlike eyes, overflowing from his face, look at her. Two candelabra, she repeats. Very well! Candelabra made of what? She must know, she must feel it now, a spring has snapped, a calm finally settles over her. She has been running barefoot along the cornices, and has returned to solid ground. She is tired. She breathes deeply, she takes her time, knowing that she can now. Silver candelabra, she says. Made of silver? he asks, he always bounces her answers back at her as questions. He thinks in stages, challenging each answer before moving on to the next stage. Silver. Who gave them to you? I cannot tell you. She is calm now, totally in control of herself. She knows

84

that they both, from their opposite corners, have begun to play the game. You cannot tell me? Very well, you will tell someone else. But the potentially threatening words do not conjure up a threat for her this time, they will not, or do not know how to, or cannot conjure it up. That fleshy mouth pronounces the words carefully, as if he were talking to a naughty child, or worse, a sulky child, a spoiled child. Someone else, you will have to tell someone else. Very…well, very…well. He gives a half smile, and erases it immediately. There is a silence which lasts perhaps a second, but to her it seems a whole minute. Very…well. You can go now. She stands up, he signals to the guard. The guard stands to attention and waits. Experience tells him that the Commandant has not finished yet. Take her away. He still looks at her, his powerful glasses study her. Do not light them again without my authorization, understand? She nods her head. She has heard. Do not light them again without my permission…that is definitely the way to treat people like that. He has finished.

People like that. Seated on her mattress, writing pad on her knee, she writes. Nothing, nothing happens, nothing ever happens. Another letter to replace the one with the dinner and the candelabra, another letter to replace the one which did not pass the censor. She is writing it now. What shall she say? I remember, mama, when I was a little girl and you… The door of the cell opens, the guard comes in. No 286, the doctor wants to see you, he says. She puts down the writing pad, smoothes her hair with her hands, and stands up. The doctor, the doctor. What will I tell him now? Wait for me, mama, wait a while… I will continue the letter later, I will tell you everything.

Will they let it through? Ah, if they do...what a letter I am going to write!

Red Indians

E gia venia a su per le torbid' onde
un fracaso d'un suon, pien di spavento,
per che tremavano amendue le sponde

Then o'er that dull tide came the crash and roar
Of an enormous and appalling sound,
So that the ground shuddered from shore to shore

Dante, *Inferno*, Canto IX

'Can you hear me, old man?' the voice shouted down the phone.

It was three in the morning the old man recounted afterwards, the phone had rung in the hall of the house where he had lived alone since his wife died. He stood barefoot on the carpet, shivering in the summer pyjamas he wore in winter. As he held the phone, he trembled.

'Can you hear me?'

It must be something important, nobody calls at three on a June morning for nothing, unless they are drunk...but this voice was clear.

'Yes, I can hear. Who is it, what d'you want at this time of the morning?'

'Hey, Chief, it's me,' said the voice. 'Marguerite is in the garden under the laurel bush. Go and fetch her!'

'Who is it, what's all this nonsense?'

But he knew it wasn't nonsense, he said afterwards, it had to be Jorge's voice because he called him Chief. And, even as he asked who it was, he knew. He knew as soon as he said 'nonsense', a word he always used for Jorge's behaviour.

'A bullet grazed her little nose and she's bleeding. But don't worry, it's nothing. Go and fetch her, keep her with you, look after her.'

The old man said afterwards that he had wanted to ask, how come you're back, what's all this about? And lots of other questions, like where's Mariela? (Mariela was the old man's daughter, Marguerite's mother.) He wanted to ask lots of other questions, because since Jorge had got out of prison and had taken Mariela and Marguerite away, he had only had a few sparse letters telling him they were in Chile and that everything was all right. But then 'the Chile thing' had happened and he had heard no more from them but thought they were in Peru and then imagined Cuba, Mexico, Sweden. And now this voice coming over near and clear, at three o'clock on a winter's morning, telling him Marguerite was under the laurel as if it were a botanical rhyme in a children's book—marguerite, laurel (the Chief was a retired schoolmaster, a former school inspector).

He did not ask any of this, of course, and hung up. He threw a robe over his pyjamas and went out into the garden, barefoot and sixty, without lighting a single light (luckily a dim moon was shining), and sure enough there was Marguerite, wrapped in a blanket, blood dripping from her nose. He picked her up and the little girl said 'Chief', as though that was what she had been taught, the only thing she was allowed to say. He took her into the house, and examined her under the light. The bullet graze on her nose was bleeding, as Jorge had said. The child was very thin, dressed in a kilt, some rather precocious black stockings too long for a four-year-old, and a dark thick jumper. He hugged her to him, the blood trickling from her nose stained the front of his pyjamas, the lapels of his robe, and his face, as he gave in to the irresistible urge to kiss her, calling her affectionately Margueritiña now that she was with him, and calling Mariela who was not, and through the dripping blood crying tears as big as those on Spanish religious effigies.

The nickname 'Chief' was another bit of Jorge's nonsense.

'Old man,' he had once said, 'you're like the grandma in Little Red Riding Hood. What big eyes you've got!' And suddenly, as Mariela laughed, 'If you were a Red Indian...,' so that was it, the Indian chief with the big eyes. Big Eyes! The Indian chief, Chief Big Eyes!

It was before Marguerite was born, but Mariela was already very pregnant and getting bigger every day. 'Big Eyes', said Mariela, laughing. 'It suits you splendidly.' And it stuck, from Big Eyes he became simply the Chief.

'A bit of an exaggeration, isn't it?' he asks with false modesty, with an old man's coquetry (because he is delighted with the nickname since his granddaughter adopted it). And he looks (he used to look, for he is dead now) out of the two enormous lanterns which dominate his face. 'No, it's not...' It would be nice to be able to tell him now (I could only smile then). Yes, it would be nice, but he can't hear me now.

The Chief wrapped her in the blanket again, got dressed hurriedly, and went to phone. He left her on his bed for a minute, the child's nose bloodying the pillow, his old pillow crumpled by a widower's dreams and sleepness nights. He called a taxi and gave the name of the nearest hospital. The driver tried to find out where the 'little one had hurt herself' but the old man had learned not to trust taxi drivers and preferred not to say. The word *haemorrhage* and the dark night had created a level of uncertainty, and the Chief thought it best not to dispell it. At the hospital reception desk, however, he abandoned his reticence. 'I think it's a bullet wound,' he said. He told them about the telephone conversation. In any case, they would know about the shoot-out, the escape, the car, and who Jorge was, long before the Chief would be forced to name him.

Jorge was no hero. When they caught him the first time, he pretended to be running a real estate office; he was actually in charge of the guerrilla files. Those fools, believe it or not, even had a filing system. So the files were confiscated, and they themselves gave away what they should have hidden at all cost. If only they had been illiterate...!

Jorge was no hero. He had talked straightaway. After that, a civil court, a few months in jail, and exile. His exile was in fact a punishment for the old man, because Jorge had taken Mariela and Marguerite with him and the Chief (yes, chief only in name) had been left alone. But now, striding up and down the hospital corridor, smoking for the first time in years despite his sore throat, the only thing that mattered to him was the little girl. Instead, a police captain came up and began questioning him. Prison, exile, the journey, the long silence and the phone call in the night. Now they knew who he was, who the little girl was, who the father was. What else did they want? If the doctor agreed, he wanted to take his granddaughter back home now.

'No,' the captain said, 'Things are a bit complicated.

There was a terrible mess, a shoot-out, people wounded. The child stays here under surveillance. We have to question her.'

'Question her? But she's only four, captain!'

'War is war', the captain said curtly, 'they were bringing money from Argentina to the MLN. We have to question her.'

'The child was bringing money?' said the grandfather with a hint of irony.

'*They* were bringing it,' the captain stressed, 'we have to question her.'

'And you think the doctor will allow you to?' ventured the old man.

'And you think...?' the captain was about to ask, but in the end decided not to.

The crackpot had been caught soon after his return. He had come back to Uruguay with his wife and daughter and bought a villa in Mar Mediterraneo Street with part of the money he had been given for the 'Orga'. He bought the house in Punta Gorda and a Citroën car, one of those flat ones. When he came back to the house one night, they were waiting for him; there had been a shoot-out. Mariela had managed to slip away in the night, and disappear. But not Jorge. He had left the child under the laurel tree and gone for medical help. When he was finally caught he denounced those who had looked after him, given him tea and aspirins. Jorge was no hero. He really was a crackpot, as the old man said. The previous day he had buried the bags of money at the bottom end of the farm belonging to his poor old Italian parents. He returned the next morning accompanied by the Major who had confiscated his house and car. So this was where his recklessness had got him. Mariela missing, the Chief unable to see his grand-daughter, he himself in jail, and the Italians watching ter-rified as their farm was searched. The Major was threatening, would he send them back to Italy as undesirables after thirty-odd years in Uruguay? That was what they thought as their own son patted their shoulders and assured them that everything would turn out for the best, thanks to the Major. He tried to calm them down, as if nothing was wrong. No, not even that, more as if he had performed a great feat and was a real hero. Totally reckless, repeated the Chief. He had presented them with a house to use for torturing, a car, and a roll of bank notes. At Easter, the Chief had another heart attack and this time he did not survive. Marguerite was delivered to her Italian grandparents, through the intervention of a juvenile court judge. They were grateful for being allowed to stay in the country, brought up the child (who was not very fond of them), and forgot all about the bags they had seen being dug up under the apple trees.

'Say goodbye to your son, who knows when you'll see *him* again. As for you, who knows what will happen to you.' That was what Jorge called things turning out for the best.

But how had the child's parents come back into the coun-try? The Chief didn't know, and the Captain seemed deter-mined to find out.

'You stay here,' he said, 'Don't try to see the girl for the time being. She is incommunicado.'

'Incommunicado?' asked the Chief, 'but she's only four.'

'Incommunicado', the Captain repeated curtly, as if the old man were deaf and was about to make him lose his temper.

And now, seated at the foot of the bed, the Captain was trying to talk to her.

'I want the Chief,' said the little girl.

'The Chief?' the Captain was surprised, he did not know about the nickname. 'You like playing Red Indians, eh?'

'She calls her grandfather the Chief,' the nurse informed him, 'That thin old man who wanders around the corridor.'

The Captain was just about to say, 'I'll be the Chief,' thinking it was a game, but the nurse's information ruined his idea.

'So your grandfather is the Chief?' he asked though he knew the answer, because knowing the answers helps people get along with children.

'I want the Chief,' was all the girl said.

'Yes,' said the Captain in an imaginative change of tactic, 'you'll see him when you tell me how you came here with your parents...'

'I want the Chief.'

'Did you come with the Chief as well?' asked the Captain. He tried another tack although he knew it was not true. 'Or just with Mother and Dad?'

'I want to be with the Chief,' was the only variation.

'It's not good for her,' objected the nurse. 'She's got a high temperature.'

'Did you come in a boat?' insisted the Captain, ignoring the remark. He was silent for a while, trying to recapture childhood memories. 'In a canoe? In a row boat?'

93

The nurse told him all this afterwards, and the old man told me, adding, 'The little girl was much more mature than Jorge. I don't know if she thought she was gaining time for him and Mariela, but in any case, she never said a word. They got nothing out of her, not with canoes or row boats or anything.'

Sitting at the foot of her bed, the Captain had pretended to row, rolling his arms like the sails of a windmill, the nurse told him afterwards, as if the bed was a canoe with him and the child in it, and it was his turn to row, and they were nearing the shore, arriving in the country clandestinely by the river delta. He assumed that that was how they had come, and it might well have been. The little girl watched him with her round feverish eyes, the huge eyes she had inherited from her grandfather, and just repeated, 'I want the Chief.'

The Captain got tired and let her be. Or perhaps they knew what they needed to know anyway, Jorge could not escape and Mariela was not that important. As he left, the Captain said, 'What terrible times! Children are born indoctrinated! Or they train them from day one...'

The nurse just raised her eyebrows. She said afterwards that she had thought of asking, 'And what about interrogating children?' but had not dared.

And the Captain, 'Well...that's war for you!' He lit a cigarette and offered her one. The nurse declined.

Over the years I have often thought about Marguerite and also, as a fading picture, about the old man. Now she is old enough to read comic books and Indian stories, will she understand the dream they tried to envelope her in as she lay feverish, the tale of chiefs and canoes and the river?

The hero would be the Chief and perhaps, as the Captain fancied as he sat at the foot of the bed, it would be a tale of Red Indians. The Chief would row her off in a canoe on a moonlit night, like the night in the garden under the laurel, sliding through the waters of heaven, where she knows that he will always be waiting for her.

The Public Prosecutor's Horse

...e disse: 'Or va tu su, che
se'valente.'

...and said: 'Go up then, thou mighty man of mettle.'

Dante, *Purgatory*, Canto IV

Tape recording of a statement made by the kidnapped
Public Prosecutor to the MLN:

Public Prosecutor — I thank you. You know I've offered
to retire, and I think I'm going to, even though you don't...

Tupamaro — No, no, we're not asking you to do that.
When you leave here you're free to do whatever you wish.

Public Prosecutor — I'm ready to leave now. I think
I'll buy a horse and go off... to the country...alone.

Tupamaro — The first step to revolution, Sir.

Release Papers

Ma dimmi chi tu se'che si dolente
Ioco se'messa ed a si fatta pena,
che s'altra e maggio, nulla e si spiacente

But say, who art thou brought by what ill lusting
To such a pass and punishment as, me seems,
Worse there may be, but nothing so disgusting

Dante, *Inferno*, canto VI

Bound. Two soldiers made him sit in a chair with very high arms and bound his forearms to them. They opened his legs, tied straps round the calves, and fastened them to the chair legs.

They were not going to execute him, however. Not a real or even a mock execution. Two days earlier they announced that they had orders to release him. Would they do it? You never knew. You had to wait. Alberto had asked if there was a similar order for his wife. No, no, said the Commandant, I'd say she still had a long time to go.

And now they had brought him to a room and were tying him to a chair. He looked around. Was it to be another session on the machine? He had his release papers but that was how they said goodbye sometimes, the bastards. But he did not see the machine or any sign of one. Only a plug in the wall facing him, and a mattress on the floor. A grey mattress with nothing underneath to raise it off the floor, as if someone had slept on it and forgotten to put it away. The mattress on the floor and the light bulb hanging from the ceiling directly above it gave that bit of the room the bare squalid quality of a stage or a scaffold where something, anything, was about to happen. There, not in the chair, not on the body tied to it. When they finished, one of the soldiers turned on the light and Alberto was startled by the powerful torrent of light over that heap of nakedness.

They did not keep him waiting long. The papers for his release had been signed, the words pounded at his temples, and perhaps they already had their orders. It did not make sense to keep a free (though bound) man waiting too long. So Ada came in quite soon. 'You can't talk to each other,' said the officer. But as he said it, she was saying, 'Alberto, darling, it doesn't matter. Nothing matters except that I love you. Listen to me, stamp it on your mind...except that I love you.'

The officer pushed her down onto the mattress, apparently to stop her talking. Alberto suddenly sensed the straps against his forearms and calves, probably because he felt an involuntary urge to stand when he saw his wife crumple softly onto the mattress.

'It doesn't matter, darling, it doesn't matter,' she said again.

Of all the things said that day, of all the things that happened, that phrase was far and away the worst, the cruellest, the one which would haunt him so relentlessly. 'It doesn't matter.' Nothing matters, she was saying, and he had simply to choose a few words of reply since the officer had failed to stop them talking.

'My release papers have come, Ada,' he chose, he could only choose something which concerned him directly, something of his own. 'Did you know?'

A dry blow struck him on the right cheek. It was not

a heavy blow, merely the officer's way of reminding them not to talk.

'That's fantastic!' she shouted. 'You'll see the girls, you'll be with them again. Now it matters even less. Now it's nothing, it's less than nothing.'

She seemed to guess what was going to happen to her on that very spot in a few minutes. The coarse robe open over her breasts, her uncombed hair, it all seemed like a parody of violence. But still her soft low voice, that weary voice which, among words he had begun not to hear, repeated 'darling'.

He knew. They were going to rape her and he would have to watch. Could he close his eyes, would he have to listen?

Ada would stay in jail. She had shouldered the blame for both their sins, and as the Commandant had said, she still had a long time to go. 'You're lucky I don't fancy your wife,' he had added. And now he understood. The Commandant was speaking for himself and for his officers. He should have said, 'You're lucky *we* don't fancy your wife.' Yes, he was lucky. For cases like this, for really lucky cases like this, they used blacks and dogs.

Which would be worse? He had begun asking himself that to draw himself away from reality. That was what he had always done (he told us many times afterwards), dissociate himself from reality. Look at one thing and think of another. That is why he had faced lesser charges, and why he had yielded to his wife's urgent stare when they were brought face to face. He had always been the weak one. When the two girls were born, when one of them was ill, when they got better, he went through everything

99

as if through a garden, a gale, a doorway. Doorways were there for him to go through safely, while Ada weathered the storm outside. In sickness and in health, as they say in Protestant weddings (although theirs was not). In sickness and in health, in the barracks and in the torture chamber. His was always first, his door was always before hers, as if the only door in sight was unquestionably there for him to go through—either he went through or nobody did. So he went through. And when they were interrogated together her eyes told him, 'Leave it to me, it's better this way,' just as she said now, 'it doesn't matter at all, darling.' Alberto, darling, nothing ever mattered, do you understand now? Neither joining her, fighting her cause with her, nor not doing it. His latest door was his 'release papers' and she had said, 'that's fantastic!' with all the naturalness in the world, one leg at right angles to the other on the mattress where the officer had pushed her, as if this time, like all the other times, she was paying the price for him. Would they rape her just to let him know, as he was about to leave, that it was all his fault for being weak?

They have brought a black, not a dog. One of those blacks from the north, half Brazilian. It was better really (once again, comfort, transference, dissociation from reality), a black rather than a dog. And he could not hate him, because he was preparing to do it as a routine job, merely obeying an order, doing his morning duty as if it were guard duty. A black was better than a dog. Dogs may penetrate less but they slobber and growl and scratch, may even gnaw, bite and tear, and in a fury they can kill.

And this black, opening the front of his field trousers as she kept her eyes on Alberto and Alberto lowered his to study his straps, this poor unfortunate black did not matter either, he was just an ordinary guy, despite the size of his biceps. A guy like any other, not overly endowed or aggressive or ferocious. He is on top of her, wielding his penis, lighter than his hand, he asks 'open up?' she opens up. She doesn't want violence, she wants to avoid it, not for herself but for Alberto; she opens up. It all seems so routine, the image of desire which a young white woman is supposed to arouse in a black rapist is totally missing from the scene on that mattress under the huge light bulb. Only the officer who said he did not fancy Ada is turned on (lust or revenge) by what he is observing so closely. He leans forward, as if he wants to make sure that the mating for which they have hired the stud is taking place. Then he sinks his hand deep into his right trouser pocket, squeezing something between the material and his underwear, as the shame and regret of not doing it, and watching it done so badly, and not enjoying it, and being there, begin to bloat his features like a stain, like wine. All the while Ada repeats that it does not matter at all, that it is useless, that she feels nothing. She tells Alberto as if this secret sign will check the black man's imminent orgasm and the one she has to curb inside herself. Now he may be thinking, to escape from his visions as he did as a boy, as a teenage masturbator, as a guerrilla, he may now be thinking that a dog would have been better because dogs do not make prisoners' wives pregnant and blacks probably do, at the very moment she shrieks triumphantly 'I planned it, I won't get pregnant' at the black's orgasm, at the slavish sob which emerges from his snout, but most of all at Alberto and—beyond him— at the obliterated

101

honour of her two daughters. 'You won't get me pregnant, you black bastard,' the words thud against the
forehead of the bound man, and against the black, who
manages only to smile and accept the insult as the end to
an impossible fear, a ghastly dream, the unfathomable
unknown. Even if she had not boasted so much, he could
never have thought it was the reverse side of pleasure,
like the reverse side of mistrust, the denial of pleasure.
The image has haunted him ever since. As for the rest,
it all happened just as she said it would, no pregnancy nor
(she assured Alberto) orgasm on her part. What did she
think of to prevent it? He has asked often over the years
but she has pretended not to understand the question.
Nothing. You think of nothing. You resist. You do not
think of paternal incest, as you probably imagine or any
other of those dirty thoughts which rot your brain. A shitty
rapist is never anything but a shitty rapist, your womb just
doesn't exist for him, and that's all there is to it. And the
officer, what about him? He must have felt his semen
escaping down his trousers under his jerking fist. The black
must have seemed a pretty mediocre tool to him because
the officer looked over at Alberto at that very moment and
said, with inadmissable sympathy and great hatred (both
together), as if Alberto were the soldier, 'These blacks
are so stupid they don't even know how to fuck.' He
shouted, 'Get lost, you pig' and the black slunk off like
a dog. But the officer did not dare approach Ada nor mount
her himself, it was as if that now silent timeless body with
eyes closed was an impossible peak to conquer and clim-
bing it would mean death. It is nothing, it was nothing,
she felt nothing, she began boasting again, sure that it was

over. She began shouting at the top of her voice, with a kind of fury which still haunts them now they are together. At times they have come close to erasing the whole thing, but it is as if the hatred of a castrated man is rekindled in him and the door no longer opens to let him through, even though an ocean separates them now, the two of them and that officer, that black, and that wretched stage (or scaffold) where the shadow of the Commandant seems to float and masturbate ('you're lucky I don't fancy your wife'), nearly founders but is not wrecked altogether. Her legs have often opened for Alberto since then, but she no longer cries out in her loving voice because he does not want any voice, reasonable or uncontrolled, sensible or surrendering, ever to invade those moments again. Her legs open but at times it seems as if he cannot go through the door and at others as if she were tearing him apart with her bound hands and drowning him in snorts, oaths and saliva. The dreams of the two little girls asleep in the adjoining room are thousands of miles away, as far as Sweden or Norway can be from that mattress, that light and those straps. In vain he sings at the top of his voice, against the long frozen night of the North, the dirty rhyme he learned from anarchists as a child *Le général était un pédéraste, le colonel était masturbateur*, because their voices do not avenge him in his bed or in his coitus, and the fjords do not understand the offence as the sea booms like a fan beyond the windows, and because it is not important to know whether the former commandant is now a colonel and has succumbed to his solitary visions or if the former officer is now a commandant and is telling another prisoner it is lucky he does not fancy his wife... He tosses

103

and turns, takes a drink almost without raising his head from the pillow, gets drunk and falls asleep. Ada stretches out her hand and it sleeps over that penis which she likes and which, yes, does make her come... A fantasy of inoffensive words and memories burns in him but she is sound asleep and he can move her hand from his consummated love without waking her. Yes, but the semen has not oiled the hinges of the door either. The door does not open and the smell of semen grows colder and colder and he knows, alone in the northern night, he knows that there will be no more doors separating him from reality, no one will indulgently repeat the illusion that things do not matter. But the truth is, Alberto (so far away, so silent), that in fact things do not matter, neither the dream of revolution nor the welcome triumph of sex matter now. Nothing matters, darling Alberto, nothing has ever mattered and time, only time, covers that heap of filth, love and courage. Do you understand now?

De Corpore Insepulto

poi disse: 'Piu mi duol che tu m'hai colto
nella miseria dove tu mi vedi
che quando fui dell'altra vita tolto'

'That thou', said he, 'shouldst catch me in this place
And see me so, torments me worse than leaving
The other life, and doubles my disgrace.'

Dante, *Inferno*, Canto XXIV

Afterwards I understood. When I saw him. Because really, what sense did it make otherwise sending me into that room (the officer turned the light on from outside but did not come in), ostensibly to look for a mop and broom to clean our hut. He turned the light on, pushed me in and closed the door behind me. You do not question orders. I learned that a long time ago, and not from them. What did it mean? Then I understood. When I saw him. 'Francisco.' He was sitting but was not seated, his body held to a chair by ropes tied tightly so that he did not fall forward and tip the chair over with the weight of his own body. Bound, like a prisoner in a film, but not gagged and with his legs dangling free. Ropes across his chest, his belly and his arms, reinforced at the joints. The chair itself was very heavy, but it might also have been fastened (nailed to the wooden floorboards perhaps?) so that the body would not drag it along. And there—not sitting because the disarticulated legs danced to a rigid tune in front of him and because no one had bothered to see that his bum was on the seat—there he was. A lightbulb hung over the figure, coagulated, yellowish, and dirty. All the buttons were buttoned, but his leather jacket was torn in several places, as if they had wanted to make holes in him and open him up (later I learned that they actually had, and how) while he was still alive. But it was obvious that they had put his clothes back on him (if he was naked when he died, that is, as I thought then, and if there was any sense in dressing corpses) and fastened his belt round a swelling waist, a swelling chest, a swelling liquid-filled body. The eyes were half-closed, the eyelids not stuck together. But because his eyes were very pale, a much too watery blue (I already knew that, I did not suddenly discover it, I knew the moment I saw his bloated but still recognizable features, the moment I saw that corpse which had been alive when I last saw it, the moment my relationship with him changed far more than he had changed in the hours since his death), there was no glassy stare or misty pupil looking nowhere, aware of no one, to be seen through the crack in his eyelids. No horror, no mist, nothing. The eyelids were slightly apart, a false dry stickiness covered old melted waxiness now that they no longer saw anyone…not his wife, nor his two daughters, not even me who, forgetting the floorcloth and broom, examined him in fascination without touching or thinking, mouthed his name in silence, studied him. How dull, how dark—yet not black nor colourless—how charred a corpse can be! This corpse was, at least. And yet, how huge a fire you would need to burn a corpse like this, still so big, or rather not still, because he was bigger now than when he was alive, and even then was pretty big. 'Francisco.' His jeans were faded, not because some rich kid had sandpapered them to make them look faded, but worn through by his motocycle and the clandestine work he did when I knew him, caked with mud, cuffs frayed, like cardboard from continuous soaking and drying out. Stiff with blood, or simply mud? His combat boots with their rock-hard laces seemed about to explode at any minute from the pressure of the blistered, bloated flesh, the soles of those huge boots almost vertical and facing the door, the capriciousness of a corpse breaking the normal perspective of a living body, the soles seen from below or from a camera angle which exaggerates their size. I was the camera and he the seated corpse in a Western, a corpse riddled with bullets because in the Wild West men do not die under torture but riddled with bullets. There he was. They had clearly dressed him up again after he died on the 'machine' (that's what I thought then, that's how I saw him). I had to absorb it all in a flash, with the ghastly knowledge that they would question me about everything later, about details registered at bewildering speed. They would already be waiting for me outside the room (how long had I been there? why didn't they come for me?) and I had to look at him rather than think, and think rather than feel or cry, because his face did not ask me for tears, nor seemed ever to have shed or asked for tears. He had always been a tough guy and there in that room he still was, his cheekbones more pronounced but no less rounded than when he was alive, the hair of a young man on his way to balding middle age, the light boring into the little round tonsure we often made fun of, as if it were the opposite of a saintly halo, a shadow over his skull. Curiously enough, he did not smell. He was not yet giving off that sweet nauseous smell which penetrates so insidiously it renders your nose useless for days afterwards, the smell I had felt near me so many times, had imagined, sensed and feared. There was no smell of formaldehyde or disinfectant either, or even a whiff of medication, as if there had not been time for medical treatment between his living hours and his death, between his death throes and his murderers' tardy efforts to patch him up. It must all have happened quickly, less than a week I thought. Yes, in fact only a few days...I had been there only five or six days myself and right up to the day I was taken prisoner... Well anyway, by then I did not know what he was up to every minute of the day, we did not live together any more, his motorbike no longer came gasping down the little sandy track to the house every night. Mireya, Miti and Tistis had long since packed up the camp they had had for a few months nearby. Everything—the way the repression intensified, the way he plunged deeper and deeper into a disjointed, ineffective and blindly desperate war, a war he by then was waging almost alone—everything made it increasingly likely that he would fulfill his own prophecy and end up 'with four wheels in the air' as he used to say with a comic gesture, raising both arms and pulling up his long legs (those same straggling legs with their boots erect before me) to demonstrate the simile of his body as a vehicle and his death a pile-up. Not the two wheels of a motorbike but the four of that unlikely chassis, clogs dangling from his feet in the air, one wheel a hand holding a kitchen knife, another wheel a hand grasping a fork, arms and legs at incongruous angles, a long frozen grin of mockery too near the truth to be funny, the pale blue eyes glinting with sad ferocity over the mechanical smile from the mechanical little piano of his teeth. And now, that little piano was shut, the eyes were badly stamped on that face. The feet sunk in muddy boots, the heels no longer waving freely in the air, seemed to put a distance between us, just as outstretched palms can ward off danger or dissuade or reject. There he was fully dressed, not in his pyjamas, unkempt, nor freshly bathed ready to sit down to supper at the end of a day which was probably even bloodier and dirtier than the day he died (yesterday? the day before? when?), a day we could not talk about, a day of fatigue we ended together because the night was another chasm to cross, the worst chasm of all. We had a liter of wine, there was a soccer match on TV, but he was no longer interested because the last stages of the war devoured all his other interests. He had a glass of wine in his hand which he drank down to the bottom (even though he was not sure if he liked it), and then suddenly he grabbed a knife and instead of sinking it into his steak, he aimed the blade at the closed window and the night of the trees, his lips and mouth shot a volley of sound against the window pane, and the knife described a semicircle of defence or agression. It was not like a joke, the parody of spraying the room with bullets was somehow really shooting. Mireya was upset, and my wife did not know whether to laugh, ignore him or cry. Mireya would probably have said sarcastically, what was the point of waiting for him all day if he was going to play gangsters at dinner and disturb his little girl's dreams with the crackle of bullets, had I not interrupted him by saying calmly as you would to a child or a madman, OK, Dillinger, OK, OK... And then Mireya, 'How long?' or 'Why?' and he, now pushing the piece of steak towards the corner of his

109

mouth, 'until victory' or 'when we take power' or some such phrase which at this point was even less credible than a volley of bullets from a kitchen knife. And she, 'Will you wait till then to see your daughters, to come home at night before they've gone to sleep and leave in the morning after they've woken up?' And he, 'Nothing is harder than making a revolution,' or 'war is war' or 'one day we'll see.' But he had not seen it one day, nor could he tell me, tied to that chair, how he had ended up with his four wheels in the air. The lips that shot bullets from the knife were getting softer, but not with words of forgiveness. He very rarely forgave anything or made jokes openly like he did that Sunday morning the girls were tumbling round his legs and the phonograph played Bartok and the summer sun was flooding the room and he had a sudden urge to move to the rhythm of the music and the beat of the light and, stretching his torso, holding aloft a *maté* he had just finished, shaking his bare feet free of his clogs, had attempted a few dance steps and asked in a histrionic falsetto voice the absurb question *'Mamma, Mamma, per che non m'ai fatto danzatore?'*; and he wasn't even Italian or the son of any mamma at all. No, a dancer is the last thing he looked like in that leather jacket, those combat boots, those jeans, and the cloud of dust and pain descending darkly over his features like a deathmask, the mask of that death in a washroom, or a toilet, or the little room with the machine in it, which was much more dreadful than a washroom or toilet although it smelt like one. Tistis was a sad little girl who asked for chocolates because of the wrappings but didn't eat them, Miti had enormous eyes (the same markings as her father's but a darker shade)

110

and, because of a problem her mother had had with her placenta, she couldn't speak although she was two and ran about the house with threadbare dirty underpants because she couldn't get upstairs without sitting on each step and pushing her little body along on her filthy bottom. And Mireya's heart scarcely beat between her two daughters, waiting for the motorbike that was her man (the man who was his motorbike). But frail, frail as she was, she trusted blindly in life beside that desperate man, protected by that lunatic who never seemed to have borne any seed except this one, his own death...only his death, or at least, his death and violence. And she believed in life, embroidering large flowers on sacking curtains, even singing at odd times and not always tangos. Where were they now? Were the three of them together...mother and daughters cornered, maybe even used to induce some impossible pity which coming from the enemy he would never have trusted and rightly so. Were they looking for him at the very moment he was in front of me beaten to a pulp. Pulp no. Shit. Shit, and surely put there as a warning. I suddenly realized that the officer had not sent me to look for the floorcloth and broom in that room just by chance, and had been waiting for me for what seemed like days or hours. Did they know we had been friends? Were they watching me through the peephole, waiting for me to give myself away with a movement, a word? I found the broom and the cloth. I stopped myself saying goodbye with some kind of gesture, or word, or even a trembling of the lips, while all the time trying to find some impossible way of saying goodbye with all my strength, I was still pretty strong because I had only been given standing torture and beatings

111

so far, not a session on the machine. One day I will see Miti again (Miti was his only weakness but she will not remember him as time passes) and she will be talking by then and I will tell her about you and who you were. I think that was the stupid promise I made him, without words, gestures, or lips. That promise or some other one bound up with tenderness, as he was bound, so that he could not reject it and the others could not take it away from me.

'Did you see him?' the officer asked when I came back. Either I had not been that long, or he had not noticed how long I had taken, or that was precisely what he had wanted, I don't know. I nodded.

'Do you know who he was?'

'No.' (Denying it did not feel good, but war is war, as they say.)

'Take a good look,' he said, although I had left the room and he did not say go back. 'That bastard snuffed it for playing the tough guy.'

The words stayed with me under my hood, they began to fill the darkness, the silence, and the stench of the place they took me to afterwards to let me dwell on him. 'Take a good look' did not mean go back and look, no, it meant remember him, but that would have been inevitable even if the officer had told me not to. 'That bastard snuffed it for playing the tough guy.' But they apparently did not know we had lived together, he had been put there as some terrifying but impersonal object, not to get anything out of me. Perhaps the machine had not made him talk and he had not mentioned me. Perhaps it was all a horrible coincidence, not set up especially for me but as a more

112

general punishment. 'That bastard snuffed it for playing the tough guy.' I chewed it over for hours and hours under a hood which was drowning me in my own sweat.

Then came the machine (and how!) but they never asked me about him. It was clear they did not connect us, he was not there waiting for me in particular but for all of us, to be used as a warning or some such... If you don't talk... How many days he lasted, between being tied up and his final decomposition, I do not know. I never heard anyone mention him in his chair, no one talked about him in the prison yard as if they had seen some ghost. No. But *I* knew I had seen him, seen him close up. Perhaps they *did* use him only for me, even without knowing all the things which had bound our lives together.

Time, time I spent in Punta Carretas, brought me the rest of the story. And it was very different from the lie which the corpse, slumped in his chair, his executioner's accomplice, was party to. The truth was that he had been killed in a shoot-out when they surrounded a house in Cuchilla Grande, an old abandoned house where he spent the night (what turned out to be his last night) when things had hotted up and he had gone to ground. The house was raided one winter morning, July 1972 to be precise, and he, dozing on the floor under his leather jacket, Luger at his side, heard them first, saw them as they got out of the truck. He gave the order to escape through the back, some of them escaped, some he did not even know, and some he probably did. But he, in the most dangerous place covering their escape, the only one to keep shooting, like Dillinger and the kitchen knife, was picked out by the truck's headlights and mowed down. A woman who tried to help him was also wounded, at first it looked as if she was dead but they were anxious to save her because she was the wife of one of the leaders. She did not die. Wounded, a prisoner. The sadists in the Military Hospital tortured her and who knows how long she will be detained because her *compañero* escaped and she will pay for him. She woke up in the night, she said afterwards, and heard him cursing, firing and firing; she hardly knew him, she saw him fall, got to him, tried to help him, and was hit as well, they kept firing in the dead of night, she knew he was dead but she did not know his name. Dead, curled up on the floor, his Luger at his side, the Luger he loved so much (that I *do* know). Afterwards I discovered who got it, in which light-fingered officer's booty it ended up. They killed him, then they must have searched his body and found the photo, and that was when, swallowing her tears and abandoning the girls, Mireya escaped. Yes, she escaped as soon as she heard, all because of the wretched photo. And now that I think about it, that is another story, one which only Goma and Flaca knew. After Mireya went away nobody else would have known because the military were bound to have imagined something quite different. His first minute as a corpse began with a lie, with the photo they found in the inside pocket of his jacket. He lied to them then, as he lied to me later in that chair. He lied to everyone, everywhere, in the end. He, who carried truth like a bomb and drove everybody mad with it.

Only Goma and Flaca knew the rest of the real story. Someone talked, and he had gone to ground because they were on to him and wanted to ask him some very important questions, and he had promised to die rather than talk, and then suddenly he got the hots for Mireya again. Mireya, so quiet and slender, his great love! He used to make her wait for phone calls in specific places to fix a time for making love, no holds barred, in Goma and Flaca's bed. They didn't want to get involved and tried to avoid him, but the lunatic used to send Mireya to wait for him at their house and then turn up, in his little jockey cap, his combat boots, his scarf, his leather jacket, everything he was wearing there on the chair except for the scarf and the cap. They made desperate love, jumping and rolling over, he never had time to shave and poor Mireya's face was red as a tomato and, sometimes, like a chewed tomato. He probably took refuge for the night with other women, but they never swapped women in places where they were known only as *compañera* for security reasons, and anyway he cared only for Mireya, so shy and frightened, with a fear bigger than herself but resolved as a woman not to deny her body, her love, and her passion, now that they were both sure they were walking the knife edge between life and death. They made love like beings possessed, like people on death row would if they chose to spend their last hours making love, in a darkened room at three in the afternoon, having crossed a city where anyone could have been following them, or hunting them, or about to. That, at least, is what Goma and Flaca were afraid of, cornered in their kitchen, drinking *maté*, waiting despairingly for the hour or ninety minutes to pass when he would leave but Mireya not, as a precaution. She stayed a little longer, even came into the kitchen and asked for a *maté*. She said nothing, but everything in her seemed to have been peeled away, in

115

the wake of a hurricane, the survivor of an earthquake which had left her alive, but only just. Yes, because the cyclone had blown away her house, her two daughters, and even the image of time past stamped on a pair of naked lovers, because they alone were the wind or whirlwind or suchlike, two mounds of organs making love with savage ferocity, with a destructive fury which left no room in their pleasure for doubt, doubt, doubt as to whether they had years or only months or only days or perhaps even only minutes left, doubt which gave their pleasure the taste of death, and contaminated them. She came out of the room soon after he left and drifted like a sleepwalker to the kitchen, did her hair, asked for a *maté* and this time began to talk. She told them he was crazy, she had never seen him like this before, he asked impossible things in their love-making, things they had never done before, things she did not know how to do, and which maybe could not or should not be done. Another crazy thing he did was to ask her to bring loads of photos. They began to look at them, remind each other of things, the two of them lying on Goma and Flaca's bed, naked with the photos sliding across the annointed slopes of their bodies as if they had been begotten there and remained glued in the semen, born or created in the animal stickiness of their bodies. And they were always—Mireya said, while Goma and Flaca wondered how many photos, memorized and discarded, they had gone through in that surge of fear which accompanied each meeting—they were always photos of themselves, never of the little ones. He forbade her to bring pictures of the girls, he didn't want to dwell on any of that again, not Tistis' thinness or Miti's sedentary silent

116

infancy. They looked at photos of when they first met and their first motorbike outings before Tistis was born when they went away at weekends just the two of them, a different place each Sunday, as if repetition was the enemy of happiness. Now, on the contrary, they wanted this repetition in time to create the home they had not cared about before, not in a place, but in the past. The house was called, 'Do you remember?' 'Do you remember?' and there, naked, bitter, unshaven, newly emptied of love, he reverted to childhood, conjuring up the story behind each photo, leafing through them with fingers smelling of sex, reliving the circumstances in which they were taken, the colour of the sky and size of the clouds, the picnic they had had that day…all the trivial details summing up his life. And that afternoon, naked, his long torso over his crossed legs hindu-style, the very last afternoon of his life, he chose one of the photos and slipped it into the inside pocket of his jacket. The photo was a pure figment of his imagination, but he called it 'The Guerrilla Girl', something poor Mireya could never have been. 'The Guerrilla Girl.' They had been camping on the rocks at Punta Colorada, it was a winter's afternoon and there was not a soul on the beach. He had made her lie down against the curve of a rock which in the event did not come out in the photo, so the ground was not important nor was the sea (he had lain on the sand taking it from below) because behind Mireya's head you could only see round clouds scurrying in the wind against a cold sky. Mireya's hair was waving in front of her face like a flag, and he was delighted with this detail, but he did not want her hair obscuring the clear outline of her profile and (as if already

117

plotting her downfall) he took her lying on the rock, her nose resting on her flexed forearm behind the Luger, as if she was taking aim. And that was the photo which on the last day of his life he had put in his jacket pocket, as he sat silhouetted against the closed blinds of Goma and Flaca's room. They must have found it, perhaps smeared with blood, perhaps not, when they searched his still-warm body. 'The Guerrilla Girl.' Impossible to explain that it was pure fantasy. Soldiers are not trained to play games of fantasy (war is war), and the photo would have been enough for them to drag her off to the machine to get names out of her, some she knew, some she did not, and operations of which she knew nothing but which would cost her many a torture session. She left her daughters with friends, with instructions for what to do when she was safe. Then she ran away. The corpse never knew that. 'Francisco' did not have time to know, nor did I when I was face to face with him that day. They had buttoned his jacket up again, and with his stiff look of dawn, mud and blood, had seated him there to tell us something, to confuse us, to make us think he had died on the machine, as others had died, as many more would die in time. 'That bastard snuffed it for playing the tough guy.' When I knew the true story, those words kept coming back to me. But there he was then, being used for lying, to give a false picture; and his woman, the guerrilla who was not a guerrilla, was trying to escape across slackly-guarded frontiers; and his two little girls were being cared for by friends; and his Luger was who knows where in the hands of some light-fingered officer. Now Mireya would have to become an activist or something, and Miti would have

118

to talk, and Tistis would have to eat what she was given without a fuss. The image that lingers with me, however, is not of the three of them. It is the knife aimed at a window with shutters closing out the night of trees and wind, firing a volley of bullets, pretending to fire something which somehow was bullets, wind and fire. 'Stop, Dillinger, stop.' It was no good, he could not stop. And the scope of his night was measured by the length of those three lives.

The Soldier with the Arm in Plaster

Mentre ch'io forma fui d'ossa e di polpe
che la madre mi die, l'opere mie
non furon leonine, ma di volpe.

While I was still that shape of bone and flesh
In which my mother moulded me at birth
My deeds were foxy and not lionish.

Dante, *Inferno*, Canto XXVII

I think there is a strange beauty, the beauty of the absurd, in the act of a man who on entering a house takes off one of his arms (a plaster arm to be precise), puts it to one side, shakes hands with the other two (of flesh and blood), smiles, and apologizes for the intrusion.

It was not exactly like that, though afterwards they talked about it as if it had been.

For fifty days after she saw him taken away, the mother had had no news of her son, where he was, or what was happening to him. She had gone to Castro Road to take him some clothes but they had refused to accept them. His name was not down at any of the desks (that's what they called the centers for exchanging clean clothes for dirty washing). 'When he's on the list we'll let you know. See all these others?' She saw them. 'They're allowed a change of clothes, some food... You'll be told what you can bring too. But your son's not on any list yet. Wait a bit, you'll be notified. Don't come back until you are.'

Nobody ever waited. They always went back the following Saturday. The officers agreed to check the lists again and then repeated 'nothing yet'. That went on Saturday after Saturday, week after week.

She went back too, of course. She was not notified but she went back. It was a Saturday morning. Young wives, mothers, sisters, queued up, they brought clean clothes and were handed dirty ones. They recognized the clothes because they were usually what the prisoners had been arrested in. They unfolded them and searched the dirty cuffs, creases, and food or coffee stains for clues. From a dirty garment they wanted to construct a whole month, two months, even three months in the life of a man, or woman, because women were there too.

Sometimes, impossible or even undesirable as it seems, a story emerged. The clothes bore rust-coloured stains, a colour similar to that of fresh blood. Naturally if there was the slightest doubt, people clung to it, they refused to believe it. Could they really be handing back blood-stained clothes, clothes with traces of torture? Had they no pity? No, it could not be blood, it must be...

When asked, the soldiers were never surprised. They even seemed to be expecting it. They simply advised people: Go to Region No. 1, at Agraciada Avenue and Capurro Street, ask to speak to Colonel Albornoz and show him the garment. They may tell you where he is.

It was an odd business, almost like a syllogism. You produce your son's blood-stained shirt and acquire the right to know where he is detained...barracks, military hospital, that kind of thing. It was not always like that of course.

Colonel Albornoz came out in his shirtsleeves and listened. He did not seem to find anything serious or unusual enough. You showed him the bloodstains, you asked him to account for how they might have got there.

121

He had no information. Were they really bloodstains? He could not say, he was not in a position to say. It was as if he were totally removed from what was happening in an army of which he was an officer, in a military zone to which he was attached, and was only attending to them out of courtesy, because he did not want to say no or have to face insults and tears. It was better to talk… Yes, of course, a blood-stained shirt kills timidity. A woman who produces a blood-stained shirt, says it belongs to her son, and has no doubt about what has happened, is someone who has lost all fear. And a woman without fear is worse than a man without fear. The building which houses Region No. 1 is moorish in style and the olive-skinned colonel's name is Albornoz. Is his inscrutable patience another feature of the style? Some mothers and wives go on about savages, murderers, human rights, justice, international denunciation, and within certain limits Albornoz prefers not to contradict them. He looks at the dirty garment, but never expresses an opinion as to why it is dirty. He looks at it again, says 'hold this', gives it back ceremoniously, excuses himself a minute and disappears under the moorish arches. He does not return.

In his place comes a lieutenant or a sergeant, also dressed in fatigues, a mere assistant.

'The Colonel has asked me to take your name,' he says.

'Mine or my son's?'

'Give me both.'

'My son's name is…. Mine is…. My phone number is….'

The sergeant writes it down.

'Is that all you have to tell me, Señor?'

'We will let you know, Señora. We will let you know.'

They never let you know, and the woman is soon outside with the blood-stained shirt again and no more information than what brought her to Agraciada Avenue in the first place.

Fortunately in this particular case, there was no blood-stained shirt, or blood-stained underpants or even a torn and blood-stained handkerchief. A handkerchief might not seem serious as it is more likely to disappear without major consequences. Every mother remembers the shirt her son was wearing, every wife remembers the sweater her husband had on when he disappeared, but who remembers a handkerchief stuffed down in a corner of a pocket? So when a bloodied handkerchief is returned, it is because they want you to know what has happened, so that the blow hits hard and the violence spreads. Sadism or pedagogy; the pedagogy of sadism, at least.

Well, in the end nothing like that happened this time fortunately. About fifty days went by, then one morning the mother was at home alone when the bell rang. Suddenly she was confronted by the soldier with the arm in plaster. She did not let him in straightaway though she was sure (she did not know why exactly, perhaps because of the softening effect of the plaster cast) it was not a raid or an act of aggression. She opened the door when the soldier with the cast said, 'Señora, I have something for you...(slight hesitation to ingratiate himself)...from Petete.'

From under the layers of dust, not of fifty days but much, much longer, from way back in his childhood, Petete re-emerged. No one had called him that since he

123

was eight or nine. Obviously he had now thought of using the nickname as a password.

That was when she opened the door despite being alone and, stranger still, closed it again after the man came in. As she explained afterwards, she must have felt the door would protect her, protect her and the man both, by protecting their relationship with Petete. That was what the message meant, no doubt about it.

'Go on,' she said simply. She did not seem too anxious to know what the soldier had to say but, wisely, was not too suspicious either, nor gave any hint of impatience or pressure.

And that was when the situation took its comical, or at least outrageously implausible, turn. Without so much as a 'by your leave', with his left and obviously good arm he took off the plaster cast on his right arm and laid it on the table. Then with his two free arms, he genially shook the mother by the hand, laughed, and still without asking permission, as if he had needed free arms and confident gestures to do what he had been meaning to do, pulled a chair towards him and sat down by the table.

'Señora...' he began.

In fact, as she realized immediately (and as she vividly remembered afterwards when telling the story), the soldier needed his two arms free to look for something. Where? In that very same inert plaster cast. He searched around in the lower part of the arm and brought out a dirty, creased, crumpled envelope.

'...a letter from Petete.'

The letter was dirty and rumpled but not bloody. She felt a sudden urge to embrace the man holding it out to her, but she remembered what her other children (and Petete too until they took him away) always said about these people, and so refrained. But the soldier, his plaster cast on the table and his arm apparently sound, seemed harmless enough. He was a short dark man, and obviously *mestizo*. The cast had come off with such incredible ease that it looked as if he had mastered the trick and did it very often. The strange thing was that his flack jacket also seemed just as casual. A large gawdy handkerchief hung loosely cowboy-style round his neck. This *bandana* obviously served as a sling for the phoney bad arm. The sudden removal of the cast and the total ease with which his real right arm now operated left all the lower part of his jacket front empty, but all the same nothing hung or pleated or fell in folds on the soldier's torso. The plaster arm lived in the jacket but was not dependent on it. Now it had come out and produced the change in question.

'I'm fine. The guy who brings the letter will tell you.'

'He says here that he's fine and that you'll tell us the rest,' said the mother.

'Well, I'm not sure I can,' replied the soldier, but he clearly did know and was merely using the pause to add interest to the account. 'The guy is fine, he is very friendly. He tells some hilarious stutter stories…because he has an uncle who stutters he says.'

The mother was radiant, soaking in all the little familiar details which brought her son back to her.

'Where is he?'

'Ah, I can't tell you that,' but he hinted, 'it's on Maldonado Road.' With that he had said it all, that and what the unfastened collar of the flack jacket told her, was enough. 'It's a good place. There's fresh air and sun, and a few days ago they started letting them out for an hour's exercise in the yard…under the palm trees.'

'So he's all right?' ventured the mother. 'Why haven't you brought me any of his clothes then?'

'Señora,' said the soldier, reminding her of the real purpose of his visit, the one which made it admirable, 'please understand, I haven't come to see you officially.'

'Oh yes, of course, forgive me. Why didn't I think of that?'

The visit was not official, his plaster arm was there and out of it had come the envelope, as if it was the only one it ever held. Had the soldier had the delicacy to carry out the operation before he came in, so that each letter appeared to be unique, the sole reason for each trip? Did he transfer it in the street or perhaps, for safety's sake, in the toilet of the café on the corner? Was he taking a risk?

In any case, apart from being undoubtedly authentic, the letter did not have much merit.

'It's not all dramatic here,' wrote Petete. 'For example, this is the type of joke going round the prisoners. A girl goes into a café, sits down and calls the waiter. The waiter comes. What do you think he says to her? (See below.)'

She looks five lines down and reads, 'Señorita, I'll take your order when you sit on the chair. I can't serve you while you're sitting on the table.'

'Funny, eh? Really stupid! That's how we spend our time here. Telling jokes like that and discussing soccer matches. Nearly everyone here supports Defensor.'

And you support Peñarol, the mother probably thought

126

fondly. There was a friendly look on the soldier's face, so she translated, 'Always joking, my son.'

'Yes, he's a real laugh,' the soldier agreed. 'There's a Captain there who loves his stutter jokes because he's got an uncle who stutters too. Every time he sees him, he says, go on, tell us another stu..stu...story... And he kills himself laughing.'

When Leonardo came home from work and did not seem in the least surprised by the plaster arm or the soldier, the mother told him about the letter and the jokes. Leonardo did not find it funny.

'He has to play the buffoon everywhere he goes. Even in jail he can't help it,' he said.

In the gesture that accompanied his reproach, the mother noticed the death of his fifty days of waiting. She did not say anything, however.

'Did they knock him about much?' Leonardo asked. His voice showed a keener interest now. The idea that his brother might have been beaten up brought back his loftier feelings.

'You know how it is,' said the soldier, extending his friendship with Petete to Leonardo, perhaps because he had been told they were very alike (and they were). 'At the beginning everyone gets it. But they didn't do him too badly because there was this fat girl called Adriana from the other group...know what I mean?...and she denounced the whole cell. So they just got him for painting "Liberty or Death" and two or three other things, and that was all.'

'And what's wrong with that?' asked the mother.

'Offence against the Constitution,' the soldier pronounced smugly.

127

'Offence against the Constitution? What the hell does the Constitution have to do with him?' asked Leonardo.

But the soldier had his reply ready.

'They don't care. They stick it on you anyway.'

'Yes,' said the mother. 'That's right, except when they're the ones who destroy it...

'...yes, and other things as well,' said the soldier ambiguously, so that no one would dare enquire further...or perhaps to encourage them to do so.

'Like the Armenian lieutenant who wanted to have it off with this luscious bird from my neighbourhood, Armenian as well, who was a prisoner. Well, she didn't want to because she'd known him when they were kids and didn't like him, so first he gave her the "bucket" treatment and then sent us to her house to get her fridge, her food mixer, her radio, everything there was. He'd been there when they'd raided it so he knew what she had. We carted it all off in a truck to the "Sun 'n Sea", a villa belonging to the lieutenant's parents.'

A question mark hung over them as to why this man, apparently such a good friend of Petete's, was mixed up in all this...

'My late father, God rest his soul, got me into it. He was adjutant to General Dufrechou, the nicer one, the one who was killed by a bowl.'

'The one killed by a bowl?'

'Yes, there were two brothers, both generals. The one I mean was passing some guys playing bowls one afternoon when a bowl ricocheted off a wall, hit him on the head and killed him.'

'It bowled him over, as they say,' said Leonardo, but

128

the soldier did not understand undergraduate jokes.

'Yes, Señor. If you say so.'

And then he told them how his own arm had been broken by a Captain during a barracks soccer match. 'He knows my arm's mended,' he said, 'but then I got into this, and since it was his fault 'cos he's such a ferocious player, he turns a blind eye 'cos he doesn't have the heart to rob me of this little windfall.'

'This little windfall' referred to the price of the service the soldier had just rendered them. The mother ventured, 'How shall we settle this, Señor?'

'Read further down,' the soldier showed her. 'Petete put something...'

It was true...amazing that she had not seen it before. 'Give the bearer two thousand pesos,' said the note. 'That is the price.' The words 'that is the price', removed it from the category of a tip, gave it dignity and—above all— made it un-negotiable. Petete was like that.

When he came to pay, Leonard felt tempted to wreak some petty revenge on the body of the enemy.

'So you think your arm's all right then? Let's see, flex the fingers of your right hand.' The other man did so, and fancied that his fingers might be stiffening up. 'Get that stupid cast off, it's served you well. Move your arm, do some exercises, flex your elbow and finger joints...every day, several times a day.'

'Are you a medical student?' His tone became more formal.

Leonardo did not reply because he was not one.

'All right, I'll take it off,' he mused, gazing at it with obvious sadness. 'And we'll celebrate it with a few jars...'

'Look how blue your fingers have gone. Just look at your nails.'

The nails were merely dirty from having lived under that flaking crust for so long and digging around in it for letters.

'It's all phoney anyway,' he was more cordial now, as if he were interested in celebrating the end of the prank. 'Go on, take it off for good...'

'Yes, I'm going to have to give it up.'

It was strangely fascinating, this mischievious bargaining in which Leonardo gave him a couple of thousand pesos but at the same time tried to persuade him to give up his plaster arm, his only source of lucre.

The man said yes he would. But apparently he regretted it later and the plaster arm stood him in good stead for yet another year.

Caragua

*El comincio: Qual fortuna o destino
anzi l'ultimo di que giu ti mena?*

*He thus began: 'What chance or fate has led
Thy footsteps here before thy final day?
And who is this that guides thee?'*

Dante, *Inferno*, Canto XV

'What about your people? Will they miss you?'
  'Miss? What do you mean?'
  'Yes, will they wonder where you are?'
  'Will they wonder? I don't know about that.'
  'Will they think you stole the horse?'
  'The colt...he'll have gone back himself by now. Or
they'll have found him. He had a strap. He got away from
me, but he wasn't difficult to catch.'
  'Is the farm where you work near here?'
  'Well, not very near. But not very far either. He'll have
gone back. Or they'll have found him. Round here a loose
colt is always found.'
  'What was it like?'
  'The colt? A bay, with a strap round his neck.'
  'A halter or a rope?'
  'A strap.'
  'And your woman? Where did you say she lives?'
  'In San Carlos...if she's still there...'
  'Have you seen her lately?'
  'Not for over a year.'
  'San Carlos isn't very far. And you haven't seen her
for over a year?'

'What's wrong with that? I was about to go…but you caught me.'

'If we let you go now, would you go straight there?'

'That's hard to say.'

'Do you know who we are?'

'I don't know…. Maybe you're the ones people call perversives.'

'What d'you think of us? Do we want to help you? What d'you think?'

'I don't know. You're not helping me much now, are you?'

'Sit over here, *compañero*. Are you tired?'

'Not yet.'

'What will your boss think if you don't come back?'

'Nothing. That I went away…that I went to San Carlos. Round here lots of people work for a while, then one day they collect their pay and leave, without saying anything.'

'Did you get paid recently?'

'Three days ago.'

He had a three-or four-day growth of beard, such as it was, since he had very little body hair. Thin and muscular, he wore baggy trousers of greenish cotton over his naked body, old rope-soled shoes, a wide leather belt with a horizontal pocket for his money and two buckles at the ends. He had no hat and no weapons (not even the traditional knife stuck crosswise in his belt over his kidneys). He worked on farms in the gentler south of the country, though he said he had been born in the north, near Cerro Largo.

Would Antonio be talking to him like this, without a mask, if he thought the peon would be free to go off and

132

tell his tale?

The farm lay alongside the highway, Route 9, near Pan de Azúcar, in the province of Maldonado. They might have been unwise to baptize it 'Spartacus', for that was the kind of name no real farmer or cattle-breeder would use. And that was the cover for their hideout, a cattle ranch.

When the Armadillo Plan was put into operation and the guerrilla war spread to the interior of the country, 'Spartacus' became very important, logistic importance they used to say in the parlance of the enemy, the jargon of war. And that was when they constructed what they called the two armadillo caves, two tunnels burrowed deep in the hills, out of sight of the road. In the biggest one, the peon and the young man guarding him, pistol in his belt, were now waiting while Montevideo was consulted as to what to do with him. Pascasio Báez. That is what he said his name was when they caught him and took him down the rope ladder into 'Caragua', as the big cave had come to be known. No one remembered when exactly but they remembered the joke which spawned the name. It was the biggest cave, and even had electric light and a long shooting range along a strip of concrete. You entered from above ground by moving a large stone, operated from inside by an iron lever embedded in a block of concrete which rotated to reveal the first steep section of the descent down a narrow pit. The stone covering this hatch into hell could also be pushed aside from above. Some called it 'sesame' and others simply 'the stone'.

The shooting range was about seventy-five yards long, and at the end against a concrete wall there was a tin puppet, which served in turn as a target, the police, the enemy.

It had taken a long time to make, mostly digging the bowels of the earth after nightfall by the light of shrouded lamps, dispersing the soil through sieves. For target practice in the gallery, they had to lie flat on their bellies or sit down since the hole was not high enough for a man to stand up in.

It was well known that in times of political friction in Uruguay, Old Herrera always threatened to lead the White Party up into the hills. 'We're going to Caraguatá', the old man would say over and over again without the slightest intention of going, surrounded by party faithfuls at his country house in Larranaga in case someone denounced him, or someone got scared, or someone came to bargain. No knives, no lances, no uprisings. Dead and gone were the days of 'fresh air and fat meat' as the famous old White Party motto said. Lost forever in time. Perhaps that is why when they finished the stone gallery, the concrete block, the lever and the lights, someone as a joke named it 'Caraguatá', in memory of that famous boast. Then it became 'Caragua' because it was shorter and sounded better. One humorist hailed the meeting of two eras with an underground sign, 'This is the intersection of two generations, two ideologies, but a single destiny: freedom' when the *El Abuso* escape tunnel crossed the *Carbonería de Buen Trato* tunnel, and the MLN and the old romantic pistol-toting anarchists shook hands briefly under the foundations of Punta Carretas.

A young horse trotting through a meadow, mane and tail flying in the wind. A lovely image, for an engraving perhaps. Freedom, sun, vitality, all that…almost like the emblem of the nation. But a peon chasing the colt, stumbling upon the mouth of Caragua, even though by accident,

134

is something much less beautiful.

Astonished, face swollen, eyelids darkened by the sun, yellow eyes lighting up his Indian features, Pascasio Báez protests his innocence, his total innocence. He is a farm hand, he says again. Why would he bother spying on neighbours, what would be in it for him?

'Tell us, *compañero*, what were you going to tie the horse up with and where?'

'With the strap, to a tree trunk. There are trees here. I've done it before.'

There is a 'hardware' group which wants the whole thing over and done with before nightfall. 'This guy is two eyes and a tongue. We don't need to consult anyone, we'll resolve the problem ourselves. We need the night for the other thing, for getting rid of the body.'

'But if he really is a peon? If he really is innocent?'

'Too bad, these things happen. We can't risk everything by feeling sorry for him. What kind of war is this? This guy is hot. This guy is two eyes and a tongue.'

They have taken him down to the other end of the concrete strip and made him sit on a wooden crate. Are they going to shoot him right there, sitting down? Whoever he is, whatever he knows, peon or spy, if he is freed and goes on living round there, one night he will have a few glasses of wine too many in a local bar and tell the whole tale. 'If he is set free, we must be prepared to lose everything...leave "Spartacus", lose the money invested in Caragua and Chico, lose the livestock on the ranch, leave traces which might lead to our capture, anything could happen. Do you want that, is that what you want?'

'What about the *compañeros* who come from Minas dur-

135

ing the night in the big jalopy with Justice Department number plates, and decipher messages about what kind of supplies to leave according to the way the three white stones near the eucalyptus tree are arranged? They'll have to be warned. All this because some moron brought a colt over to graze on another farm—just supposing it's the truth—all this because of that oaf.'

'We always say we're fighting for people like that, however stupid they are. We say we're doing all this for them now, that's the whole point of the Armadillo Plan. But at the first problem, must it be so obvious that it's pure rhetoric?'

They have taken him to the other end of the shooting range, made him sit on a crate and wait, although even if he heard them he probably would not have understood. Who knows! Do we know what goes on in a peon's head? Do you have to have been to university to understand? Is our concept so elitist?

Well, they will never know for sure. They see his rope-soled shoes, his baggy trousers, the colour of his skin, the suntan of a field hand, not of a tourist at a beach resort. But they cannot see further than that. Even the simple language of a farm hand could be a trick. He gave the name of his boss, of his woman in San Carlos, but there is no time to check it out and it would be no use anyway. The problem is not he himself but what he could say. 'Tomorrow they'll realize he's missing and start looking for him, especially since the colt is missing too and we have him. They'll look for him to find the colt, the colt is what matters to the boss. It'll be worse if we let the colt go. If they both disappear, in the boss's mind it will all be clear...he stole the colt, sold it or rode off on it, and disappeared, so help him God. If the colt shows up alone, it will be obvious that something has happened to the peon, that he drowned, dropped dead in the fields, fell down a ravine, or something. They'll start looking for him, and there are people here in the countryside who can track animals across fields. They'll follow the tracks and we're done for.

It was not hot down at the bottom of Caragua, but Pascasio took off his shoes and put them on the concrete floor either side of his bare earth-coloured feet. Touching the ground must have made him even more aware of being a prisoner hanging on the decisions of others, because he looked over at them without hearing, saw them silhouetted against the light from one of the bulbs. An air extractor started up and its noise came between him and the figures in the circle. It was impossible to tell what they were saying to each other.

The woman in San Carlos, the colt running towards the edges of the night...what time was it? Impossible to tell, down here is only earth, only prison.

'What if we send him to Cuba?'

The question, the suggestion, came from Marcos, one of the oldest *compañeros*. He was wearing the mouse-coloured felt hat he used for working in, his shoes were still covered in dung from inspecting the fields at the very end of the ranch, the corner ones furthest from the highway. He had not taken part in Pascasio's capture but had heard about it at midday when he went back to the house. His old anarchist instincts moved him, as far as possible, to consider man's fate over and above anything

137

else. And man was not only the poor peasant, the worker, the social victim; he could also be the enemy, the repressor, the policeman, the soldier. For him, the *compañero* on his belly taking aim and the tin puppet he was shooting at had, in principle, the same worth. Both were representatives of the same human condition. He accepted unwillingly that in war you had to kill, for the strict exigencies of the war, if there was no other way out, no other solution. But not for any other reason, absolutely not. For statements like that, and especially for those kind of sympathies, the younger *compañeros* called him the Priest. The name made him smile. He was not a pacifist, he protested. He had chosen direct action, and action forced you to certain irrevocable extremes when the time came. Being more merciful did not mean being softer. The others knew (and that is why they respected him so much) that in his case this was true.

'You can never be an executioner,' he had said once, 'if someone else's death is a moral question for you, a matter of conscience. For the executioner, it never is...that's why he is an executioner. We could not be. Could we? I, at least, don't think we could. Someone who kills fighting does not execute. He just kills, no more, no less.' They were used to this kind of reflection. They accepted it from him, more in Marcos than in themselves. They accepted it because his life reflected his words. He had courageously covered some famous retreat single-handedly.

One night, long ago, looking at a photo in the Cuban magazine *Bohemia*, he had begun to philosophize on his favourite subject: the greatness of the Revolution and the

size of the man who makes it. The picture was painful
not only for someone like him, when he illustrated it with
reason and passion; the others found it painful too. They
all had the same anxiety. They feared his power of per-
suasion, however, and afraid he would convince them,
argued against him—the disadvantages of purity and
absoluteness they said (or perhaps only thought). The photo
shows the speakers in a meeting room in some Cuban province. A long platform, as wide as the front of the room,
runs from wall to wall. On it is a table almost as wide
as the platform and behind the table facing the front, pos-
ing for the photographer, are a dozen or so seated peasants
with cowboy hats and oppressed expressions on their
impassive faces. Their enormous hats come down so low
they almost bury them, erasing their foreheads, resting
on their ears, the brims flattening their heads as they try
to take flight. Those small swarthy faces, swallowed by
those enormous oppressive hats, look out towards the
reader as if trying to share with him the misfortune and
the glory, the tenacity and the fear which flow out in a
single stream from the words (human tenacity, supernatural
fear) covering the fluttering banner suspended in the air
across the width of the meeting room (like the image of
a great wind frozen by the flash of a camera). 'We have
made a revolution greater than ourselves' proclaims the
sovereign phrase, over the heads of those illiterate
peasants, so poor, so astonished, so crushed—crushed by
their hats, crushed by a mission of transcendental misfortune. We have made a revolution greater than ourselves.
And now what? We have made a revolution greater than
ourselves. Tough luck! Like those little bubbles in comics

139

which float over the characters and descend in little wedges to their mouths speaking for all of them at the same time, this banner proclaimed that those people had made a revolution greater than their poor, meager, individual lives, exalting them and destroying them at the same time, freeing them and making them responsible. What does their tiny size matter beside the size of the revolution which they have made together? We have made a revolution greater than ourselves. Yes, and what do we do with it now? It is no use, the Priest had insisted that night. The revolution should be on the level of those who make it. If it is not, it will not work. It should express everybody's highest achievements, of course, but nothing else, no more than that. The highest level, but no higher. Everything for the revolution but also for the man who makes it. Because the ideal and purpose of revolution is to diminish the power of one man over other men. (The former anarchist background is there, he could not give that up for anything in the world.)

And now, when the subject is Pascasio Báez and not a humble actor in a drama larger than himself, when the subject is the fate of a man who lost a colt and stumbled by accident on the entrance to the tunnel, these same humanist considerations lead the Priest to propose a way out.

'What if we send him to Cuba?'

Although much younger and less complex than the Priest, Antonio did not want to be thought any less pure. But he is interested above all in revolutionary efficiency, so for him the praxis is more important than the man himself, a pre-eminent revolutionary value, beyond the private individual human condition.

'Getting him to Cuba could create many problems for us, *compañero*. I don't know if we could do it for a start. You know that...'

But what he is suggesting is another way of looking at the matter.

'Is the risk we would run in proportion to the best possible result?' he asks. He says it is.

But this was not a simple dialectical training session, they were not simulating exercises in logic. At the other end of the concrete strip was a man, immeasurably distant from them in ideas and perhaps in destiny (or perhaps very near them but in different tempos of the same destiny, who could tell?) A barefoot man, with feet the colour of earth, a man waiting, a man no longer master of his own destiny and deep in the unfathomable world of his own thoughts. Do they know that world? Do they know, have they any idea, what this man could be thinking? Do they know, at least, who he is? Could they get near his thoughts, simple as they believe them to be?

Sending to Montevideo for advice had relieved them of the burden of decision-making. But it did not make them feel any better in the end. Raúl had left on the five o'clock bus. They had agreed to outline the facts but give no evaluation apart from an appraisal of what was credible given those facts. For instance (in Báez' favour), the belief that he truly was what he said he was, a farm hand who had arrived through an unfortunate accident, and not a spy, nor an undercover cop, nor anyone's agent. Also for instance (to Báez' disadvantage), how risky it would be to release him and let him go on living there (or anywhere else in the vicinity) no matter how many promises he gave. What had happened to him, like the banner of the Cuban Revolution, was greater than he was, it went beyond him, it transcended him quite terrifyingly. That and a glass of wine would sooner or later be his downfall, and theirs, despite his prudence. Releasing him there, or in San Carlos, would mean abandoning the tunnels and losing the money invested in them, leaving 'Spartacus' and everything they had done there, risking the lives of many *compañeros*. Solutions? Raúl had left that afternoon to find them, taking with him these options: indefinite detention, exile abroad, elimination. No one had wanted to say 'death' but including that option was unavoidable. Raúl had gone to Montevideo, he was expected back the next day with the decision endorsed by the executive committee. Meanwhile, one barefoot man was about to succumb to sleep, while other men keyed up by their own responsibility within an ethical process of revolutionary precaution, waited for time, other heads in higher places, and a more balanced appraisal of the situation (Could they get a prisoner to Cuba? How? Across which border? When and by which means could they do it?), to bring them the answer.

Here, where the matter would not be resolved, they had already listened at length to the Priest's arguments.

One. An execution in an ideal order, however abominable, is carried out either to punish (like Morán Charquero), to set an example, or for publicity (like the adviser). This execution, on the contrary, would be secret.

Two. An execution must presuppose a crime, not

142

ignorance and innocence. This would be executing an innocent man and, what is worse, precisely because he was
so innocent.

Three. We say everything we do is for them, for people like this man, as deprived as he is. But as soon as they
threaten our interests and safety through their ignorance,
we choose our safety over their lives. (He could have said
but did not that this comes from making a revolution
greater than ourselves, a lack of proportion which robs
us of choice and delivers us up to fate—the greater of two
mercies, the lesser of two evils.)

Four. When in extreme cases we have legitimately
chosen a man to be executed, we have recruited him from
the ranks of our most disgusting enemies (again Morán,
or the *yanqui*) not from among those for whom and in
whose name we said we were fighting. The truth is that
we do not consult them, and in the Armadillo Plan we
presume to know, only from our own perspective however,
what is good for them, and how they can be liberated.
We act for them, invoking their greatest well-being, and
that is that. But, at the end of the day, can we calmly
choose for them their own death?

Five. A death imposed in this way is shameful for two
reasons. First and foremost, because it is unjust. And
because it means accepting our dialectical failure. We kill
someone because we abandon, with little apparent effort
on our part, the possibility of convincing him. To this
extent we are acting in accordance with the ugly bourgeois
conviction that men are not equal. We had to trust common criminals for a jailbreak simply because we could
not do without them. Why then are we incapable of trusting

143

a simple farm hand? We believed in a thief enough to escape with him because when the risk was over we lost sight of him. But we cannot lose sight of this man because he already knows something permanent and concrete about us. I don't suggest we let him go just now, I propose we keep him and convince him. Time will tell if we made the right choice. Why do now what, if the worst comes to the worst, we could do later, unless we are impatient for our own safety. Impatient for our own safety? Is that a revolutionary value? Does it have sufficient revolutionary purity? (Again he could have argued the point here, but he did not, about making a revolution smaller than ourselves.)

Six. We have not renounced, in extreme situations, all dialogue with the enemy. When it comes down to it, we recognize a common language. On the more humble level of those we say we are protecting, are we not rejecting the possibility of a common language with them?

Seven (and this takes us back to the beginning). For an execution to be morally defensible, it must be an offensive action. This would be a defensive execution, besides being secret and shameful. An execution should settle an account, this would open one because if we kill a man in order to keep an important secret, are we then ready to die before we reveal it whatever the circumstances? Do we realize that we are swearing to die for the same values for which we are now prepared to kill? Because whoever denies that commitment to save his own life, or to stop his suffering, is assuming that his life is worth more than his fellow man's, and this difference automatically makes him a murderer. A murderer is someone who values his

144

own life over his fellow man's. We believe we know what a madman is, we believe we know what a sick man is, we believe we know what an enemy is. We cannot refuse to recognize in advance what a traitor is. Whoever confesses one day the whereabouts of Caragua after taking a man's life to ensure his silence, first murders him and then betrays him.

And finally, *compañeros*, and this seems very important to me, there is the problem of human legitimacy (apparently he did not want to have to say 'morality'). From where do I get my right to decide? In what sense do we have to accept that the 'Orga' is an omnipotent institution, which creates its own scale of values and, without bothering about guilt, imposes its punishment. I would not do that...!

Surrendering to his fate, Pascasio looked at them for the last time and pushed aside the crate they had given him for a seat, assuming (with good reason) that he would be spending the night there. No one had told him otherwise.

They decided to let the Priest guard the prisoner as if to condemn him to spend the night awake with his own arguments. They put a gun in his hand, and reduced the number of lights in the tunnel without making it too dark. The Priest sat on the fruit crate now that the peon no longer needed it. It was preferable to reduce conversation to the minimum. A communion of time and tension would unite them, that was enough. The Priest sat alone and sleepless with his arguments; Pascasio Báez sunk in the earth and his weariness.

Of necessity, men are never equals.

...Paradise on Earth

...e caddi come corpo morto cade.

...and, as a dead man falling, down I fell.

Dante, *Inferno*, Canto V

He walks along the middle of the street, if that fuzzy meandering line can be called a street. Here and there the beach resorts thrust out long inverted sandy tongues between the grassy dunes and hillocks. These are the streets, sometimes no more than trails. He walks along them, it is three o'clock on a late autumn afternoon, June 13, 1972. He goes along the clear swath that slopes gently down towards the sea, no foliage ahead but edged with trees, trees that turn to watch him from behind as he passes, walking with a contemptuous indolence which looks nothing like desperation, like gestures of desperation, although that is perhaps what they really are. Trees that suddenly appear in that little circle of vision through which his pursuers trace the shape of the man's head, moving down along his shoulders, coiling around his waist, following him. It is as if the telescopic sight of his pursuers, who a few short yards further on will become his executioners, that sight, rigid with intent, demanding to know *when* rather than *where*, were pruning away his surroundings, slashing, parting the foliage to clear a path for the bullets. If it were not for those almost motionless conical shapes that form a background and cloud the expanse of sky beyond him, he would look like a hobo fading into the distance, into the bare landscape of the last shot of a Western. Gary Cooper or somebody. Someone who seems not to want to make it hard for them, someone willing,

146

as it were, to help them take accurate aim, a suicide by omission, a lazy suicide. There is no face in the sight, only the nape of a neck, shoulders, a torso, legs. He walks slowly, heading for the tang of the sea, as if nothing else in the universe matters. The tang of the sea, only the tang of the sea, only the sea, knowing full well that he will never get there, will never sink down into it, sure that they will shoot him first. Bullets in water glance off, ricochet, are uncertain, and they won't risk that, they won't wait that long. Everything depends on the pace of his steps towards the shore, as if he were carrying inside himself the stopwatch of his own death and forcing it to go very slowly.

There is no autumn in beach resorts as there is in the countryside or in city parks with their avenues and lawns. There are no russet branches, no tiny slaughtered flowers, no autumn leaves nodding off before gusts of wind or asleep in heaps on the ground. In that resort there are only pines, seasonless trees, trees like sharp-beaked hens, feathered all the year round. Three p.m. Thirteenth of June. Within a week, without his seeing it, it will be winter. But there is no winter in beach resorts either. Solitude and a wild sea, yes, but not winter. Nor will there be, by then, the mark of a corpse on the dunes, nor the track made by his legs in the sand if they drag him away by the hair, nor the cratered, dirty, oscillating, jolting trail of a head or the blurry hollow made by a backside bumping along the sand, the flattened buttocks and the wavering brushstroke of shoulders if they drag him by the feet. There will be no trace of anything. Is that what the telescopic lens is seeking? Winter is coming, the tides may be high

147

enough to make him disappear, a tidemark ribbed with damp, rotten leaves in the dent where he fell (what does a thin body weigh on soft sand?), if they wait until he gets to the bit past the edge of the stunted grass and as far as the sandy clearing which opens up between the last of the pines and the sea. They will have watched him, studied and restudied him, perhaps photographed him. The first heavy sea of winter will wash all that away, the killers' cigarette butts, the spare spool from a roll of film, all turned to jetsam, a chorus of footprints, the imagined circle trampled by their boots if they have surrounded him and are continuing to insult him and spit on him, waiting for his death throes, watching him die. Nothing will be more fleeting than the spilled drops from wounds on the dune, nothing so unlikely as that blood. In the meantime, for now, they will continue watching him from a distance, measuring him, making sure of their moment. They don't shout at him or give him any warning, they don't want to give him the chance to turn toward them, to raise his arms, to plead with them. And he won't raise his arms, he won't plead. To hell with them. Perhaps, involuntarily, he will just part his lips to catch the mouthful of air which his lungs can no longer give him, just that and the light shining for a second on his perfect teeth. Neither his cry nor their yells will be heard above the boom of the sea, while everything continues and they keep watch and he walks. They will howl, yes, once they've fired and he has fallen; then there'll be insults and curses; by cursing him they'll curse their own fear; they'll wait a while longer, they'll spatter the beach with strafing shots before coming close to his huddled, still body, curled up and gathered

148

in on itself, they'll riddle him with bullets again, just in case he's been cunning enough to feign death and crouch down in wait for them with a grenade, maybe (brought from where? carried on what part of his body? hanging from what place that doesn't need hands?) They'll fire at the likely spot, so the grenade will explode before any of them gets near: strict instructions, a plan for every contingency.

He walks as though about to stop, but without ever coming to a definite halt, without quite ceasing to move forward, ignoring them; for now they know that he knows, now they are certain that he is aware of the ambush, of the order (suspended for the moment) to fire and to keep firing without respite until they shoot him down, the order to take aim at that zone which the little circle of the telescopic sight, oily and somehow cloudy like sea-water, never abandons as it comes and goes, roaming up and down, head, shoulders, back, buttocks, thighs, calves, flicking at the unlaced shoes, taking hold of the undone shoelace tracing a tiny snake in the furrowed sand, thinking it has discovered disgust and arrogance in those untied laces, in the deceptive carelessness of negligently swinging knees, trousers, arms, in the rowing movements of those empty hands.

He walks with his arms well out from his body, and the body itself is slender and straight, the legs and buttocks tightly encased in very narrow gabardine trousers, soiled and shabby from the days at the resort leading up to today. Trousers so tight that if they delay afterwards and let his body swell up, the undertaker's assistants will have to cut the cloth off him with scissors. Stovepipe

149

trousers, a cowboy shirt that was once blue but now even the telescope can't guess at its colour. And when another motionless backdrop of trees appears in the little circle, pines hardly ruffled by the lightest breeze in the midday sun, the unkempt fair hair shines like a halo, luminous for a moment and always dishevelled, as if that cloudy eyeball reserved for him a pocket of wind that blew nowhere else in the world, not even between the crests of the pines. A head tousled by a wind that exists for it alone, exists to brush from time to time against a hatless forehead. No felt beret or panama, no hiding-place between a hat and the crown of his head, where he might be concealing a grenade.

In San Quintín, in October 1968, El Viejo was with him and Rodríguez Ducós, and they were carrying a grenade in a briefcase; but it all happened so fast and so suddenly that they had to get out of the van with their hands up, without time for El Viejo to open the briefcase and for them all to jump out. But anyway, this time, the advance of the struggle has transformed the battle orders. For them, the order is to shoot without checking first, to shoot without encircling, without going close, without exposing themselves to anything. For him, there is time to know that everything is over after the 'vacation' in the beach hut. Better this way, yes, maybe it's horrible to say it, but it would be better this way for all of them: preferable to torture and mutilation, the vengeful settling of accounts, and only at the end of that rosary, death. Clearly, they will have been watching him from a distance, presumably with a military telescope, and so they'll know that he's unarmed. That he's obviously carrying no weapons and

150

that even if he were he would have decided not to use them. Not through shortage of time, as in San Quintín; through languor this time, a deliberate, parsimonious languor with no backward glances. He won't use a gun, but for them it will be the same as though he had: they are going to write this part of history as though everything had happened in a rush, as though they had suspected there were more people lying in ambush and could not discard the possibility that they'd be fired upon from the shoreside or from the other side of the pines. That's how it will be, and no one will be permitted to deny it aloud, either in a newspaper or in a report. Besides, they know the press doesn't count any longer; and once the autopsy has been carried out, no one will get involved and the case will be closed; the doctors at the military morgue have never been inquisitive.

His arms are held well out from his body, his shirtsleeves rolled up to his elbows, the skin darkened by the days on the run (the hideout in sun and saltpeter, if it's not too absurd). The skin of his forearms is almost coppery, but often he deliberately turns his palms backwards, facing them, and the palms flash white. They flash white in the curve of the lens and this warns them that his hands are empty, open, carrying no weight and exerting no effort; there is nothing hanging from them, nothing held against his sides—no weapon, no package—nothing. It might seem excessive to attribute to him a desperation so frozen in its purpose, so scrupulous, so fiercely detailed. Impossible to say whether he is doing this so as to accentuate the abandon of a suicidal disdain, or whether he has given up noticing and can no longer tell caution from

151

recklessness, in that zone where everything is confused and scrambled to embrace death.

The telescope jumps from one of his hands to the other; both hands have been turned backwards, towards the clearer signal made by his back, and show that at this stage nothing matters any more, it doesn't matter whether he hides or presses forward towards a hidden entanglement, towards traps for the hands or feet, with untied shoelaces and hands with the fingers spread, like ungainly fallen stars, like teats on a parched udder. They would find him anyway; it might be even more agonizing to die surrounded than to die out in the open. Either separate shots (between ever-shortening morsels of silence) or a blinding curtain, a squall of machine gun fire sending up clouds of sand, broken twigs, splinters from the tree trunks, then a single, longer silence this time, without those snaps of gunfire. They know that now there's no one else there, that they needn't waste another hail of bullets. Are they afraid of killing others without knowing who they are? What does it matter to them?

They must know very well that as soon as they have located him and he is within range, it must be final. When they escaped from *El Abuso*, the tunnel began right there in his cell. And then, even supposing they had negotiated for him in advance, and he was part of the exchange for the British Ambassador, the opening for the escape was very limited, covering only a few days and within the terms of that particular situation. Negotiations with *them* rarely guarantee anything, not even at the time. It's 'the next time we get our hands on you ...' And now they have got their hands on him, and he walks more and more slowly, within the little corral of the lens which doesn't miss a single step he takes. The next time they got their hands on you they wouldn't forgive anything, however you confronted them, be it with armed resistance or naked flight, it makes no difference. No help will come from the sea. Jay is still there, with her leg broken, on the steps of the beach hut; the door and windows are open, and through them the sun pours torrents of light behind the figure of the seated woman, who has reached the cottage crawling, with her leg broken. Or maybe they've already got her, already raped her and hurt her, despite the injury; or they might have left her there, besieged by guns, till they brought her the corpse of the man from whom—is she pale from physical pain, or because her mind is numb?—she has had to take her leave almost without looking at him ... *Paradise on earth*.

When Jay was a child, some Chilean businessman started up the beach resort and the Uruguayan Insurance Co. set about selling plots of land with no other attractions to offer but the sky, the sea, the quiet, the pines. The Chilean baptized it River Plate Park and organized a local competition for an advertizing slogan. Hold a competition like that and it's inevitable: there's always some office clerk at the other end of the radio announcement, some mousy bureaucrat with a wife and three kids, living on a pittance. In the back room of his hovel with its dingy partitions and one fly-spotted light bulb hanging from the ceiling, this unknown poet dreams of the sun, the sand, the waves, the clouds, and his need to make ends meet. So he takes a torn scrap of office headed paper and he writes: *Paradise on Earth*. He likes it, but it could do with something more;

he thinks a few minutes longer, corrects it and punctuates: *River Plate Park, a paradise on earth*. Yes, that doesn't go beyond what's called for, it's fine. He sends it off. The jury meets, he wins, there's a big public gala, he signs the deeds to the shack, it's photographed in all the papers, eight columns wide. But the clerk didn't win the shack so he could lounge about at the seaside: he has more urgent needs, his own hell on earth to deal with, no paradise. He puts the place up for sale and along comes this fat guy who's young and more impressed by those three magic words, *Paradise on Earth*, than by the shabby ceiling with its bare rafters or the flimsy wooden walls. The clerk shows his talent for words again and Fattie becomes the owner of the cottage and starts to clutter it up with kitsch, majolica dwarves dotted about the sandy yard, a little Gothic castle in wire (pure rust by now) as a cage for a canary long since dead. Jay was still a child when she stopped spending summers there; now she returns as a woman, with false documents. The fat guy doesn't recognize her, but does he believe her story? Two simultaneous honeymoons...out there, exposed to the wind, on the verge of winter? Fattie doesn't seem to question it; but he charges a very high rate for a cottage that can't have cost more than a thousand pesos twenty years ago. He refers to it in falsely grandiose terms, as if suggesting he could get an even more scandalous price for two neglected, creaky rooms at the beginning of the low season. 'This *bungalow* would qualify all by itself for the title of "Paradise on earth",' he says. (*Bungalow* has more class, house is such an ordinary name, not at all suitable.) The deal is struck, the fat guy takes the credit for inventing the phrase, the office poet fades silently into the shadows. The lie is twenty years old, as Jay knows: Fattie has got fatter, older, greyer. The canary cage is a wreck of smashed bars, the noseless dwarves recall the infancy of the fattie's sons, people whom Jay knew once. She knows nothing of them now; she wouldn't ask after them.

Owners always ask too much, a price absolutely disproportionate to what they offer; they demand to be paid in full before handing over a pair of rusty keys. And when they get what they ask they begin to complain, and a week later, to avoid blame and make sure they don't lose out, they denounce. Or rather they 'communicate their suspicions, in view of the circumstances'; thinking about it later, they realized what was happening, so they're denouncing. It's the most drastic method of eviction: for the tenant it means prison or death. And in prisons and cemeteries no one ever pays back rent advances. The house is up for rent again, vacant possession, and a good citizen gains credit in the eyes of the authorities. Long Live Democracy.

In this case, Fattie waited more than a fortnight, if in fact it really was he who did it. Did he spy on them on his own initiative, until he was sure? A storm lantern, to give back to a non-existent sailor, a beach umbrella, left behind by mistake and now returned (even though it would be winter in a few days). They were blockaded, out of contact with everyone. Every night, El Nito ('Carlos' to the Organization) would say, 'What are we doing here? What are we waiting for? We don't know what's happening to anyone. None of the other *compañeros* know what's happening to us.'

And Jay would say, 'We're waiting. We just have to stick these dreadful days out. It'll all become clear later on.'

'When is "later on"?'

Milka would go to the kiosk every morning to fetch the paper. On Thursday, when they read there was a search on for a group in Las Toscas, Carlos and Milka decided to leave, and he and Jay decided to stay. 'I think you're getting apathetic, you're giving in to weariness, it's stopping you going on,' Carlos reproached them.

'And what if we are?'

'If you are…', but Carlos left the sentence unfinished. That Sunday it was Jay who went to the kiosk and bought the paper. It had news of the 'clash'. Carlos had died the previous afternoon in a shoot-out with a military patrol in a house in La Unión, Milka had been captured, slightly wounded. The paper carried photos of them both, the dead man and the prisoner, old photos, but near enough to their actual appearance to be recognizable. If he hadn't already done so, that was when Fattie must have denounced them. And that very afternoon Fattie came back, officiously, this time to replace with a gas lamp the storm lantern, which he took away with him. He couldn't fail to see that there was only one couple in the cottage now. Jay talked to Fattie, the man said hardly a word, Fattie must have noticed that the foursome, the two simultaneous honeymoons, was reduced to a one honeymoon twosome. But he asked no questions.

They'd been in the cottage nearly twenty days; ten to go. And then what? Fattie didn't seem to want to know that either.

When night fell, they held each other in the closed shack, without lighting the gas lamp. The fat guy had just left, perhaps he still lived in the resort and it was just an unlucky weekend. They embraced each other in silence, not mentioning Carlos, not naming him, without exchanging questions which would only have been useless phrases. La Union, La Union? Could it have happened? Yes, it must have, because it had been published. When they didn't hush these things up, the result wasn't distorted either. Clashes, ambushes, manhunts, surprise attacks, the result was always the same; and of course they lied about that. Every time it was the same. For months now, it wasn't *they* who had been dying ; the *compañeros* were dying, never *them*. It would have been impossible to forget Carlos's face; not the face in the photo, the face of a few nights ago. He'd said nothing to them about La Union, only reiterated their intention of leaving, he and Milka, on the last bus on Thursday night. He didn't even seem to think there was any particular urgency. The urgency seemed to be hers. As if he were doing no more than reading out the last words of a telegram. Carlos had just said, 'Luck', one word was enough, no other word fit. Carlos hadn't had much luck, and certainly luck didn't seem to be on the cards for Jay and him.

Jay is an exceptionally beautiful woman. There aren't many as beautiful in the 'Orga'. Jay accepted his *nom de guerre*, but he refused to use hers. 'It's awful,' he said, 'I don't like it. I love you with your own name.' A long time before that, long before Paradise on Earth, there had been another *nom de guerre*. 'And what does it matter if you don't like it? That's how the cell structure works, isn't it?' 'Yes, but we're with Carlos and Milka this time, and they know us already.' So, they negotiated and came to an agreement.

Jay: he would call her Jay, keeping the initial of her real name, he rejects all other disguises for… 'No, don't say it!' (her hand across his mouth). 'OK, so it's not the name you picked out of the hat; let the other *compañeros* respect that name, I won't.' He was tired and let his arms drop. Very, very tired. He lets them drop again, alone and away from Jay, this afternoon on the sandy path, this afternoon of sun and almost no breeze among the pines. If the rules of organization in cells have broken down utterly, then it was idiocy to have met up again. But there you are, it's done. Now it seems no time since Sunday night, when they broke apart from each other, loosening their embrace, and he tried out the gas lamp; at first it caught light along one edge, then burned white almost at once. Carlos (the memory of Carlos? the ghost of Carlos?) was silently between them, like a bat among the rafters. And on Monday night: would Fattie come back? He didn't. And they, did they light the gas lamp again so that Carlos wouldn't speak to them, so as not to speak to him, so as not to name him? Luck, just that one word: luck. Milka hadn't even seemed to want to say it, she seemed to have known that it had run out for all four of them. Only her great emotionless eyes, watching them fixedly, that moment on Thursday afternoon as they left for the bus. And the two of them, in their turn, watched the other two depart, standing in the doorway of the shack. No one was to accompany anyone else, of course. Just 'Bye' and 'Luck' (Carlos again). But now (Monday night) Milka is

158

not there, not in the window-curtains (Jay had drawn them as soon as the little spike of light leapt up from the gas mantle), nor in the walls nor at the portals of that dream of death. The living can wound and be wounded, the dead cannot. Prisoners hold out as long as they can, cry out from wherever they can; death is the final bolt on the door. It's all there, in the choice of going or staying. Not in those now-ruined lips saying 'Luck', not in those big eyes that kept on watching as long as there was a flicker of light for others to see them and measure them by. And now it would be no use either, to talk to each other, to toss questions back and forth between the two of them. They were tired and this was another barren vigil. Months ago now they had decided not to have the child which she had given up asking him for and which he had not wanted to give her. War is not the time for it, and a hideout not the place. Later...Yes, later, you can never tell with whom. Not with him, who had now decided to let his arms drop, to push the pistol away under a far corner of the mattress, put on some old worn-out shoes without tying the laces and go down to the sea, exposing himself to them as surely if he were swimming on his back... Luck, luck, what luck? He would never again undress himself (Sunday night) never again undress her nor call her by that reminder of that name, as beautiful as herself: her name. Luck? Yes, it's still possible to think of it: that they won't bother about her, that they'll keep their eyes on him: he continues to be very visible, he won't disappear. Isn't that how it is, or haven't they understood yet? He turned down the lamp gradually, lowered the flame steadily into darkness, made the circular glow of his cigarette wax and wane between loose, horizontal lips. Jay's hand touched his shoulder for a moment, as the gas mantle stopped flickering. Two hours more, in two hours and a few minutes the hands of his watch would embark on the quadrants of an infinite day, Tuesday, the day convention calls 13 June 1972. Tuesday the thirteenth! A fine day for luck! When the time came, he would not put that watch on his left wrist, nor get out the pistol. By then nothing would get any better, nothing could get any worse. Luck.

It is incredible how the chalets, the houses, the trees, the sea itself die when one has turned one's back on them and does not intend to look at them again. That too is death—to lose oneself, to cease knowing, to postpone to the end. Finally there's no going back. And nonetheless, even so, we accept death without giving it a meaning, in the case of those who mean nothing to us. The other person to whom we say 'See you soon' is already a dead man to whose death we have consented, a deceased person even while we are contemplating him. As soon as he has closed the door, eternity will settle itself between us and him. And the same thing happens with objects: this cane arm-chair, that window, that sloping piece of ground, which helped us to meditate for a while, at dusk. But the too unforgettable is inconvenient, once the pursuers' moment arrives: the too memorably beautiful face of Jay is not convenient to the Organization.

The days in the beach hut (*bungalow* is something else, a *bungalow* is a log cabin, El Nito had insisted) appeared now, now that all was lost, like a time tucked away into a corner, and in another sense like something floating, weightless, expectant and swollen. Nobody can believe, nobody can admit that they may have to pass their last hours in a trap. 'I'm staying right here, they can come and get me,' Jay had said. Her right leg was fractured, the bone exposed; she had fainted after falling into a deep ditch, in her small, truncated, curtailed attempt at flight. The ravine was carpeted with old cans and empty bottles, but the rubbish wasn't theirs: they had always burned or buried whatever they could. Tins and bottles (sardines, beer, that kind of thing) and him kneeling at her side, not to ask her forgiveness but to go on loving her, promising to let himself be killed there with her, clinging to her. At first there had been many gunshots, then, abruptly, the explosions stopped. What were they waiting for? She would not let him stay there with her; she knew, and said, that he, with two good legs, need not stay there, inviting the killers to shoot them both together. 'Bye' and 'Luck' as Carlos had said. 'They know who I am,' the man argued, 'and that's invitation enough for them. I'll stay here.' But she made him go. 'Two of us here, trapped together, it's certain death.' Wouldn't she think of herself, didn't she want to save herself? They had to separate. He carried her in his arms onto the flat ground, from where she could crawl, using her good leg, until she gained the door. And once there, would they take her alive, or would they pepper her with bullets where she lay, or tear her with a grenade? The chance had to be taken. He kissed her once, one last time, distraught, as he laid her down again on the pine needles at the edge of the ditch. And then—just as she could not suppress a cry, as shafts of pain stabbed her again—only then did he begin to run, to put distance between them and disperse the pursuers' fire

161

if they came. He closed his door, a door wrought in air; the door that made him a corpse for her. An eternity is knotted up in this act.

Yes, this has been the only course he's tried. A short one, in terms of distance, but long enough for him to disappear from her. She wasn't able to cry out. She hadn't the strength to cry out, nor should she have done so. Silence was not yet eternity, but it was beginning to serve them for eternity. It served, it lasted, it beat in seconds, in the minutes that were parting them from each other, minutes that for her, perhaps, were life itself.

...*Paradise on earth*. His fall was a void. Where might he be now, what might he be thinking of? Of his flayed ankles, when they had tortured him in the Central Prison in October 1968, that time when there was no time to set off the grenade at the corner of San Quintín and Garzón? That was a year before others had bled to death on the outskirts of Pando, trapped in a circle of boots, the boots of the Metropolitan police, who were waiting and watching them die, preventing anyone from getting near them. He was not to die that time; he (motionless, spreadeagled, strapped down at ankles, knees and elbows) was lying in the chamber of mirrors. From beneath the hood he had seen on the floor pools of the water used by his torturers, glinting with a quicksilver gleam. And almost at once the *picana*, the cattleprod, and the ring of cops in shirtsleeves, shouting rhythmically and clapping, *rock-rock-rock*, buttressing that surrounding wall of deafening music, against which cries seemed to dash themselves, his own cries, the cries of his *compañeros*, keeping them from hearing the ebbtide of solidarity flowing back from the whores, which

162

they did hear later, from their cells, when others whose ankles were ulcerated, whose joints were flayed, whose ribs were broken, dancing and howling with pain, almost electrocuted; and the *rock-rock* and the clapping, louder and louder, and the other chorus, from the prison-load of whores, mingling with the ROCK-ROCK-ROCK and swelling the whorecop bedlam, the coprotten pandemonium, with their part in the whole chaotic ritual.

People say images like this don't occur to one at such moments (how do they know?); that at such times people tend to think of their childhood, to remember some toy or some episode from infancy—a doll, a favourite tree, a swing, a cup—when they know that they have only minutes left, less than half an hour of life, for instance when one senses the final onset of cancer or has checked out the usual time of day for the firing squad. Do you believe that? Wouldn't it be more likely that an individual thinks about the things he is never going to see, that he wants to hurl himself into what he has to leave unfinished, that he strides forward, giving a shout destined to be lost, since he himself is being carried off anyway, and is lost?

He walks on, to distance himself, he walks in the opposite direction to the path that would bring him round to meet her again. He is sure that they aren't feeling panicky, because he knows that when they are startled, when they catch the whiff of their own death in the death of another, when they begin to fear that they will burst apart themselves in the act of disembowelling their victim with gunfire, then they go mad, they shoot wildly in all directions, they shout insults, leap, run, they turn their fear into hatred for others, something animal, desperate,

163

a mixture of cowardice and fury. They fire on anything that moves, anything they fear is moving, they rage against the thing they have just vanquished, they vent their fury once they are sure that they are winning and their victim is finally defenceless. Yes, in that kind of tumult they act, in that kind of tumult they dare act.

First there will be his fall, a thunderous commotion in the air and the afternoon overturned; the fall and the bolt of lightning and a sudden flight of birds. Like a smear of soot, like a scrawl scribbled in charcoal by a clumsy hand, like the extreme, oppressive nearness of a dirty finger, like a greasy stain which will in time give them back their passion, their anger and their laughter: someone else's death.

The blow, so long expected/unexpected, impels him forward like an axe blow, a searing, it burns more than it hurts, it flames, it envelops, it darkens, it blinds, it asphyxiates.

He opens his arms.

Opens his mouth.

Falls.

Caragua (II)

Ver me si fece, e io ver lui mi fei

So he advanced to me, and I to him

Dante, *Purgatory*, Canto VIII

They are there and the night is there, surrounding them. Pascasio has slept for perhaps a couple of hours to compensate for his initial weariness. Now he is leaning on his left elbow, his naked feet still on the ground, horizontal, one across the other.

'Is something bad going to happen to me?'

He does not look as if he suspects what bad thing it will be, or what he should be afraid of. He looks at Marcos, who just shrugs his shoulders, a gesture which does not exacerbate the prisoner's fears but does not dispel them either. 'Who knows,' he seems to be saying, 'who knows.'

He had been told not to talk to him too much. Shrugging his shoulders was not talking though it did suggest something; perplexity, ignorance, suspense. The peon had not caught the substance of that conversation held in the circle at the other end the cave, but he had heard the murmur of their voices and no doubt thought that it gave him the right to expect a better answer.

'I haven't done anything.' he insisted. 'Why are you holding me prisoner?'

'It's not up to me,' replied Marcos. 'I'm just obeying orders.'

His answer was very much like a policeman's. Wasn't he ashamed? Wasn't he shocked? How could a guerrilla give an answer like that? In other ways as well their conversation seems like that of a prisoner and his jailer.

165

Pascasio had summoned enough confidence to ask him questions but not enough to call him by his name. Marcos did though. He talked casually, his words were meant as encouragement, to convey a human interest in the life of a fellow man. Yes, but the cops were often interested in us too, and not only to get information. No one thought they were good guys just for that.

'What's your family like?' It was that kind of question. But Pascasio returned it, rejecting the opportunity for intimacy.

'What family, Señor? I don't have a family, only my woman.'

He could have asked him not to call him señor. But the situation made it morally unacceptable to encourage him to say '*compañero*' or 'friend', or to make the conversation more intimate, more friendly. Can the prisoner and his jailer be *compañeros*, can the victim call the man holding the knife by name? Could he criticize his aloofness, could he say 'don't you feel we're equals?' No, because in all honesty they were not. And his apprehensive question, is something bad going to happen to me? marked the extent of that inequality. It was dishonest to invite false equality in that situation, to encourage intimacy at the gates of death, especially if the executioner wanted to see that false confidence to absolve himself of the weight of his deed.

The prisoner kept his replies to the minimum, 'I don't have a family, only my woman.'

'Haven't you even got a dog?' It was another silly question because this was no time to show him how poor he was, to prepare him to hate.

166

'There are dogs at the ranch,' replied Pascasio, 'but they belong to the boss.'

A peon is a man who cannot even have a dog, even if he found one lost and hungry in the fields. In the absence of words, the pause seemed to bring a reflection, not a complaint. 'My own dog? The boss doesn't allow it.'

'But it's the same thing,' he was reassuring Marcos now. 'The boss's dog is your own dog in the end.'

If that was so, could there be a dog out looking for him in the night at this very moment? Yes, but when you do not feel the dog is yours, perhaps the dog does not miss you so much. From Pascasio's position on the ground, those yellow eyes seemed to ask another question, his head raised just enough for his gaze to reach his jailer, sitting on the fruit crate, his felt hat unnecessarily tight , his pistol slanted in his belt. But, what were they asking?

Marcos himself must have noticed the difference in their positions. The barefoot *mestizo*, raising yellow dog-like eyes towards him, asking nothing with urgency, not exchanging tension for boredom in the vast expanse of the night. When it had been his turn to guard the kidnapped banker, Marcos had had to wear a hood with two slits for the eyes so the guards always looked the same, like Chinamen. No one had told him to put a hood on this time, as they had for the banker, the public prosecutor, and the ambassador. Wasn't that the first sign that this time there were no potential revelations? The banker was now perusing dossiers with photos of subversives as he prepared to leave for Italy, the public prosecutor was fingering them reluctantly as an occupational hazard, the ambassador was claiming diplomatic immunity and not doing it. And now, in Caragua, did the physical proximity of mutually uncovered faces mean the silent prophecy of death? Or were they sure that Pascasio would be incapable of picking out a face or describing features at an identification parade, even after they had spent a whole night together. Again, once again, we always start with the assumption that men are not equal. We do not feel their equals, we do not consider them our equals, we do not behave as if in theory they are, however much we sometimes say we do.

This was the second time Marcos had been made to think. The first was when he had asked a really stupid question. They had been talking about the peon's woman and Marcos surprised himself by suddenly asking, 'Would you like to write to her?'

'I can't write, sir. And she can't read.'

The reply ended the risk which for a moment hovered suspended between them, a risk created by such stupid curiosity. Because, if he could write, would they let him? Surely not. The letter could have been posted, of course, but what lies would he have been allowed to tell? That he had gone to Brazil without explaining why. Sent from Rivera, from Santa Victoria, from Chuy. That would have forced him to lie about his own death, a despicable and unnecessary lie, and a dangerous one besides. Or, otherwise, offering to write a letter for him, of reading it to him, and then when it was all over, burning it right there or burying it with him. Luckily, those yellow eyes had not been interested, it had not occured to him to ask. A peon is a man who cannot have a dog nor say goodbye to the woman he is leaving. Everything is cruder and simpler with this kind of man, and it is senseless to deceive him because you feel sorry for him, want to comfort him or help him. He did not ask, he let the opportunity pass without the slightest intention of asking for it. He was not a banker, the terms of his ransom did not enter his calculations as they had in Nino's case. He had no bank he could ask for money, no family or friends to turn to, no one whom he could extort through fear and guilt. For a farm hand there is no relationship between his person and the trappings of power. But despite all this, a more imaginative man might have suggested, though he might not have known how to make use of it afterwards, that they let him write a letter, a letter to the wife he had not seen for more than a year, of whom he knew nothing. Yes, but he could not write and she could not read, and that was the end of it. Silent separations are for people like that.

Nino had given him a letter written in Italian for Laura, his wife. Marcos understood Italian and could have read, 'Cara Laura...', but he preferred to fold the sheet in two and take it to the *compañero* in charge. He did something silly, however, and said, 'Laura? Like Petrarch's Laura?'

Unlike Marcos, Nino was not wearing a hood. His eyes dilated in amazement.

'Ma come..?' He had just been writing in Italian and the language stuck to his tongue. 'I'd have never thought a man of action...' he searched for a way to praise rather than offend by his choice of words, 'would know who Petrarch was.'

Marcos chose not to take the offensive. He could have retorted that *that* was a bourgeois cliché about a man of action, an ignorant statement unworthy of his intelligence.

But instead he muttered something vague, folded the letter, and went out to take the message. He had committed an indiscretion, he had left a cultural clue by which he might at some later date be identified, a clue which was much more reckless in the Italian's case than his naked face against the light in the peon's. He asked to be relieved of guard duty on Nino, and exempted from any future contact with him. They assumed he hated him and agreed. He knew it was not true but took advantage of their misconception nonetheless. He could never hate a prisoner, no matter who he was.

Caragua (III)

Cenere o terra che secca si cavi
d'un color fora col suo vestimento...

Colour of ash or earth dug dry, agrees
Well with the sober vesture on him clad

Dante, *Purgatory*, Canto IX

A man's death should always be central to any drama. That is why, among other reasons, wars are so stupid—they waste and sacrifice at the same time thousands of central plots. The machine gun, the bomb, kill indiscriminately; there is no individual fate for each death they cause, no private reference to the destiny of the man caught up in the destruction of his body. That is why that form of death is so blind, so horrible, so stupid. To rescue any meaning, we have to search for difficult doors, perhaps impossible doors, as though they lie within walls which (in the absence of God, in our case) we know to be invulnerable.

Marcos had just been told. It was mid-morning. The executive committee had decided, without looking at Pascasio's face (without ever having seen it) that the only possible safe solution (in what way safe? Safe for whom? Safe for how long?) would be death, for the time being, Pascasio's death. Two *compañeros*, experienced in giving injections, would be coming from Montevideo with one of the 'Orga's' leaders, who would be responsible for the operation. Responsible as far as they were concerned, that is, because the judges would see it differently and hold more people responsible. Marcos had spend the night with the prisoner but had been relieved at dawn. He had not

171

slept at all, preoccupied as he was by the crisis of his own responsibility. Not the responsibility the judge and the public prosecutor would probably discuss, because some day someone was bound to talk even if it was not the peon. Marcos did not care about that. Nor the responsibility (there would be no more discussion of the reasons) which brought the 'Orga's' man from Montevideo, because *he* was merely responsible for the details of the deed; the bus trip, the box containing the phials, the timing of the injection, maybe choosing the site for the grave, for the pick and shovel.

Marcos was just about to let the calves out when Antonio came over to tell him. He had seen Raúl get off the bus a hundred yards from the proper stop. He came walking along the road, looking to see if anyone had got off behind him, making sure no one was following or watching him. When he was within ten yards of the *compañeros*, even before he spoke, he raised his right hand to the middle of his chest and turned his thumb downwards. The width of his back, acting as a wall between the others and the road, protected the gesture.

'No one in Caragua seemed pleased with the decision,' said Antonio. He himself was looking contrite. The *compañeros* on the executive committee were not happy either, neither with themselves, their lack of imagination, nor the problem they had had to resolve. That is what Raúl had said and Antonio repeated it.

'But it was what you suggested last night,' Marcos reminded him gently, trying not to sound offensive.

'It was and it is,' replied Antonio. 'But I'm not happy about it. I wasn't trying to win a bet.'

172

Marcos squeezed Antonio's left forearm. His hand, framed against calves jostling each other towards the gate, went up and patted Antonio's shoulder. It was as if he wanted to express his condolences and solidarity precisely because he *had* won the bet. Antonio understood and smiled wryly.

'...sometimes things just have to be done,' was all he could say.

'But *I* won't do them,' replied Marcos forcefully.

'Won't do what?' asked Antonio.

'I won't soften him up with lies about going on a trip and, call me the Priest as much as you want, but I won't help give him any injections. I'll offer him my suit, that bit of mud-coloured rag I've got, because we have to pretend we're moving him somewhere else. But I won't help bury him, and I won't throw a handful of earth on his grave. I'll dig the hole if I'm told to, he wouldn't be there anyway, but I won't throw my handful of earth on his grave,' he repeated.

'And if you're ordered to?'

'I'll try to avoid being ordered to, I'll talk to them. It's senselessly cruel to tell me to do that after making me spend his last night with him. In a sense I acted like the priest you all think I should be.'

'The suit...your suit,' Antonio hesitated. 'Why give him your suit to wear?'

It was Marcos' turn to smile.

Slowly, in the ambiguous tones of a sermon, Marcos began to reproach himself. He expected no sympathy from Antonio, whom they always called the 'hardware' man.

'Last night I suggested he join us,' he said. 'I can't have

173

done it with much conviction though, because he didn't even ask what ''join us'' meant. It's at times like this that I realize we also speak a kind of code. I finally explained although he did not ask, and he shook his head. Was that when he sealed his own fate? What d'you think?'

'And who authorized you to suggest he join us?'

'I knew he wouldn't accept, he'd be more frightened of that than he would of dying... But if he'd have said yes, I'd have talked to the others just in case they agreed to consult Montevideo...and I might even have asked to go myself. After all, we wouldn't have lost anything by putting the decision off another twenty-four hours. In any case... But he didn't, he said ''no'' twice, he was quite sure. He said it was none of his business, that it all had nothing to do with him. And the worst of it is that he's right...'

'It would've been a disaster letting him join,' thought Antonio. 'Remember what happened with the thief that time? We'd have had to kill him afterwards, in cold blood, when all the urgency had gone.'

He was thinking of the case of a common criminal whom they had invited to escape with them from *El Abuso*. The man had agreed, seemed to have joined, and had been given special tasks in three or four operations. But one day they got suspicious and discovered he had been keeping ransom money for himself. They confronted him, and told him he would be tried. He then threatened them, he said he had people notified in case anything happened to him. You'll have to let it pass, he insisted. They tried him *in absentia*, and decided to get rid of him. When they came to carry out the sentence, he saw them coming, realized what was happening, got up from the chair he was sitting in, and made a move to defend himself, but they did not give him time. That was somewhere else, not Caragua, Caragua did not exist then. But Antonio and Marcos had both been there and that time they had both been of the same mind.

'Remember?'

'How could I forget,' replied Marcos. But that had been different. The guy had cheated them, betrayed them, was almost certainly an informer who would turn them in at any moment, and to cap it all, he had had the gall to threaten them. What Marcos was saying was that there had to be a reason for killing someone. In the thief's case there was a reason, he argued. But not in the peon's. That time, Marcos had helped choose the place, on the bank of the river in an area washed by the tide. That was the end of him.

'That was different,' he insisted.

But it was kinder not to ask, not to keep asking him to explain the extent of the difference, since the outcome had been the same—death.

'And besides,' said Marcos unexpectedly, 'that time we tried him ourselves, we took care of it ourselves, and did everything ourselves, right to the very last...'

'That was what I suggested yesterday,' replied Antonio, he too made sure there was nothing offensive in his tone. 'And you were the one who wanted to consult Montevideo and receive orders from there. I don't understand you, why change your mind, from one day to the next? Did something happen last night?'

'No, nothing,' Marcos lied, in the desperate hope the

175

other might understand. 'It's just that yesterday I could see that the majority supported your argument. So I took the chance that in Montevideo they'd come up with something else.'

'You lost your bet,' Antonio said now, but without arrogance, with no sense that there was anything in his victory to boast about.

Marcos was conscious of that fact that he should have gone up to the peon and said, I want you to know what I think, I think they are wrong, but I cannot disobey an order, nor the 'Orga'...because, in the end, I'm not my own man either. But am I less guilty because I didn't take the decision and am telling him that I disagree with it? No, it's the same for all of us... But they had decided to pretend they were taking him somewhere else, and would make him get dressed for the journey. We'll be putting you to sleep, they added. So, compassion, just as much as discipline, prevented him from speaking the truth. And of the two values Marcos far and away preferred compassion.

He was up to his knees in a hole which was beginning to take shape. Raúl had chosen Marcos and two others because the *compañero* from the executive committee had been delayed. Had Antonio asked Raúl to choose him? 'He wouldn't be there anyway.' Raúl had taken them down to the old river bed which was now dry and surrounded by trees and, marking the spot, said, 'Dig a hole this long and this wide.' 'How deep?' One of the others (not Marcos) had asked. 'Say a yard and a half,' Raúl had said precisely. He was in charge until the *compañero* from Montevideo arrived. A yard and a half, they were nearly

176

there. It was two o'clock, the hole should be ready by late afternoon. It was clay soil, difficult to dig. They had abandoned the shovels and were finishing the sides with the curved edges of bricklayers' trowels. Marcos seemed to have got over his anguish and was strenuously tackling the job in hand. No one had mentioned what the hole was for, but Marcos knew from his conversation with Antonio. And besides, the measurements were unmistakable. Marcos compared them with his own body because he and Pascasio were about the same size.

There was a particular kind of debate he was very interested in, which dealt with extreme points of view. That is why Marcos had often said he would find directing his own version of *Dirty Hands* fascinating. Yes, his own interpretation of the play. He had also said many times, however, that it is not a question of dismissing a particular version because it differs conceptually from ours. We have to be impartial, put ourselves in the artist's place and judge it from there. The results will differ considerably. Otherwise, we have to go the whole way and create our own version. He had not brought his books with him, there were none in his hut at the end of the paddock. It would have jeopardized his credibility and he had to be very careful of that. A *real* man who tends pigs and cows would not be reading Sartre, just as a *real* cattle-breeder would not call his ranch 'Spartacus'.

But if he had brought his old books with him, he would have run to his hut yesterday in search of *Dirty Hands*. For him, Pascasio was a variant of Sartre's Hoederer. And Hoederer was the only character in the play he was really interested in. Not for nothing (and this was probably to

177

do with his anarchism and distrust of imposed disciplines) would he have directed the play concentrating on the character of Hoederer rather than Hugo. And for that same reason, he probably would not have been allowed. Was Hoederer objectively a traitor, as his old friends in the theater would say? If Hoederer was objectively a traitor, Pascasio could objectively be an enemy. If one accepts the outer limits of the categories of intention and guilt, it all becomes one monstrous jelly. But Hoederer, at least, was a voluntaristic actor, his behaviour had purpose and meaning, while the peon was the exact opposite. Barrault's Hoederer was Marcos' most memorable theater experience since the night he saw the French actor in performance at the Solís. It was like an age-old memory of another life before we tried to change the world, a time when we could go to the theater, have a coffee in a café, read a book in a park, discuss ideas without having to take action, learn about ourselves and not about set circumstances which denied our own individuality. All that was destroyed by our experience of action and clandestinity. But even in the midst of it all, with no emotional conflict, Barrault's Hoederer was unquenchably alive. Trofimov, the student in *The Cherry Orchard*, and many others were only characters, creatures who existed because of someone's talent, mere creations. But Barrault's Hoederer was more than that, and that is why it was possible to conjure him up while helping dig another man's grave—while in the very act of collaborating in his murder. When Hugo appears, the play says that he is thirty-three and is standing in the doorway. It says absolutely nothing about Hoederer, but Barrault put a white sweater on this bodily nothingness. There it is, it cannot be anything else, he cannot be conceived in any other way, it is a bit of real life which comes into play and will not go away. He no longer belongs to fiction and the realm of probability. It escapes mere artistic creation, mere fantasy; Hoederer wears a white sweater, it is impossible to imagine him in anything else. To talk about Hoederer without having seen the white sweater is like saying 'a farm hand, about thirty-five years old, appears at the mouth of Caragua one morning.' But suddenly that farm hand begins to exist. His name is Pascasio Báez, he has earth-coloured feet and yellow eyes. You have to assume that or you cannot know him, judge him, take decisions about his life or death. He is now real, like the white sweater. He is Pascasio Báez, he cannot be anyone else. They would have to deal with him. Yet in Montevideo they had just condemned him to death without even having seen him. Could they take Hoederer's white sweater away? Besides, Hoederer was Barrault's age just as the peon was the same age as Pascasio Báez. Hoederer had (he would always have) Barrault's bony, taut, painful face, his high waxy cheekbones, his elusive eyes, his dry slit of a mouth. These are facts impossible to alter, they transcend dramatic illusion. One can imagine the rest, but by itself it is not enough. Is Hoederer objectively a traitor as Pascasio Báez is objectively an enemy? It would be possible to discuss these questions in an abstract, speculative way if the characters in question (Hoederer in his white sweater, Pascasio with his earth-coloured feet and yellow eyes) had never existed. As soon as they are there in the flesh, the argument is different, it changes. Guilty or not, traitor or not, enemy or not,

179

this all has to be debated, of course, but other factors have to be taken into consideration now: those high cheekbones, that voice, that sweater, those earth-coloured feet, those eyes. It is impossible to go on inventing something real.

And there he was, Marcos, shovelling earth out of the grave, following orders, orders from others who had never seen the earth-coloured feet, yet believed they had the right to pass sentence.

And so, to give the matter its true colours, he had taken his mud-coloured, rust-coloured, worm-coloured suit from his hut (would someone who tended pigs and calves be likely to have one?) and had offered it to Raúl. That was before he had been chosen to be one of the gravediggers. Earth, rust, worm, impossible synonyms for life, but not for death. Earth, rust, worm, equally gratuitous detritus..destiny as refuse, or the other way round, refuse as destiny. He went up to Raúl with the suit and said, 'Dress him in this, our bodies are the same, he and I.' 'Do you want to put it on him?' 'No, you do it, to disguise the reason for the trip. I don't want to.' He had said, 'Our bodies are the same, he and I.' But atheist and ignorant of the subject as he was, he could not have been referring to the sacrament of the Eucharist or to either of them as Christ. It was only a question of the same height, width of shoulders, size. Again, the real world, perhaps for the last time.

Raúl held the suit in his hands for a moment without a word. Then he took it away but came back a few minutes later, called to Marcos and the two others and asked them to dig the hole.

He looked up and said, '*Compañeros*, it is done.' If

Antonio had asked him what he meant, he would have answered, 'the worst of it is, he was right,' because we wanted them to join before we stopped to think who they were, because we invented the Armadillo Plan before bothering to find out what went on in these people's heads, how their minds worked, how they functioned, in other words, whether they wanted for themselves what we wanted for them. And now, perhaps, other people will be wondering what is going on in our heads, urban guerrillas turned rural guerrillas. At the beginning, when we robbed the Monty Finance Company and the San Rafael Casino, we were Robin Hoods, we wanted justice, we were crusaders against injustice, defenders of the poor. But after that, after we had been forced to kill, we became, in the minds of the majority, murderers, wild animals cornered in their dens, teeth and claws at the ready. And now, for logistic reasons, that transformation was complete. We were digging the grave of a man whom we would never ever have reason to believe was anything but innocent.

'*Compañeros*, it is done. And I now realize who it is we are burying.'

'Who?' they asked, allowing him to exercise his fantasy for a moment (was he going mad?).

'We are burying Robin Hood,' he said.

At four o'clock the two doctors and the *compañero* in charge of the operation arrived. Raúl's orders had been carried out and everything was ready. The *compañero* from Montevideo did not have the power to change the instructions he had brought, so nothing depended on the good or bad impression Pascasio made. The case was closed. The *compañero* asked the doctors to proceed at once, he

181

himself would see the prisoner only when he was dead.

The elder of the two doctors was to attend to Pascasio, due to his long experience of dealing with the sick in hospitals. The assumption was that Pascasio was sick.

'Brother,' he said to him in the farmhouse kitchen (two *compañeros* had brought him from Caragua because they had agreed that it would have been obscene and indiscreet to carry a corpse up), 'you're being moved. We've come to get you...'

'Moving where to?' asked Pascasio, suspiciously rather than fearfully.

'We can't tell you, brother. You'll find out later on, not now, we have to put you to sleep for the journey for security reasons.'

The repeated word 'brother' smacked inevitably of Cain. The doctor decided not to use it again, and softened his tone still further.

'Where are you taking me?' Pascasio insisted on an answer. 'Will something bad happen to me?'

'No, nothing.'

Marcos was not there to hear the question asked the previous night come out intact. It was clear that the idea of being put to sleep really alarmed him. But instead of saying so, he asked,

'And the colt?'

'Forget the colt.' The doctor adopted a kindly tone, intended to inspire medical confidence, because his imagination did not stretch to any other.

'Fucking hell,' exclaimed the peon, encouraged by their sympathy to show his anger, and as if he wanted to make a joke to cement their friendship. 'Asleep, and with no

182

colt. Dammit !'

The doctor could not resist a smile. He took advantage of it to say, 'We are going to have to give you a little injection.'

He said 'a little injection' to ease his own conscience because if he had said 'a lethal dose' the peon would not have understand it anyway.

He was oddly dressed, as if for a ceremony...brown two-piece suit and a faded but clean white shirt. The doctor probably imagined he would not have come running through the fields after a colt dressed like that, but instead of asking about it, he said as the younger doctor passed him a syringe of pentothal, 'Roll up your sleeve a bit. Take your left arm out of your jacket.'

They helped him do it, and the doctor saw he did not have to roll up his sleeve because it only came down to the elbow.

The first dose was very slow, and Pascasio's eyes showed he wanted to say something but could not. The young doctor held the patient's left arm, in case he withdrew it violently, but he did not. He might have wanted to say, 'I'm dying,' or perhaps, simply, 'I'm falling asleep.' Neither phrase reached his lips. The second injection was given to an inert body which had slumped over without falling off the chair.

The older doctor went to find a stethoscope in the bag he had hidden in the darkest corner of the room where Pascasio could not see it. He took a long time examining him, granting him his kindly, detailed, yet remote attention as if he had not used the instrument for ages. A long time seemed to go by, minutes, too many minutes, but

183

only those necessary for him to be able to say what he finally said.

'This man is dead.'

The *compañero* from Montevideo came in from the next room at that precise moment. He refrained from looking at the face. The doctor had just closed the eyelids in a tardy, ambiguous caress.

'What's that suit?' he asked. 'Does it belong to one of the *compañeros*?'

Only when the answer came did the doctor break free from the surreal image of the man in city shoes, trousers, jacket and shirt, running over the hills after a runaway colt.

'Take it off immediately, before rigor mortis sets in,' he ordered.

They knew Marcos had wanted to give the peon a present to take with him under the earth, but since it was the first order the *compañero* had given, it did not seem wise to argue.

'Do we know his name, and how old he was?' he asked next. They told him. The *compañero* dismissed the other details they wanted to give him...his wife in San Carlos, the ranch where he worked as a day labourer.

'I think the less biography we have on the enemy the better, except for information which gives us some advantage over him and helps us act against him.'

It was clear the *compañero* wanted to appear tough, since he had come a long way and was older than the rest. The word 'biography' sounded clumsy, as cruel as the word 'enemy' and the need to 'act against him'. Pascasio's body contradicted it all.

Meanwhile, they had begun undressing the body. They

184

took off the laceless shoes (a gift from whom?) slipped on earlier over dark, bare feet, without socks, the white shirt, and the worm-coloured suit. They had not found underpants for him.

Someone brought a length of sacking doubtlessly prepared before Marcos' gift of the suit. They wrapped him in it, naked but well covered.

The small horse and cart they used for ferrying the milk churns was waiting outside. They put the bundle of sacking in it. They chased the dog's curiosity away with a stone and the old nag trundled off very slowly as if recognizing the unusual the nature of the load.

'There are *compañeros* waiting down there,' they replied to another question.

Antonio preferred not to climb onto the narrow plank which served as driver's seat. He lead the way on foot, holding the nag by the reins.

'This old boy wouldn't have got away from him like the colt,' he said.

Karonicki

Ma voi chi siete, a cui tanto distilla
quanti' veggio dolor giu per le guance?
e che pena e in voi che si sfavilla?

But who are you, whose cheeks are seen to teem
Such distillation of grief? What comfortless
Garments of guilt upon your shoulders gleam?

Dante, *Inferno*, Canto XXIII

I'll always imagine Karonicki the way he was described
to me on that freezing rainy night in mid-autumn, May
the 18th. Karonicki, enormous, stripped to his underpants,
standing in the middle of the cobbled yard of the prison.
It's raining, and water runs down his face and shoulders,
down the rest of his body; but by some strange optical
effect I can see it running above all down his face, streaming down past the corners of his mouth as if to give the
impression he is crying. He is not crying, however, as
though the relief of tears were not granted him, and he
had known this fact for more than a generation now. He
doesn't cry. He confronts everything with a fathomless,
timeless resignation worse than tears or shouted protests:
the attitude of a Jew caught up in a pogrom. There is a
famous photograph of a boy, who must be about ten years
old, during the burning of the Warsaw ghetto. The boy
with the crooked cap. He's wearing a jacket and short
trousers, has bare knobbly knees, and his cap is tilted to
one side. The boy of the Warsaw ghetto. This he knows
is death, and his face says it. His face offered to an

186

unimaginable photographer, chronicler of fire and looting. Another Jew, a Nazi? We'll never know. Probably a Nazi: they documented everything, set up filing systems for the worst barbarism, for public and private infamy. The wonder is that this photograph is so unemotional, yet so chillingly full of terror. The boy knows that death is at hand, but he's a Jewish boy and by this time, death has lost all meaning. It has nothing that can frighten more than the horror he has seen, nothing to wring a fresh reply from fear, whose voice has already been rendered speechless. The Jewish boy stands there, houses are burning all around him, the people with him until just a moment before are most likely dead, and their deaths have transformed what's left of the world in his eyes, in that precise moment when the photographer has caught him, into a desert of absolute indifference. Who was that ten-year-old boy? Nobody ever laid claim to that chance moment which made of his face the symbol of martyrdom. Nobody ever came forward to say 'Here I am, that was me twenty years ago, look at me.' He never did so, no doubt because five minutes after the photograph, his own death overtook him. And yet it is possible to imagine a more pathetic fate than that of this child: that of the child living on. That incredibly sad and empty face had nothing at all left to say. 'Hands up', and he hardly raised them above his ears. Nothing to say, nothing to beg for; the Nazis had wrung him to the bone, had said everything for him. Impossible to imagine Karonicki, huge and naked, as that boy. He couldn't have grown so much, from those wretched knobbly knees to this enormous bulk. His parents (Karonicki wasn't yet born) lived through the Warsaw ghetto fire. His grand-

187

parents helped to fill the sealed railway trucks, and went to their deaths. Karonicki seldom talks about that; it happened so long ago for him, it has been talked about so often. And yet one can imagine that, since childhood, this image of naked, rain-swept horror has been with him, and that in this very moment, in the dawn of May the 18th, it is somehow happening again.

One May 18th, in 1972, in a vicious attack that was as stupid as it was desperate, a commando from the MLN gunned down four soldiers guarding the home of General Gravina. It was their senseless and brutal way of affirming that the battle was continuing, when in fact it was being lost. On a cold and rainy night, that other May dawn, the soldiers, wrapped in their cloaks and huddled in a jeep, were keeping watch over the commander-in-chief's sleep. They had been drinking maté—there were empty thermos flasks around them. Machine guns ripped them to pieces on the spot; one of the victims hadn't even time to open his eyes. It was so senseless that some people thought the whole thing was a fake, that the bodies had been placed like that for propaganda purposes. No: it was a real crime, that of madness, a last convulsive effort, the desperate need to do something because everything was falling to pieces.

May the 18th, dawn of the anniversary of Las Piedras, Artigas: impossible to pick a better day for martyrs, with four humble almost anonymous names redolent of the North: Saúl Correa, Osiris Núñez, Gaudencio Núñez and Ramos Jesús Ferreira—jeep 229 and its cargo of shrouded bodies will live on in the posters of institutional vengeance.

That was a year ago, next year will make two, and how is the army to commemorate it, in what way does it respond, what values does it call into play? Panic, panic on a set date: you knew they would come and they did so, you knew they'd return, and on the night of the battle of Las Piedras they came back. That's how they celebrate Army Day. Fort Gluck has prepared some terrifying posters. A huge pair of eyes with deep irises staring out of a murky background with the inscription: the Tupamaro guerrilla is always watching you. The gleam of a knife blade as it buries itself between a pair of shoulder blades, a heavy drop of blood rolling downwards, shining with the light of the universe: the Tupamaro stabs you in the back. A tiny little old woman, apparently all generosity, offers a basket of fruit: the Tupamaro is everywhere. The typical posters of a fisherman concealing his gun among the fish: the Tupamaro is always lurking, the Tupamaro is laying a trap, the Tupamaro is spying on you, pursuing you, the Tupamaro is waiting for you, the Tupamaro is coming to get you, the Tupamaro know your movements and leaps on you, the Tupamaro has got you. One couldn't expect too much imagination from the artist at Fort Gluck. Enough to instil in him two or three ideas (so that he could in turn instil them in others): there can be no relaxing, your life is in danger day and night, wherever you may be, whatever is happening; because the Tupamaro is treacherous, merciless, and always on the look-out, the Tupamaro never sleeps, he is waiting, panting, like a wild beast crouched to spring, he's after only one thing—your life. To fall on you, tear you to pieces, murder you. Why? Because you are who you are, because you defend your country, because you love it and are willing to give everything for it. This is what the artist knows. All of it

189

portrayed in the sordid style of *Rosemary's Baby*. Defend yourself from them, kill them at every opportunity, don't allow them any breathing space, don't give them the slightest chance, because then you offer them life, and that will mean your death. Defend yourself from them as you would from a rabid animal, from a wild beast lusting for blood. You must attack them, kill them whenever you can. Don't worry, the Order will protect you.

But on the night of May the 17th-18th they turn to something stronger than the effect of posters or warnings or goading. On that night a new element is brought into play. It's probably not marijuana, because that affects the smoker's nerves. First it makes him thoughtful, dreamy, and sleepy, and they're looking for something else, for violence, lack of control, aggression. That's the way they celebrate. The reasons for celebration can be deduced from the way they do it. Something upsets the fragile everyday balance, and that something smashes through boxes and tears off hinges. It may well be that the means are no more refined than those employed by common criminals to rouse themselves into their orgy of shouting, stampeding, bells, alarm sirens and knifings: mandrax and Coca-Cola, disorienting stimulant of barbiturates and coca so that all hell breaks loose.

It's three in the morning, and everyone knows already. Three hours before the army's ominous dawn, which must be used to good advantage. Here they come, piled into three or four trucks. The usual guards of the prison disappear, leave things to them; the gates of Ellauri must be (the word has gone round) left wide open, since no one can be sure of the drivers' reflexes, or of their brakes, or the force of that carefully stoked screaming rage flung into action on this precise date, the anniversary of the four soldiers. The Saúls, the Gaudencios, the Osirises and the Jesuses are dead, and this is the best way to serve their memory. This first year it will go unnoticed by the whole neighbourhood of Punta Carretas. They will learn later on. It's not an escape, or an alarm; it's a raid. Not a mutiny or plot, but a pogrom. The guards open Ellauri's massive gates. For a brief while security inside the prison is suspended, because in any case it's from outside that it is to be broken. The troops' whooping screams in the night—a sound meant to be raucous, ridiculous, and unnerving—accompany them as they burst in. Their party begins before dawn of May the 18th, with the ridicule of the prisoners in the political wing. The soldiers leap from their trucks, form up noisily and press forward. No one is to stand in their way, because one of the rules of this absurd game is perhaps that of no surrender.

The wailing of the sirens splutters to a halt, the search-lights on the trucks play for a moment on the chosen section of the prison's grey walls. All the lights inside are switched on in reply. The guards hand over all their duties, give way before the monstrous break-in. They give way and disappear. Still stronger searchlight beams, and shouts—their shouts, aimed into the unresisting air, shouts which meet with no reply from the prisoners, who have been waiting for the attack for several hours now. Everybody line up in the yard—that's the order. Or more exactly, it's not an order. It's a mixture of insults, curses, an anger chewed on for so long it is spit out into nothing. 'Bastards, fucking murderers'—that's how the order

191

begins—'line up in the yard.' Only one person stays in each section of the prison, the one who will hand over the belongings, the one who will tell them where they are although, in any case, they would find them wherever they were and destroy them. Bayonets rip open woollen and flock mattresses, spear the small cardboard panels where the prisoners pin family souvenirs at the top of their bunks. The destruction is also a symbolic pogrom against the faces of the children and the smiles of the loved woman and the serene countenances of parents, everything that conjures up normal feelings in prison about hearth and home. Perhaps the shouts are merely to lend some justification to the stabbing bayonets. This is the military's party, it's their night, it's their dawn of the long knives wielded against idols, images, landscapes of lives patched together on wretched pieces of cardboard. 'Bastards, degenerates' shouts the short chubby lieutenant, who seems to be one of the most excited. 'They kill our men but they've got to be respected. Don't touch a hair of the bastards' heads, they're sacred.'

Everyone is outside in the yard now, on the cobbles. It's raining. 'Take your clothes off, strip to your underpants, bastards. So it's cold, is it? Too bad, the people you murder are colder still, fucking butchers.'

Lines of barefoot prisoners, lines of underpants and cold. 'Bastards'. On the top floors of the prison, small vents open in the darkness, letting out shadows, a smell of acidity and sweat, rancid sleep. The common prisoners are watching. It's not their turn, this has nothing to do with them. When the whistles, the alarms, the bells, the cudgels, are aimed at them, then they run. Not now. Now they don't even move. Between the floors of the Tupamaros and theirs are long nests of wire, like the skeletons of mattresses or nets used by acrobats, a network of springs laid over emptiness, a net in which from time to time some poor wretch runs like a cornered rat while the guards, better trained, also run across the bouncing coils dealing him blows, whistle, run after him again, shout through their loudspeakers, rain blows on him. Yes, then it's their turn, with the regular warders and their heads streaming blood, split open by blows from knives or truncheons. But now it's someone else's turn, the Tupamaros' turn. This time it's not them, and they don't interfere. They don't talk, mutter, say anything. You might think they are asleep, sunk in their layers of grime and silence, indifferent. But they aren't; they look on in the night. Without sympathy, perhaps without hate, they look on. They can see the line of men stripped in the cold, dripping in the searchlights, the line of men in underpants in the dawn rain. It's not their turn.

In the cells of the political prisoners there is milk. In their cells in the civil prisons—which the military are trying hard to do away with— there are portable radios to listen to the news, there's sugar, there are small kerosene heaters, yerba to make some maté in the afternoons, the second time for maté each day. Soldiers and even their officers, bayonets in hand, smash open containers, pierce bags, happily pour out the green stream of yerba, or mix it with ant-killer; they pour kerosene with the milk, plunge the transistors into the kerosene. The aim is to destroy these tiny hoards of foodstuffs, which it seems revolutionaries have no right to. They are in jail for seeking to bring about a revolution, but they behave like the petty

193

bourgeoisie, storing their saved fruits: yerba, the gestures of their children, the benign smiles of parents, radio news, the fight against cockroaches, soap powder, insecticide, somber sexual longings in their own eyes and those of their women. One of the officers goes over to one of the plastic containers of milk, opens his fly, and begins to urinate in it with slow purpose. In its two quarts of milk is floating a transistor radio. He doesn't need to urinate, but forces himself. The soldiers smash things only when ordered to. As if the initiative for such action needed a command, as if they felt they had no right to revenge unless expressly authorised. A soldier, on his own account, cannot: those in charge rob, those in charge smash, those in charge do the beating.

Now the chubby officer thinks he's made the great discovery, and howls: 'And this Tupamaro star, who's the bastard who put it there?'

He's standing at the head of Karonicki's bunk. When he learns that Karonicki is responsible for it, he has him brought out into the yard, and begins to hit him laboriously. The biggest prisoner of them all, barefoot and naked in the rain.

'It's not the Tupamaro star, officer,it's the star of David,' Karonicki tries to explain, while dodging the stupid blows, which don't really bother him that much anyway.

'Say "Lieutenant, Sir" when you speak to me, you bastard.'

Karonicki repeats, in the correct way, that it is the star of David , but the Lieutenant doesn't appear to be listening, he merely turns on him and hits him again.

'You tell him,' the giant figure protests, without

194

apparently any pain from the blows. 'You all know perfectly well. Tell him once and for all, don't play games.'

Nobody says anything, while he, hunched in the rain, tries to make them believe him. 'It's the six-pointed star, Lieutenant, Sir. Just take a good look.'

But the officer's rage knows no bounds, and won't be satisfied with just one object: 'Bolshies, Zionism, and Cosa Nostra,' he shouts... 'three things that will destroy us if we don't put a stop to them first. Three forces that will destroy the world.' He pauses for dramatic effect: 'We must fight to the death.'

It seems that to go on believing that it's the Tupamaro star is of no great importance to him. His rancour moves on rapidly to focus on the Jews.

Karonicki had talked it over on various occasions with his parents during their fortnightly visits. Their plan was very simple. They would get their son the most expensive lawyer (the most expensive, they would repeat, we can afford it). Have him set free, then all of them leave the country quickly. We have seen how this sort of thing starts, a quarter of a century ago, in another place. We know how these things begin...that's why we don't want to stay...to wait a second time.

'Go tell that to your Jewish friends who don't want to know and are collaborating with these filthy Nazis,' Karonicki would reply blandly. 'Don't say it to me, I'm already in jail.' (And one couldn't escape from the fact that it was to the other child with the crooked cap that they would have liked to have been saying it.)

After his parents had gone, he would add that he didn't

want to leave the country either. 'I must have a streak of the ancestral longing for martyrdom in me, but the truth is I don't want to leave. This is my land, dammit.'

Yes, but Poland had been their land, and their fathers' and grandfathers' land before them, and what use had that been, when the time came?

The old Jewish couple didn't hesitate in trying to win over their friends: 'Please, tell your son to persuade our boy that he must leave the country. The two of them are friends and perhaps he'll listen to him... We're Jews and we've already been in one concentration camp. We didn't die because we were young and strong, like he is now. But who knows whether this time...'

I often think of Karonicki. He wouldn't listen to them, he smiled gently when his parents talked of selling their business in Andes Street, finding him a good lawyer, securing his freedom in that way (secretly, discreetly, they couldn't think or believe in anything but buying it, on any terms, whatever it might cost). And then straightaway— to get out—out! Where to? To the United States, they would reply. 'A Tupamaro in the United States, you must be crazy!' Yes, the United States, they had rich relatives there, whom they could count on. I wonder if they have gone?

The tubby officer who blamed the Bolshies, Zionism, and the Cosa Nostra for everything, saw them as wrecking the world if they were given the time. He was getting more and more hysterical. But nobody dared contradict him, either in his apocalyptic judgement or in the mistake which started it all off, the confusion between the Tupamaro emblem and the star of David. He hit the young man two or three times more, until he was finally convinced it was useless to continue. Karonicki's circumcised penis had slipped out of his underpants and swayed from side to side with the blows; the little fat officer appeared to consider that even more offensive than the star.

When he had to give up, presumably because his companions plucked up sufficient courage to explain to him, he would not back down; apparently it was he who was leading the whole operation. He ordered his men to return to their trucks and the prisoners to go back to their cells. 'All except this one,' he said, pointing out Karonicki to the prison warden. 'I want this one left for another hour in the rain, for being a bastard and a Zionist, so he'll remember me.'

The warden didn't obey the instructions. He merely waited prudently until the noise of the trucks had died away completely.

It was raining still harder. From a latrine on the fourth floor a common prisoner took advantage of the situation to shout (the anti-semitism of prison): 'Judas, it's your turn to pay.'

His was the only laugh to be heard.

The Judas, moreover, seemed to have turned to stone. Water ran from his face and shoulders. The strange nighttime optical effect in the cobbled prison yard made the water seem to dig great channels in his face creating the impression that he was crying. His eyes crying, and his penis pissing, from the crumpled soggy mass of underpants.

'Everyone to their cells—and you too,' said the warden. 'So you'll have something to say for us later on.'

The massive Jew, streaming water, didn't appear to take

in what he said. He didn't hear him, until he was pushed.

'Just one thing,' he asked his cell-mates afterwards. 'Don't anyone go and tell my folks what happened last night...they'll just go on pestering me to leave the country.'

Nino

Io era gia disposto tutto quanto
a riguardar nello scoperto fondo,
che si bagnava d'angascioso pianto

I now stood ready to observe the full
Extent of the new chasm thus laid bare
Drenched as it was in tears most miserable

Dante, *Inferno*, Canto XX

Every man has an image of himself for normal times and another for extraordinary circumstances. It is merely a question of altering the image at precisely the right moment.

I, for instance, was not born a banker. When did I become one? I have forgotten the exact date. My father was always involved in finance and was one of Mussolini's ministers in the Social Republic of Salò. Then things started to go wrong and the Duce owed his political survival solely to the exploits of Otto Skorzeny.

I am in the pit, I do not understand. Is it a parody of Dantesque suffering? Is this how revolutionaries imagine the bankers' purgatory?

I have spent days and days in this dark pit,
I feel my hands with my hands and with them
discover my face,
a face like mine, alien hands
that touch it, want to pinch it, and take
the stench of the pit to my mouth

199

the decency of those hands to my lips
and dead saliva to my eyes.
I have spent days and days in this dark pit
                              but, still, I am alive.

Am I imagining, am I writing? Did I used to write poems?
Perhaps, but not that I remember. I wonder if I did not
compose them in my mind while on a journey, at the wheel
of my car, at the rail of a yacht anchored at dead of night,
or in my mind wandering from a crossword puzzle on a
plane. Yes, I must have composed them and let them fly
away, free. I have read Ungaretti, Quasimodo, Pavese,
Montale. I learned their poems by heart, although they
were never mentioned at home. Northern Italy is said to
be less poetic than the South, but those are silly distorted
notions, meaningless clichés. Laura knows I never had
to kill the poet in me, because I never really let him be
born. Curiously enough, my pit prison filled me with
worm-ridden dampness but also with an absurd nostalgia
for poetry. I began to think, for the first time in my life,
that there are certain things you can say only in verse,
just as there are things that can be resolved only by letters of credit. I was dangerously inclined to dream this
kind of dream; a bank director is thrown into a foul-
smelling crevice in the earth, exuding murky water and
sweating thoughts of darkness in clods and slime. It is like
an allegory of death and the world beyond the grave, earth
showing through one's own skin, like muscles without
epidermis in anatomy charts. What remotest possible connection did the life I had led until then have with that liquid
oozing out of the bowels of the earth, with myself as I

200

was now, dressed at first and later, at my own request, almost naked, sitting on a bit of soaking wet sacking?

Once they put a hood on me and took me to a place where they questioned me about the procedures of the Banks' Association. Back in my hole, the guard asked me, with no particular aggression or politeness, 'Have you always had flat feet?' 'I don't have flat feet,' I replied. 'It's a wound I got in the war.'

That was all. The guard showed no interest in the details and I did not give him any. My situation was detailed enough as it was. My fantasy was not, however. Some time later my fantasy composed, clumsily, some lines of verse. And deep in that poem my memories of the war in Salò fused with the stale smell of a prisoner's socks. I wanted to write it down, I took some paper and began to draw lines on it. 'Do you have permission to write letters today?' asked the same guard who had not been able to comprehend the greatness of a hunted Fascist, just because he was a Fascist. 'No, it's poetry,' I said. Under the hood, his voice betrayed his incredulity. 'Poetry? Do you write poetry?' (As if he really wanted to ask, is a Fascist capable of that?) 'Sometimes,' I said, casually. I wrote the poem and gave it to him. He read it, twice I think, but gave no sign of having understood it, of approval or disapproval, nothing. 'I suppose it's allowed...' 'I suppose so too, but you'd better ask anyway...' I never learned the outcome, I don't think he even raised the matter, and I wrote no more poems while I was a prisoner. Therapy like that is unexpectedly cut short.

They asked me if I have flat feet.

201

No, I said, no I don't, but once,
lying on my belly defending Salò
a stray bullet wounded the sole of my foot.
It hurt me, ripped my flesh, tore out a piece of me
I should wear inner soles but... Now they listen to me
but do not want to know if it is true. What do they care?
They would rather I did not take off my shoes and risk
the smell of my feet in that pit,
the smell of a foot which has spent a month
in the mud of that pit, enveloped in a sock
which I do not take off even to sleep.
They want to believe me, not suspect me. After all,
what is a scar on the sole of a foot to them?
No, I repeat, I do not have flat feet,
I have an old scar, a pleat in the center of my foot.

I should use inner soles, but they rub the edges of the
wound,
the edges are always vulnerable.
No, inner soles scrape the skin off, better to
limp along the corridors of the bank without sores
No, I do not have flat feet, don't think it is that,
I am a war cripple, caused by a cause
(I repeat the word) a cause I no longer believe in...

I am writing this in Milan, ten years after it happened.
I don't know if there is a ten-year statute of limitations
for what I lived through, but it is long enough ago in any
case. You are all wherever you may be...and Italy is the
same old Italy. All the details, all the bargaining, are
luckily fading from my memory; the hollow trunk of the

202

tree in Villa Biarritz, the letterbox used for negotiations...the lawyer says that he passes it sometimes (he still lives near there) and is tempted to collect the last letter which remained there, forgotten. Perhaps the ghost of his cocker spaniel who died ten years ago accompanies him on his walks. I am tempted to do just the opposite, to write the letter which no one came to collect, which no one knew was there. I would have said things much more clearly, things I still believe today. They did not persuade me, as some cynics believed. They did not persuade me, just as I could not persuade them of the ultimate greatness of an outlawed and hunted Duce, former lord of an empire in ruins, hung upside down near where I am writing in the Piazza della Repubblica. The man, discredited, alone, dead, with his beautiful young mistress crying in the face of a gun barrel. They could be moved by Che Guevara, they told me, but never by a Fascist, never by the Duce. Pity is only linked to particular sympathies, it is ideologically and emotionally conditioned. It no longer carries credentials of its own. Not long ago, during the Aldo Moro kidnapping, I relived a time I thought was past. Moro might have changed a great deal in that time, but all that was left of him was a handful of letters. I certainly changed. And what was left of me?

During the last ten years I have often dreamed of the people with whom I spent those long months. I lived with them. Did I understand them? Did they understand me? Was our relationship antagonistic, contradictory, fundamentally hostile? Was that the only kind of bond we established? Could I say we hated each other—I the prisoner, they the guards—if not deep down, at least in

203

a kind of suspended truce, a frozen animosity? I would like to be honest, but I can't say because the truth is that I don't know for sure myself.

But etched on these dreams, which have flowed for a decade, comes another image. I remember the night of November 20th, 1969, when they made me get out of the car on the bend by the Oceanography Museum, between the last rocks of Puerto Buceo and the open horseshoe of the beach. They had given me a tranquilizer and were setting me free. Still, they seemed strangely nervous. The police might be trailing them, that's what they felt (that's what they said), and if they were ambushed then, we would all die. They sensed that the police might have been tipped off, might be watching. The police could kill me to discredit the Movement—see what we mean, they take the ransom and then they murder him. This, in the end, was what frightened me most. I discovered a bond of solidarity with my kidnappers, I would feel safer if we were attacked while I was still in their hands, than if the police came for me when I was sitting on the wall alongside the ocean drive, near the shore, on the bend by the *Cabaret de la Muerte*. Alone, at their mercy. Because, I thought, they could riddle me with bullets just to screw their enemies...kill me and pretend I had been executed by guerrillas. After all, they had no reason to like me very much. A sacrificial victim would be better for propaganda purposes...to prove that you cannot make deals with subversives. That was the worst moment. They told me to get out. They said that the friends they had been negotiating with would be coming for me, they were probably nearing the beach at that very moment. Meanwhile, they said, do not leave this spot. I sat on the wall, my back to the flashing lights of the passing traffic, like someone out walking at night who momentarily stops to rest, lights a cigarette and looks out to sea. I think I made out the horizon, as if the skies of Italy stretched behind it and with the certainty of imagination I could see them. They came, they finally came. I will never forget the first face I saw, that noble, aquiline face. He was beside me, then I lost his face for just a moment as we embraced. He did not share my ideas, nor I his, we met across an abyss but I felt safe, paradoxically even more safe, because he was there. The years went by. I was in Italy in May, 1976, when I heard he had been kidnapped, killed, his body abandoned with others in the boot of a car in a Buenos Aires suburb. I return to his face again and again, his image blots out all others. His blue eyes, sharp nose, tumbling lock of blonde hair never to turn grey, and big toothy smile, pound and push the waters of the night of November the 20th behind that memory. From the very depths of pity, clouding its purity (as from the crevices at the bottom of the pit), emerge obscure clots called gratitude, companionship, sympathy, protection, intimacy, world. What are these things called now? I would like to know for sure, so that I can grow old in peace.

Julio and the General

E io: 'Maestro, i tuoi regionamenti
mi son si certi e prendon si mia fede,
che li altri mi sarien carboni spenti'

'Master, for me thy teaching is so true
And so compels belief, all other tales'
Said I, 'were dust and ash compared thereto'

Dante, *Inferno*, Canto XX

The 'disappeared' do not gradually slip away from us like a drowning man in his last futile, fruitless effort to save himself. There are no eddies, no submerging heads, no whirlpools in which an arm waves desperately then disappears. We do not watch, helpless, from a distance as the drowning man loses the struggle and with it his life, swept away by the current, after a picnic. The water that shelters him till morning then returns him, bloated and nibbled by fish, to the calmest stretch of the bank or entangled in the rocks, has never actually taken him away. We always know, though perhaps not where or when. We are there. Night falls as we walk along the river bank and watch the darkening horizon. The somber mass of the sea swells, grows enormous and impenetrable, but the drowned man is part of its fauna and we can recover him in the morning. The 'disappeared' of our times, however, falls already dead from the torture factory, naked, broken and often mutilated, tied to a block of cement, or bound with wire at feet, wrists and knees. He may have drowned in a sinisterly small pool of water in the *submarino* tank where they ducked him either to suffocate or talk, it doesn't really matter; the fundamental aim, the real objective, is never clear. If he survives, and comes out, and talks straightaway, he may live. If he can't bear it, and his lungs burst, and he dies, he begins another journey, the journey of the 'disappeared'. In Argentina, their corpses waft along on winds of the estuary. Sliding and bumping out of a helicopter, they are delivered up to the currents, destined for remote beaches and the final calm of decomposition and anonymity, to the ambiguous, almost sarcastic, mercy of a brief burial in a foreign land (nobody knows who anybody is, nobody recognizes anybody, nobody asks questions, nobody claims the bodies). This is the story of the 'disappeared'. The currents carry them away from us, rocking them among islets of driftwood, flotsam and jetsam, and sheets of slime. Chinamen killed in shipboard mutinies (they say) knifed on the high seas, fugitive Koreans, mercenaries on pirate fishing boats, characters out of Conrad...yes, a sea-bloated body gets slanted eyes and might look oriental to one who did not know.

Julio's case was very different. On August the 1st, 1977, a Monday morning, Julio went out to do a few errands round the city, driving on his own. After that he was supposed to go to the funeral of Petit Muñoz in Buceo at 11 o' clock. He did not arrive. So, the time and manner of his disappearance were defined quite precisely; some time before eleven, someone had got into his van and forced him to drive on or had taken his place at the wheel. From then on...nothing. There were reasons for being cautiously optimistic as his wife preferred to be—Julio had promised to tell them his medical history before they touched him. 'I could go at any time, I've already had two brain haemor-

207

rhages, I'll be sixty-eight in a couple of days.' He was a risk, and what information could they want from him anyway? Nothing very important. Julio had been a school teacher but he wasn't now, he had been a journalist but he wasn't now. He had friends abroad, lots of them. In Unesco, in Venezuela, Ecuador, Mexico, in all the places he had been posted. The telegrams began arriving as soon as the news filtered out, but the army obviously did not believe Julio, the telegrams, or anyone. Certain forms of brutality cannot allow anything but the very image of health. They like it this way, perhaps because they need to destroy. What they tried to get out of him were mere details (whom did he send the cassette to abroad? who recorded it? who took it?), life was a detail too but it would be all right because *they* did not deign to think about it. They took no precautions, and ducked Julio's head under without more ado. But it was not all right, death knows no reasonable half-way measures. So Julio was dead and Venezuelan senators asked about him, and Unesco asked about him, and even the North American black leader Terence Todman asked about him when he passed through Uruguay. It was impossible to give a frivolous reply; death, gentlemen, sometimes comes in such futile ways...they could not say that.

They had to say he was not there, he had never been there, nobody had ever held his head under water in the tank at the marines' barracks. That is the answer they had to give, and pretend that his Indio van had vanished into thin air on that lone journey from Pocitos to the Port.

A woman's hope surpasses the limits of reality. At first his wife imagined him in some remote barracks; then as

208

time went by, in different forms of captivity abroad. Letters, inquiries, friends interceding...nothing. And then, towards the end of September, the General took over as Commander-in-Chief in an interim government. It was an amazing opportunity. Julio had been his teacher during his last year of primary school, the Sanguinetti School in La Unión. He had taught the sixth year boys in that part of the school which took up half a block on the corner of October 8th Street and Felipe Sanguinetti. And she knew (she thought she knew because she had been a teacher too) how long the effects, or loyalties rather than effects, of those golden years last.

A boy of nine and a general probably have nothing in common; forty-five years of devastation, nothing else. Even Julio, despite his long country boy's memory, could only conjure up a white tunic, a silhouette among the still fragile *paradisos* in the playground, those slim *paradisos* planted in freshly dug holes in the reddish gravel. Now they were big and strong, but the image of the boy, once graduated, had not returned to enjoy their shade, nor had the general's battledress. Julio always talked of him as a good pupil, he remembered a boy, as teachers always do, but inside the boy a man had grown. Teachers hold the secret of freshness and innocence in their memory and their smile. They sometimes fondly pinch a cheek no one would dare touch now, or pat the head of a boy now on his way to becoming another old man (like the teacher). Julio had led an interesting life and time had never stagnated round him. After the boy, he had visited other countries, lived in them, made friends with no tangible childhoods, seen the years go by. He no longer called the

209

General by his first name in the presence of a long lost schoolboy; he knew these two people as individuals—separated by time—and it would be difficult to fuse them now. But *she* could perhaps, especially at the very moment she took up her pen to plead her womanly desperation and solitude.

'Señor General: You are a very important man and I am merely a woman who spends twenty-four hours a day, waking and sleeping, looking for her husband. Julio disappeared more than a month and a half ago. I have learned nothing of his whereabouts during this time, but I have not given up hope of finding him. Against all advice I address myself directly to you. All I ask is a few minutes of your time. Surely you have not forgotten the teacher you had in your sixth year of primary school? He often mentioned you. More than once over the years, as you rose to not unexpectedly important positions, he talked to me about you, and I can assure you that his memories of those days and of you were very pleasant. I imagine you will be aware that nothing has been heard of my husband since August the 1st. I wonder if you, in your present position, could obtain some information for me. That is all I ask, I implore you in the name of the many years which have passed and the pure innocent affection of those bygone days.'

She had purposely sought not to provoke emotion, and so elude the secretaries, *aides de camps*, assistants, and all those other openers of letters which never arrive. Better a few sober lines, and know that they would get to him for sure.

That same night the phone rang and the Chief of Police

210

himself came on the line, not through a telephonist or operator. He was a colonel, he introduced himself with rank, serial number and duties.

'Señora, you sent a letter to the Commander-in-Chief.'

'Yes, Señor. Today, this very afternoon.'

'And the Commander-in-Chief called me straightaway, he is very concerned. He assumed his new duties only yesterday and knows nothing of the case you describe...'

'Nothing at all?'

'They had no reason to inform him in his previous post.'

'But people in Caracas and Paris know already...'

'In any case, Señora, he asked me to contact you immediately. For my part, I'll ask you to be good enough to receive an official who will call on you tonight. He is of the utmost confidence.'

The official was a police inspector. He kept on asking questions.

'Did you report the disappearance at your local police station?'

'The same day.'

'Did you do anything else?'

'We took a medical certificate with my husband's clinical history to the Navy Mechanics School so that they would know about the risk to his health. But apparently it arrived too late because they denied holding him in any of their sections and returned the certificate to me.'

'When was that?'

'August the 8th.'

At this stage, towards the end of September, the inspector suggested publishing a 'wanted' ad in the newspapers and asked for a not too old photograph which he took away

211

with him.

The photo appeared the following day but, not unexpectedly, nobody came forward with the desired information. A couple of days later, however, the police inspector reappeared. He brought with him a type-written file headed 'routine investigation'. She read Julio's name on the cover, opened the file, and skimmed rapidly through the several pages. The investigation had come up with the information that the person concerned had travelled to Buenos Aires on Uruguay's official airline exactly two days before the Commander-in-Chief had taken up his duties. There was a number corresponding to an airline passenger list. Would she consider herself informed and be good enough to sign? No, she could not have a copy.

'Don't think I'm going to believe any of that,' she said.

'I am merely communicating to you the result of an investigation carried out by others,' the official refrained from adding anything more. He obviously did not care whether he was believed or not. He took pains to maintain the facade of his credibility: *rara avis*.

'What about the van?' she continued. 'Did they put it in the plane's baggage compartment?'

The inspector shrugged his shoulders in reply.

'He disappears on August 1st, turns up travelling to Buenos Aires on September 20—something, and there's no trace of the van. Who could believe that?', she insisted.

Perhaps the General thought that only a failure could afford the luxury of a childish gesture in later life. Only an inept man, a man in whom the passing of years had registered nothing, neither responsibilities, obligations, disenchantment, nor new memories. In his case, a lot of

212

water had passed under the bridge. Too much perhaps. For him the conventions of the system were much stronger and truer than a simple childhood memory. A person knows he is important when the system which envelops him prevents him from saying yes to a memory, a past feeling. If he is stuck in the past he is no use. For the General, nothing is further from the here and now than his schooldays. Come off it! One would have to be a fool, a softy, a weakling, a hopeless romantic. Days of blue drinking fountains, packed lunches, sweaty games at break, then at the sound of the bell hurriedly lining up to drink the trembling vertical jet spurting from the bottom of the porcelain bowl before returning to class. Sometimes the electric bell did not work, and it was Julio who rang the little hand bell, the punishment bell, the games bell, and by ringing it louder and longer but paradoxically less threateningly, announced the end of playtime. Did the General remember, or had years of guard duty, boots, strangled cries, and drums deadened his mind to the sound of the bell?

Julio was dead, that much was clear. The General had not had time to ask for official confirmation (luckily the matter had not gone through his office), but he had known about it for a couple of months at this stage. How could he dig it all up now? Ask how he had died, where, who, incur the Navy's wrath when he'd just taken over? Only a failure or a dreamer, qualities of no use to a Commander-in-Chief, could start asking questions like that for the sake of a few memories. As for Julio, had he ever asked his permission to think as he thought, conspire as he surely had conspired, want what he had wanted, act how he had

213

acted? The General represented a certain kind of order, Julio believed in quite a different kind. The General wasn't about to burn his fingers by asking questions within his own order, a world where he was somebody, and have others accuse him of sentimentality and weakness, and criticize him for being wishy-washy, luke-warm, unreliable, pusillanimous, according to the scale of values by which he would really be judged. In that other strange world, the world of Julio's friends, he was already irretrievably lost: he did not feel alone because they, the generals, had power, authority, the silence of others, and strength. That was why Julio was dead. And even if he were alive, he would probably never ask something like this himself. The desperation, faith, and pitiful practicality of women was different, they leave no stone unturned, knock on every door just in case someone, the most unexpected, might open. Julio would never deceive himself like that. And if he had agreed to ask something, it would surely have been to trap him, to find a way, some day who knows when, of making him pay; simplifying from convenience and pleasure, so that for one last fictitious moment he could see a child where for years there had only been a soldier, a school uniform instead of battledress, a childish fringe instead of a kepi. The school bell does not ring in the barracks-yard, so why go on asking to hear it?

Julio is dead, but something of what he was fills cards and telegrams, raining greetings, concern, incredulity, condemnation, questions and more questions. The General is alive, and for another year he will be the Commander-in-Chief. After that, if things go well, he will hope for more power; if not so well, for embassies. Who knows.

214

Perhaps one day, as in the story of Rosebud, the name of a sled will drop from his lips in the murmured words of a coma and no one will understand them; and another day, the day his puny glory is over, someone will watch the sled go up in flames. But it will not be a sled. It will be a little bell. And perhaps the image of the schoolboy will try to prise it out of the hand ringing it, so that the hand will stay still, will not open its fingers, will not raise its forefinger and point at him and accuse him...you... the member of a certain order, you...the man who must have known yet did not want to, you...the good pupil.

But it is not the hand on the bell now, it is his own right hand, lying taut on the file on his desk. Only failures, or incurable sentimentals, only cowards, receive orders from their own memories...

The hand journeys towards the pen, takes it and writes: Case closed.

Mar Mediterraneo

...che sotto l'acqua ha gente che sospira

That others he plunged deep in this vile broth

Dante, *Inferno*, Canto VII

I've come to the conclusion that the most important things in my life have always been connected with the sea. I should have been a captain in the Navy, not a colonel. Yes, when I was about to die all I did was count the waves between myself and my son. I imagined being shot on the rocks along the shore and falling backwards into the sea, like a battle scene. Ever since they set up that kind of fabulous torture mansion bang in the middle of the residential suburb of Punta Gorda, people started imagining executions like that in the early mornings. Perhaps they were really only mock executions (that's what I think now). Who knows. From time to time (three in the morning, let's say) they stopped traffic down Coimbra Street and along the coast road. They probably blocked it off higher up at General Paz as well and from Coimbra towards the center and all the side streets. Two or three hundred yards from every intersection were soldiers warning cars away (it was said) with round cardboard signs painted red or simply by swinging lanterns like pendulums. 'Road closed, stopping prohibited.' 'Turn round and go back.' 'How do we get through?' 'Round the other way,' ordered the soldiers. 'You can't go this way.' Rifles cocked. 'Try Italia Avenue, further on, anywhere up there. You can't go through here.' It only took a matter of seconds. 'Has there been an accident?' 'Drive on, don't ask questions, don't stop, it's dangerous.' This last warning was very convincing. 'Was

216

it a bomb?' But nobody asked in case the soldiers became suspicious. 'How do you know? Who put it there?' Wide awake early risers and half drunk night owls had fueled the legend. During more lengthy questioning (or had the officers drawn it out on purpose?), a volley of gunfire sometimes came from the direction of the sea and the little bay of the Playa de Los Ingleses. The soldiers became strangely nervous, and signaled the cars blocked by the searchlights round with their rifle butts, 'Come on, drive on, don't get us into trouble.'

And so the legend of the Major's nocturnal beach executions was born. Propagated by himself no doubt, because it wasn't hard to imagine his being proud of the terror instilled by his person, his house in Mar Mediterraneo Street, his name. Fame does not pay its price when it should. The Major had been promoted and his macabre international operations spread from one country to the other, crossing the estuary to torture in a garage in a Buenos Aires suburb, killing Santucho's brother there, or bringing 'Victory for the People' (PVP) guerrillas over to Uruguay and pretending to surprise them in a house in Shangri-la, their coming out with hands up, in front of the TV cameras, to the Major's greater glorification. The regime thought the moment was ripe to propose the Major for the Interamerican Defence Council, but the U.S. denied him a visa and that was the end of his glory. The Yankees create people like that and then jettison them after they have served their purpose: that's the story and whoever doesn't want to understand...

The mansion's history bears witness to the Major's operations across the River Plate. Someone had obviously been following that fool Jorge in Buenos Aires when he was picked to bring the money over to Uruguay for the Tupamaros. First he bought himself a house in Punta Gorda, in Mar Mediterraneo Street. Then he bought a Citroën. But the Major obviously held all the cards and when he was ready, he intercepted Jorge's car, shot him, arrested the people who tended his wounds, jailed him, dug up the money (buried beneath the apple trees at Jorge's parents' farm), and kept the house. He set up the torture mansion (he might not have chosen that neighbourhood perhaps had it not been handed to him on a plate), crying it aloud to anyone who wanted to hear from his newly acquired balcony overlooking the sea, crying it from someone else's house with screams wrenched from the guts of others. Clever!

The Major's house was not just any dirty old torture chamber. His was superior among the genre. During the PVP affair, his most famous publicity coup, the Major must have hesitated between the advantages of discretion and publicity. But the whole thing was hard to keep secret. It was beginning to leak out that members of the 'Victory for the People' guerrilla group had been captured in Buenos Aires. Some were killed outright, others appeared a few months later among the corpses in the pine grove, children were taken from parents, the parents were dead or in prison, or presumed dead, or anyway 'disappeared'. It was time to bring things out into the open, to put paid to the idea of *another* land, *another* freedom, *another* life. People like the Major did not recognize national boundaries when it came to hunting subversives. Something eventually had to leak out from people involved in these toings and froings, and leak out it did. But by the time Enrique Rodríguez Larreta spread the news from Paris about the torture sessions in the Buenos Aires garage, the signed confessions, and the ferrying of the whole group across the river, the Major was already one step ahead. He had had his film (no credits) screened on all Uruguayan television channels. He adopted a neutral position; his voice-over in some sequences, his unidentified face in a corner of the screen in others. The story of the PVP was told for the first time. A commercial product (a spray, a detergent) was invented to introduce it to the market. A lot of money was spent. The Major had to put his own money up at first. A cycle race advertised the three letters PVP on the shirts. Once the product was established, the mystery of the initials was revealed. Yes, the Major had known all this because he specialized in 'confessions', and now he used it. First he filmed the mock cycle race. Uphill stretches, the coast road, Malvin, scenes well-known to the audience. The Major had decided where the plot would be hatched and where the authors would gather: in a summer resort in Canelones, in Shangri-la. He had notified all the TV channels, gone to the villa, knocked on the door, and the subversives had come filing out, hands over their heads (all at the same angle, the show had to have a minimum amount of staging), and had surrendered without visible emotion to the Major. Clever, too clever perhaps!

In January of 1976 firecrackers exploded under the quays in Punta del Este and this was used as a pretext to re-arrest those army officers who had been jailed, then released, and were living in the area. The General, for a start. And several others, myself included. I was always prone to foolish illusions that made me follow events without ever catching up with them. I knew about the Major's famous torture techniques but I would never have believed they could be applied to colonels. However, many basic principles changed in so short a time, and that was one of them. When it came to the crunch, we used to say, army officers would treat one another like gentlemen and that might mean execution but not the 'machine'. As I hung from a huge pulley, exposed to the sun and buckets of water, my shoulders splitting, wrenched asunder, I knew that now this was not so. First they had stripped us of our rank, made us civilians again, the worse kind of civilians, those who had been army officers and had been deemed unworthy of this honour. We civilians were then hung in the patio of Mar Mediterraneo from our shoulder-blades and armpits, from beneath where our officers' stripes had been ripped off.

Our case, just for the record. Naively trusting in an impossible electoral victory, we had been afraid that our success at the polls would not be recognized and had organized in a rather primitive fashion to resist a coup. It was known as 'Operation Counter-coup' but in reality it was little more than words, a dream on a blackboard. The Major had apparently been told to change its name, to give it a more aggressive character, and force us to accept it. He wanted it called 'Operation Takeover'. But that changed its whole significance, and if there was one thing right about our crazy little enterprise, it was its name. We stood by it.

Yes, *we* would stand by it as long as our armpits stood

220

it…if our chests held out and our ribs did not crumble.

The Major wanted more people involved in the plot, retired majors, colonels, others loyal to the General. 'Operation Takeover' as he insisted on calling it, was a bag which, in his opinion, could hold a lot more cats. It was a waste for it to be so empty. The faces of some former comrades-in-arms may still be smiling at me from the mists, I have earned their smiles forever. I did not allow them to be dragged in for the simple reason that they never had been in.

The Major put hoods on us. I'm referring to myself and a naval officer whom I had never met before. Mar Mediterraneo, like the bag of cats, had room for lots more people. The navy man was interrogated in a different place, but they used to bring him out into the patio for some specific operations. From beneath our hoods we quickly exchanged signals; I now think that they probably pretended they did not notice.

Even while I was hanging there, I never imagined that similar things were being done to the General. Now I know that they did not in fact hang him, but made him stand to attention for hours, beating him to keep his back straight, and that more than once a soldier kicked his ankles, until they swelled, to keep his legs open at the correct angle, or what the soldier judged to be correct. To a general! When he was thirsty, after two or three summer days without a drop of liquid, they gave him a glass of hot water and left it on the floor (he did not drink it); and when he was hungry they left some stew in a plate on the floor, with no fork, spoon or knife (he did not swallow that either).

I also learned afterwards that when they were taking a statement, they put a big electric fire almost touching his skin, meaning to burn it. The Commander of the Maldonado garrison came in, wearing a hood, to guarantee the General's safety while he made his statement. The General said that any commander of a military unit degraded himself by wearing a hood in the presence of his inferiors, and that anyone who denied his own identity both to them and to himself was in no position to give guarantees to anyone. The Commander found no answer to this charge in the repertoire prepared for him. He was silent for a minute, then left.

The General was in Maldonado and we were in Punta Gorda. We had no news of each other then, as we now do from time to time as we carry out our umpteen-year sentences.

This business of hanging us, majors and colonels alike, was particularly dreadful and don't think I say that because I think an army officer is any more privileged, more worth protecting than anyone else. It was dreadful because the order in which we had lived and believed for our entire lives had been ripped asunder even before we were. There is something at the root of it all, however, that really intrigues me. Why this kind of abject hatred, so solid, so urgent, so absurd, irrational, and at times hysterical? What fears lie behind such hatred?

The Major did not wear a hood in Mar Mediterraneo. Yet he must have known that even though we were hooded there were times when we could see him. His philosophy, if one can talk about a philosophy of torture, was demonstrated by an episode which he was obviously not

222

trying to hide since he did it at the top of his voice in front of everybody. There was this lieutenant assigned to the electric shock machine. He was a huge man with a mane of rebellious hair, locks as thick as feathers which stuck out of his canvas hood and made him easy to recognize, even if his size had not already done that (and it had). He asked to be transferred to other duties. He had to fill out the prisoners' file cards before interrogation sessions and the first question he asked was: Name, address, phone number, and person to be informed in case of death, injury or accident. 'Look, Lieutenant,' I said, 'this isn't a plane trip...' 'Who said I was a lieutenant?' 'Well, whatever you are,' I said, 'I've got a hood on. I was a soldier too.' '*Was*,' he replied with visible contempt, 'not any more.'

The main reason for his request was the problem with his hair. We were lined up in the patio, waiting for what they euphemistically called 'exercises' to begin. Then they separated us into sections; hanging, wooden horse, electric shocks, submarine. The Major chose that precise moment, in front of all of us, to humiliate the Lieutenant. 'Don't you think we're here for a more important reason than whether or not we're recognized?' 'Yes, that's true, Major. But there's no point in giving oneself away...' 'And what if they recognize you because you stink of sweat?' 'Yes, Major. They could recognize us. They're like dogs, these people.' 'They could recognize *You*, lieutenant. *I* wash.' 'If you stink, you stink, Major. They say people stink when they're afraid, and in this job you *are* afraid, sometimes very afraid, even if you don't realize it yourself, Major...' Silence, and the Major said, 'Consider yourself under arrest, Lieutenant.' 'Yes, Major...but why?' 'For disrespect to a superior. And now for asking questions instead of obeying orders.' But after five days under arrest, the Lieutenant with the electric locks reappeared with a larger 'hair proof' hood, and took up his former duties again where no one except newcomers could fail to recognize him.

But all this is a much too voluminous prologue to the unique, brief and true story of the death of Major Brezzo.

Sometimes in shoot-outs or moments of madness, police and soldiers killed one another. Commissar Rodríguez Moroy shot Police Chief Silveira Regalado when he went into the shack where Mario Robaina lived, and caused his suicide. Naturally, Robaina was reported as having killed Silveira before taking his own life. In the Club 20 affair, the group of soldiers and police that raided the club and killed the eight Communist militants, also shot Captain Busconi. He took a month to die in a web of lies. In Cuchilla Alta, police killed each other and the judge convicted a Tupamaro. But now, suddenly, Major Brezzo's death seemed totally different. One day at six in the afternoon, there was a great hubbub at Mar Mediterraneo. The Major arrived in a fury, totally beside himself, and sent for us. Hooded, the naval officer and I were taken to him. He did not disguise his voice, in his anger he forgot all precautions. Major Brezzo, his old friend from the Military Academy, had been murdered by two subversives, 'two of those cretins whose heads you have filled with filth. With ideas, you would say, murderous ideas. Because that's your creed. Hate, kill, destroy,' he repeated, and the verbs seemed more like his own code than ours. 'This is *your* doing, your traitorous generals, your gangsters disguised as intellectuals.' Standing handcuffed and hooded, we seemed in danger of being blown over by the torrent of words. As the Major's shouts or whimpers of resentment rushed at us, we could feel his gasping breath. 'Brezzo,' he shouted, 'a good man, a fair man, a gentleman, a true officer, not an extremist in uniform. Brezzo!'

It was not a moment for thinking, wondering, or doubting. Brezzo had been murdered, the Major said, by a couple of subversives, and that was all there was to it. We were no doubt older than Brezzo but, still, it was strange that neither of us had heard of him before. Brezzo. Brezzo. Who was he? What branch of the armed forces? What unit did he command? In what operation had he been killed? Some men get so slow-witted at the height of emotion that they become even more obtuse just when they should be explicit; in their grief they can't come up with a single meaningful detail, merely a pile of set phrases, funereal clichés, and commonplaces. Long live Brezzo! The gamut of idiotic expressions floated round his memory but not a single profound, unmistakably individual reference. Brezzo seemed to be an entity murdered by other entities, not a man executed by other men. The Major was on the verge of drowning in his own eloquence. He asked for a glass of water, and they brought one. It was getting dark and our hoods prevented us seeing how many people were out in the patio. Then with a calmness more threatening than his rage, he announced his decision: we were the intellectual authors of Major Brezzo's murder. People like us, people whose creed put guns in other people's hands, did not deserve to live. We would be shot at dawn, right

225

there (he did not say if in the patio or on the rocks). Someone had to be guilty, and it was better to look for the guilty party among the treacherous ex-high ranking army officers who preached hate, than among the sad degenerates who had actually done the deed.

It had been a hot day but our hooded faces were turned towards the sea breeze. Yet still we were sweating under the burning canvass. We sweated an acrid, stinking sweat.

He turned to us for the first time. 'Prepare to die, if there is anything left in you of the soldiers you used to be. You will await execution here, standing to attention till dawn. No one will be allowed to speak to you, nor will you be allowed to speak to each other. Your families will not be notified, you may not write, and you will remain handcuffed. You will face the firing squad handcuffed.

Over a year earlier, five young people with no police record had been executed in reprisal for the murder of Colonel Trabal in Paris. That was the proportion established beforehand: five for one. Brezzo was not so well known as Trabal, a different price would be paid for him, a lesser one; a retired colonel and naval officer, or rather a colonel and naval officer in the process of being reformed. De-graded, as they say. That was us. After all those days of hanging, wooden horse, and electric shocks, my body ached all over. Now that the hour of my death was fixed, the dangers became, to a certain extent, trivial and absurd. I stood, hooded, to attention beçause I felt the guard at my left side. On the other side, the right, I sensed my companion on death row. It was still hot, night had fallen, you could hear the lazy, languid, repetitive boom of a lone wave coming back again and again, changing nothing. Would we die there, in the short, throbbing, repetitive ebb of that wave?

There were still several hours left, however. Brezzo's family might be coming, invited for the satisfaction of revenge. Well, I thought, revenge is usually sweeter when the mourners don't have to leave an unburied corpse, when the funeral rites are already over, or when the other is sacrificed on the dead man's funeral pyre. Can you imagine Brezzo's mother coming to see me die before her own son has been buried? And who will mourn Brezzo at the end of the day? Children? A girlfriend? Probably not, given how old majors usually are. Parents? A grandmother? I realized I was playing a game, thinking of my own family. I had only a middle-aged wife and a young but already adult son to think about. No grandchildren yet; I might have some in the not too distant future and never see them. In relative terms, not having grandchildren did not bother me. I was playing with the time I had left. I had to squeeze the last drop out of it. There were still hours to go. I could continue creating characters, subjecting them to Brezzo's judgement, and if it were not too much to ask, to his memory. Brezzo's grandmother, for instance, to someone who held no memories for me, since I did not know her, but nonetheless interesting, in the circumstances. A doddery old lady who might come for my execution and confuse it with her grandson's. Or she might cry for me and her grandson both.

There was time, time to peel all that fruit. When there was only one hour left before dawn, there would be no room for lost imaginary grandmothers, or fantasies of that kind. With one hour to go, all sixty minutes would be for my wife and my son. With relative calm I discovered that the most horrible thing would be to leave this world at an age when your son would not remember you. The deadest of all dead men in the cemetery is the one who's son can only say 'they told me he was...' But I was lucky, I had a grown-up son, a son who had gone to Spain so that my being in prison would not affect his life too much. That was what I had wanted, had desired, had asked him to do so many times. Would I now die with him so far away? And my wife, a middle-aged woman, at the age when a woman resigns herself, makes changes in her life, and opens new doors, looks after grandchildren and all those things. Perhaps Brezzo is leaving small children, children too young to remember him. No matter how much hate I felt, I would see this as a tragedy too. The wave boomed again, the same eternal wave.

I don't know what time it was by the clock, but it would have been good to make a note of it; the time the patio lay still, when we agreed silently that the guard had left. A father's fear when his child is young is his own fear of disappearing, of not having a future he can see with eyes open, either because he cannot see, or because his child has closed *his* eyes. It is so remote, yet it would be so terrible...

In barely audible murmurs, my companion and I agreed to let our bodies slide until, hands tied, we were sitting backs against the wall, our backsides coolly resting on the patio stones. We did it with a ludicrous sense of adventure (ludicrous because what possible punishment could dissuade a man awaiting execution?) and no one appeared

228

to chastise us, insult us, or stick a bayonette in our ribs. We did it.

The physical reality of being a little more comfortable paved the way for an even more daring idea; we were alone, abandoned, and certainly without Brezzo. That was when my companion said to me, 'Perhaps this Brezzo is just a sinister joke.' He called me by name for the first time. 'I bet you anything this Brezzo never existed...'

This was a truly revolutionary idea. In one fell swoop it not only wiped out our guilt, but also the whole story. Brezzo never existed; *ergo* he had no mourners. No one would come for us and fix a time for any ceremony; therefore, it would not take place. Brezzo had never existed; ergo the Major was a consummate playactor and his fury pure parody. In this new light, certain things became clearer. That was why Brezzo had no colourful anecdotes, little witticisms, or anything that makes a person out of an entity. It is strange. A moment ago it had seemed incongruous that the world should stay the same now that Brezzo had disappeared. Now, on the other hand, we accepted without any proof at all that Brezzo had never existed. You had to hand it to the Major, his imagination was not bad...

With all that, there was still a big risk. If Brezzo was an imaginary martyr, he could still be the pretext for a very real act of cruelty. He could be used to prove that the Major hated us and that we were in his power. Worst of all would be if Brezzo did not exist but that his death did, through us and only through us. We had another three hours before dawn in which to put our memories and farewells into some kind of order. Three hours to invent

229

a role and a future for those who would go on living. I had now discovered to my relief (the relief which comes from knowing that at least the torture is over) that my relationships and feelings were, naturally, in order. I was neither excessively indebted nor too much a beneficiary.

'There's no such person as Brezzo, my friend,' the naval officer repeated more confidently. His tone was increasingly familiar. 'I've been through every year of the Academy, I have a good memory.' he added. 'The Navy is not like the Army... No, there's no Brezzo, I'm certain of it. What we *do* have, however, is that shit, that gothic torturer...'

I must admit I liked the 'gothic torturer' bit. But my answer must have seemed crazy to him.

'I'd hate to die for a Brezzo who didn't exist.'

A moment ago, when there was still no question of Brezzo's existence, my main aim had been to liberate myself from the image of death itself, first in Brezzo (how had he been killed?) and then in me (how would they kill me?). Liberate myself, that is, from imagining the physical pain caused by a firing squad in the very act of firing. Oh well, I thought, if we close our eyes and change substance, how can we suffer, what do we care? Everybody has a bird in his head but only bishops believe it is the Holy Spirit. I was never religious but I began to imagine, I don't know why, that the shots would liberate that bird inside me and it would fly away. If, at that moment, I could stand aside and watch myself, I would feel it wrought from deep inside me. From under my hood in the darkness, I wanted to look. My wife began to smile at me from some invisible place in space, almost as if she

230

were there. I interpreted it as proof that she did not believe in my death either. And surely that was the only thing my body was waiting for, for neither she nor I to believe it. The wave, booming now and again, and the darkness. I began counting, counting sheep, like they do in story books. I don't know at what stage I fell asleep. My companion woke me with a soft nudge. 'You're snoring,' he had returned to his previous formality, 'and it is getting light.'

My ears began to penetrate the silence. There was no sound of footsteps or people or cocked rifles. Only the boom of the wave. It seemed more intense to me, the first light of dawn would be shining on it, glittering on its crest. I raised my hooded head, scratched my right temple against the wall, and the hood slipped enough to let the light through, yes, in fact, the sun was coming up. This was perhaps the most dangerous moment of all. We might be fooling ourselves, like when planes land. We heard steps. Were they coming for us?

'On your feet,' said the guard, with false hostility. 'You're not allowed to sit on the floor. How did you manage it?'

My muscles ached all over, the navy man's too, I could tell from his groans, but we managed to stand up. Another whole day was beginning, a day of suffering. Or would it be shorter, more radical, more...? It might look as if I were playing the hero if I said I did not really care, but, with the first warm rays of sun in my eyes, it was true, it really was.

'Let's go,' said the guard. 'It's daylight.'

'Go where?' I asked.

I never found out if he was in on the night's game, of Brezzo and awaiting execution.

'To your cell,' he said, 'Where were you dreaming of going?'

The Pine Grove

...e pronti sono a transpassar lo rio

So eager to cross the river and be gone

Dante, *Inferno*, Canto III

And now we had chosen a Devout Man to govern us. After all those years of the Boxer, we had made an effort to become more spiritual. However, by this stage the Devout Man was already hand in glove with the military, and they had effectively held political control since the 1973 coup. The Devout Man had gone on making money and children. He had inherited a cattle ranch. And he also had his own personal confessor, indispensable since he needed near him an intelligent and sensible person who was a member of the Curia and not of the communist wing of the Church so in vogue in those days. What we now need to ask the confessor is whether he was consulted about what happened on that particular day. I don't know anyone who knows. I don't know anyone who said he did.

The news that Colonel Ramón Trabal had been murdered in Paris on December 19th, 1974, arrived in Montevideo around midday the same day. It was not broadcast on the radio of course, because in Uruguay we make a practice of not broadcasting news. The censor sat on it for a while. Or rather, he took time to prepare the official version. People heard it on Argentine radio from noon onwards, but all we knew here was that the President of the Republic would speak to the nation on all radio and TV channels at 9 o'clock. What about? They did not say. Meanwhile, out in the streets, the purveyors of unofficial scoops were delighted. A phone call to the news agencies in Paris had

233

ascertained that a certain Raúl Sendic International Brigade claimed the dead, carried out by two anti-imperialist Frenchman with shotguns. Trabal had been riddled with bullets in the garage of his home as he put his car away. There was no question of the Devout Man providing these details, he was not a newsreader, he was the President. He merely made a statement, the traditional ingredients of which are (or they were in this case, given the Devout Man's personality) a moral condemnation, a prayer and a tear.

The President has no gift for oratory, or anything else for that matter. But others write brief or detailed statements for him according to the occasion, and he, albeit with little flair, faces the cameras behind his solid Queen Anne desk, puts on his glasses and reads. A small national flag watches over him, and the national emblem yawns behind his head.

Colonel Ramón Trabal was a controversial man. Young, able, ambitious, and from 1973 on, with no larger dose of scruples than appropriate for furthering his budding career. He had problems because everybody mistrusts everybody in the Army, and those most intellectually endowed provoke the most envy. 'We must face the fact that torture is an evil impossible to avoid,' he once said, 'and that being so, we should make it work for us, have clear objectives.' His objectives were clear enough. He believed in the Peruvian Army ethos, if that meant anything in the Uruguay of 1973. He had no shortage of potential enemies, from subversives he had tortured to ultra-rightwing groups within the military. It was not, however, the subversives who sent him to Europe, nor they who ignored his requests to return and be considered for promotion to general. There are dossiers reserved for military tribunals which hint at the existence of a 'Lodge of Eight Brothers', mentioned in connection with the murder. The Uruguay of censorship lives on rumours.

With the corpse far away yet very present, the COSENA meets—the National Security Council, where the generals take the decisions and the President always arrives on time. The terms had been set out years ago, as a threat. Five subversives for every officer killed. The wall of the Uruguayan Glass Company in Asamblea Street has proclaimed it for ages. Every motorist taking this road out of the city sees it, or rather, cannot avoid seeing it. Graffiti so huge and visible (or any graffiti for that matter) couldn't last more than a few hours unless the authorities permitted it. If they don't like it, they bring soldiers and prisoners to give it a coat of whitewash; soldiers from the barracks and prisoners from Cilindro jail. Or sometimes the owner of the wall is ordered to get rid of it or face charges. That graffiti which survived for months, years, was painted one night by the army (everyone knows and says so under their breath).

For every officer, five subversives—5 to 1, a dose to dissuade hostages. Kill us and see, it seems to warn.

The equation was officially formulated four years earlier in July, 1970. An organization, self-styled MANO. (the Uruguayan Nationalist Armed Movement) warned that 'For any policemen, soldier, taxidriver, or honest citizen who is killed, we will take five useless lives.' Even though extending the service to taxidrivers, and offering it so broadly to all honest citizens, authorized a kind of reprisal production line, time passed without it showing any sign of life. MANO—wasn't that the name of the death squad in Guatemala? Why so little imagination from such supposedly well-emunerated people? Or was it, on the contrary, that they wanted everyone to understand, clearly and unequivocally, what you and I imagined at the time: that there was a centralized counterinsurgency headquarters working along the same pattern at all latitudes. Wherever it was judged necessary. If an armed movement really was Uruguayan, really was Nationalist, would the CIA need to use such a crude pleonasm? There are words which exist only as initials, and initials which exist only as acronyms.

Another acronym, the COSENA, is meeting with the Devout Man in the gothic chair. The Secretary goes over the news briefly, accepts its authenticity, and does not even question whether the 5 to 1 'clearing' system operates in foreign exchange. A death in Paris compensates for a death here, according to the rate. We have a dead colonel, killed, obviously, by subversives (if not, by whom?). The formula must be applied or it will be like the bogeyman, only good for scaring children. There is no middle way. No, there is not, the generals' faces dispel any possible doubt.

But what about the raw material? Do we have it or shall we go out looking for it now? Yes, fortunately, we have it. On November 8th, about forty days ago, the police arrested five subversives, two couples and a woman, at a house in Sarratea Street in Buenos Aires. They are already here, they've already been ferried over.

Read the names out. They are read out; they are unknown, not one of them is notorious. Is that good or bad? The discussion is opened. Supporting the thesis that it is better for them to be unknown: 'they are unimpor-

236

tant and that emphasizes the algebra of the reprisal (am I right?)' 'You mean the arithmetical proportions?' 'Yes, thank you: 5 to 1, no beating about the bush.' 'The five include a woman with no police record.' 'Better still, how did the slogan go? "Useless lives." ' ' She's the wife of one of them, she's the same breed.' One woman has no record, they'll say, none of the five are actually wanted by the authorities, they'll say. Yes, they'll drop it in, casually, so people will get the message that you don't even have to be on a wanted list these days. Anyone in the subversive stockpot is our enemy. That's reason enough. Wanted or not, record or not; it doesn't matter. And this lot have actually been in Chile, they all went to communist Chile, they lived there. Isn't that enough?'

It seems enough. At least, nobody objects. All right. Let them be found with their 'bought in Buenos Aires' clothes, their 'bought in Buenos Aires' cigarettes, 'bought in Buenos Aires' matches. So people can see, so people will know. Dress them up, load them down. It will come out together with the news of the Colonel's murder. Let people see that too.

The Devout Man does not feel comfortable. His message has already been approved and recorded with its allusions to piety, to the tears of Uruguayan mothers, all that. And now? Will it seem a good flag to cover those five bodies? There are still no bodies, but his statement has already been recorded. Isn't that rather...? They are in no mood for opposition and sweep it aside. What about the Uruguayan Revolution? What will happen to the Uruguayan Revolution if there is dissent here, today, on this matter? He feigns a sore throat, takes a fistful of lozenges, and remains silent.

No arguments are put forward for the disadvantages of their being unknown, at least no one comes forward with one explicitly. It is put to the vote...

Votes in the COSENA are secret, of course, but this time secrecy is probably not even needed. All the generals vote yes, it must be done, with the necessary precautions to be taken and certain ones not to be taken. Shoot the five hostages, and move on to other matters. This is the reality of Uruguay today, they all seem to agree. 'There is no death penalty, we know that.' (The Constitution has no provision for a COSENA either, but here it is voting.) 'There has not been a proper trial, we know that. We must be tough, there will be no hypocritical official regets either. Is that clear? We will mourn our own dead.' Consulted, the Devout Man's chin confirms that the civil response has been given and will come on the air at 9 o'clock. 'We will mourn our own dead before the fuss begins and will confer the rank of general on Trabal posthumously by decree.' Unanimous agreement.

'If there is nothing else...?' The Devout Man requests and is given permission to speak. 'I want it put on record that I do not agree with the executions... That's all.'

The generals look at each another, until one of them suddenly figures it out. His Christian beliefs, naturally. Oh yes, of course, his Christian beliefs, his Christian beliefs, his Christian beliefs...

The fact is that there is no time to consult his personal confessor. The facts, the facts. Such are the facts.

At nine that night, the recording made at four in the afternoon is screened. The Devout Man gives the news, he

238

is indignant. International subversion recognized no boundaries. But the Devout Man promises to continue fighting it to his last ounce of strength. He offers up a prayer for the dead man, and invites every Uruguayan mother to shed a tear with the Colonel's family. (End.)

He has just finished listening to it at his home, surrounded by his children. Yes, but he dare not tell the full story; tomorrow at dawn five other bodies will appear. Where? He had preferred not to know the exact site. His concept of innocence and quilt seems to bear a strange relationship to details known or not known. He prefers not to know. Between him and them is the night. But he will have to talk about it with his personal confessor. Tomorrow morning early, before breakfast, when the news starts to get out? When? When he confesses and asks for absolution? When?

The isolated grove. A little pine grove near Soca, about 50 miles from Montevideo, at the intersection of highways 7 and 90; visible from there, I mean.

The five bodies. The bodies of five young people. The bodies of five young people killed by machine gun, shot, scattered. Fully dressed. Brought there to be shot in the night or brought dead through the countryside from the barracks and thrown, there, under the dark vista of the pines? Who, which officer, which fat colonel with memories of a happy picnic, had chosen it as the appropiate place?

'Useless lives.' No one had thought of writing it as an inscription on the forehead of the bodies, any one of them. And anyway, could we agree on what would be a useless life for a sixty-year-old general?

Journalists are summoned in the early hours to cover the story. The bodies of five unknown young people have been found in a copse near Soca. 'Yes, Señor, five deceased persons, that's the news, move along now.' (On the police pages the word 'deceased' has a meaning all its own.)

Patrol cars come speeding up, to a certain schedule. They keep on coming (camera, action!). There is the local police chief, he is in charge of investigations. 'Yes, the clothes, the smokes,' (he says smokes not cigarettes, TV cop's jargon) 'and the matches are all Argentinian brands. It seems these people came from there and were caught by surprise...' 'Is that what he had been told to imply?' 'All right,' the inspector corrects himself, addressing the journalists, 'put that the things are from over there...' He dictates, clothes labels, cigarette brands, all from Argentina. 'Write it down!'

'Some things are still not clear, the local police chief continues to redress the effects of his mistake. 'Was it one of the guerrilla organization's clandestine death sentences, a settling of accounts right here, or was it done somewhere else and the bodies brought here to the wood?'

'Here are some empty .9 and .45 caliber shells. It looks as if it was done right here...'

'What about car tracks?'

'No, it hasn't rained for quite a few days. You'll see these three M's made with a pointed object by the side of the road. Anyone any idea what that means?'

The bodies are lying there, the sun begins to touch their faces, and army truck will soon be coming to take them away. When the judge in Pando authorizes it, someone

240

says.

'Any names, documents?'

'No nothing, absolutely nothing. But it's certain they came from Argentina.'

For the journalists it's easier than usual. 'And, anyway, there will be a communiqué...with the names perhaps, we're working on that now.'

'From the fingerprints?'

'We're working on it, that's all I can tell you. It's enough, isn't it?'

The sun puts unexpected movement in a dead mouth, it abandons another. 'They must be between 25 and 30, they're young,' they murmur as they pass by—they are leaving, not writing it down. They are young, they're young, no doubt about it.

No one mentions Colonel Trabal. No one forgets him. 'Hey. tell me, is there anything new on the wires?'

No, there is nothing new. That group is also unaware that a little boy of three, son of one of the murdered couples, has 'disappeared' from Sarratea Street. He has been reported missing at police stations in Buenos Aires.

If the Devout Man told the story to his confessor, this may be the moment he looks at him, waiting upon his ecclesiastical lips as never before. But can anyone believe that COSENA will tolerate any recourse to personal confessors, any instance of Canon Law?

The trucks are coming, you can see them from the road, they are at the turnoff, 'No, no, of course not. No photos here, no way... For obvious security reasons, let's say.'

Contrary to that kind of prudence, I know, I hereby write their names and ages. They did exist. They were executed

241

by the generals, with a confessional qualification from El
Señor Presidente. They were:
Héctor Daniel Brum, 28
Mará de los Angeles Corbo, 26
Graciela Estefanell, 34
Floreal García, 31
Mirtha Hernández, 29
In memoriam. A formal phrase which to devout people
seems as good as *For Reasons of State*.

...Over Those Dead Bones

Fer la città sovra quell'ossa morte

O'er those bones they built their city

Dante, *Inferno*, Canto XX

We should say goodbye to a book as we do to a person. But we never do; our original relationship with it has been so corrupted.

The book then becomes a harvest of dead or living people beyond our reach. We don't even feel needed to share anything, to die in the pages where the characters die, to have loved or hated when they have.

I sometimes write, sometimes ponder on a landscape. I go to a window and it helps me feel. It doesn't matter what abyss or cavern I look onto, which faces or absences I come up against. Any landscape will do, but I'm especially drawn to the sea. The sea has strange ways of talking with time, death, and even impossible distances...impossible because at the end of the journey there are impenetrable doors or beaches where those doors rot and creak like old splintered prows run aground on the sand. And that image, a door stuck in a sand dune, is the living expression of exile, even in the land which the word and the sand deny. There is no door, there will not be, we will never find it again. A window is good, whatever the landscape it opens on. Because what is important in the end, O God of writers, is having stopped looking at the pages, to have gazed into space, air, distance, memory; to think.

Did budding poets die? They most probably did. But others stopped writing perhaps because, their youthful passion past, this impetuous and generous vocation proved irrelevant to their lives. Did someone say that intellectuals died? That is adhering, despite ourselves, to the petty notion that adolescence is the age of poetry and maturity the peak of the intellect. There is nothing more absurd or odious than to talk of rebellion and reason as naturally consecutive ages of man.

I do not think that either promising poets especially, or intellectuals especially, died when the guerrilla organization was wiped out in those years. *Young people* were destroyed; that is, men and women, examples of the human condition, people with something new to say, many of them with no place to say it. *Fer la città sovra quell'ossa morte*; that is what is left for us in the years to come. Build the city over their dead bones. Not on the cast-off skins of poets who fell silent and changed, but on the bones of men and women who had a passion for life and were sacrificed to the Order of the Barracks.

SALERNO. The quaint side of the story came at the beginning, with the phoney funeral, the wreaths, the Martinelli Company hearses, the procession from Montevideo, the parody of young mourners weeping. And the terrible bit was the end, especially when their escape route from Pando was obstructed because they chose the wrong road out of town and the Metropolitan guys came in ready to shoot-to-kill. Nobody was shot by subversives in Pando but the police attributed to them the death of one of their own men killed by mistake, recklessness or panic, by themselves. In Toledo, however, Ricardo Zabalza, Alfredo Cultelli and Jorge Salerno, though unarmed, were shot by the

Metropolitan police before journalists arrived. They and their photographers came just in time to record the death throes of the three youths. They received no medical attention; Salerno bled to death, Cultelli bled to death, Zabalza bled to death. The Toledo landscape—an area of small farms and houses, not a battlefield. There, under some fruit trees, young men fell and died, surrounded by Metropolitan police, the toe of a boot photographed beside a mouth which opened to die. Che Guevara would not claim this sacrifice of youth like some pagan god; but he was receiving it on this the first October 8th since his death, not with hallowed rites dedicated to him but on orders to the troops, given either then or some time beforehand (we will never know for sure). For Jorge Salerno it had been a bit of a sentimental trip, a mixture of Western and picnic. His girlfriend now a prisoner, the final tragic ending gushed from his body and stared from his half-closed eyes.

Not for Salerno's father, but for everybody else there in the house, the dominant feeling was one of stupefaction. 'They kill young people just for the fun of it,' said some. 'They occupied a whole town, for half an hour they occupied a whole town,' said others in astonishment. Each person chooses his own sorrow or fear and stands there like a bird on a post. Behind the ingenuity lay an audacity which had sinister overtones. They began to suspect what it was. Behind the three deaths lay a brutality which in time would become a law unto itself, and it was debateable whether the idea appalled them more than it reassured them. They were middle class, some were rich. A Catholic and a just man, Salerno's father questioned himself in the presence of his son. A world was clearly crumbling (that comfortable world in which the figures in the picture keep moving because the décor always changes afterwards). He wanted to understand rather than love, since love somehow threatens to come close to hate, and before understanding fully he did not, as a Christian, feel allowed to hate. His old school friend (no, he was a friend anyway) the Monsignor was there beside him in an ordinary suit, his collar closed.

'Look, Father...,' said Salerno's father.

'Don't call me Father, call me by my own name, like always,' objected the Monsignor.

'I'd rather call you Father today, I need it somehow.'

'As you wish then,' conceded the Monsignor, 'if it helps you feel calmer.'

'No, I am calm, don't worry... But there's something I've been asking myself for hours. I don't know if my son was a hero or not. I don't know if he died bravely or cowardly (the rumour that Jorge might have been shot had started round, but his father had still not taken it in). I don't know about that. But I think he made a choice and died for it... I believe God cannot see that as bad. What do you think, Father?'

And the Monsignor (looking deep into his eyes and with an inevitable tone of authority since he was having to interpret a divine sentiment):

'He cannot see that as bad.'

PUCURULL. The autopsy gave the cause of death as suffocation brought on by haemorrhaging and, according to the pathologist, suffocation occurs within a minimum of four minutes. It was not in the written report but he had

246

added verbally, (…and it can be prevented by quick action in the case of a young man like this one.) He had said it, but it didn't figure there. 'Death by suffocation, brought on by haemorrhaging', that's what the report said. Nobody could take the Army to task when these things happened. But Hernán Pucurull was alive for a lot more than the four minutes indicated by the pathologist, gasping and writhing while the soldiers merely took the precaution of stopping anyone going near him, touching him, moving him, and above all giving him medical attention. Usually when an operation is planned, the Medical Corps waits at the ready. But in cases like this, when it's only a subversive of little interest who is wounded and not a soldier, no one uses the walkie-talkie to call the ambulance, no one worries about getting assistance. The autopsy report only refers to the outcome, it does not judge whether it could have been avoided. Hernán Pucurull was the son of a deceased judge, and that's how his family had been able to find out the little they knew. Naturally, there was nothing on paper. It was some sort of backhanded consolation; her son could still be alive if he had got medical attention in time. His only brother had sensibly preferred not to tell her. The autopsy did achieve something, however; the various procedures delayed delivery of the body. The funeral was to be in Durazno, that was where they were from, and the almost 150 miles, the journey, the opening hours of the municipal cemetery…the authorities calculated all that. It was Sunday, the morgue caretaker's day off, and the pathologist had no special keys. Each person plays a minimal part and disappears, no one wants to be suspected of collaborating with subversion.

But there is always an old school friend to be found. In this case it was not a Monsignor but the undertaker in Durazno. He knew the dead youth, and more important he knew the person arranging the funeral. He reluctantly agreed to take it on, as a duty incurred in childhood.

'As long as you don't implicate me, my friend.'

'How can burying someone implicate you? A death certificate, a hearse, one accompanying car, and you charge the full fee so no one can accuse you of doing favours...'

'I'm sorry, but you know how things are. It's a very compromising funeral.'

When he was being paid, the school friend said he had been given the following instructions: there was to be no wake, the coffin was not to be opened, there were to be no speeches, no responses either at the graveside or anywhere else, the procession was not to stop, and there were to be no flowers. Understood?

For the mother this was horrible, as if on top of his death there were to be more horrors.

'They kill him, let him bleed to death by a barbed wire fence and then won't even let me see him...'

But she stopped in mid-sentence and added, 'We have to look at him before we bury him, just to be sure it's him we're burying. How do you know they didn't give us another body in the morgue?'

'No, Mama,' objected the brother. 'It will be him. It's bound to be.'

But he could give her no rational proof which would convince her. She wanted to look.

It was the first of June. It was drizzling. The chauffeur said they had to drive slowly, the hearse's tires were bald

248

and with the bad road, worse today because of the rain, it was dangerous to go fast.

'Why don't you change the tires?'

'The one in Durazno has good tires but there wasn't time to bring it. This one is from here, it's not used very much.'

The childhood friend was with the two of them in the accompanying car, explaining things. It was sad for the mother to hear them, and in fact the whole afternoon was sad; a twenty-year-old as corpse, the beginning of autumn, intermittent drizzle, windows steamed-up, less light in the sky and less time before dusk encroached on their journey. When the mother said again that they should look at him before burying him, the schoolfriend gave his reasons why not. 'It might not be allowed. They must have sent the same instructions to Durazno as they gave to me, and I am responsible.'

'Yes, but I must know if I'm burying my son, or someone else...'

And there it was left, for the time being.

As they neared Durazno a couple of army motorcyclists stopped them. They seemed to want to delay them on purpose. 'It's late now, you'll have to leave him in the funeral parlour, and this gentleman (meaning the undertaker) will bury him tomorrow.'

'I won't leave my son until he's buried...and I won't bury him without seeing him first.'

Grudgingly, or because they had difficulty reading, the motorcyclists lingered over the funeral papers, the military authorization and the death certificate, and they asked for the autopsy records which the mourners did not have or need. Finally, insisting that they would be too late, they let them continue.

She knew the town by heart, she had been born there. She noticed that the blinds were drawn as they passed because people did not want to run risks.

'No, Mama, nobody will have heard about it,' said her son, wanting to keep a sense of proportion.

'Wretched town,' she said, 'but I'll have to keep coming, for the anniversaries at least. Your father's and now your brother's.'

The rain continued, heavier and heavier. On one side of the cemetery wall (they had not been let in) a handful of students were waiting in the rain. They did not know Hernán but he was a local boy and *they* had murdered him, and as students that concerned them to some extent. He was a hero, if only because of the way he had died.

The mother must have regretted having proclaimed it so categorically a 'wretched town' because those students were there at least and when the hearse stopped they had begun singing the National Anthem. A couple of civil guards watched them, with no general imagination and no specific instructions about whether they should be allowed to sing or be prevented from doing so. The mother acknowledged them by bowing her head, but they did not know who she was and did not respond, especially since at that moment they reached the verse, 'Freedom or die with glory'.

Encouraged by the reception, the mother said 'Let's look at him now.'

Don't implicate me, Señora, implored the funeral director, though he could see that the civil guards were the only figures of authority around. 'Don't implicate me, my brother.'

But the brother, who was not his brother but the victim's, turned provocatively toward the group of singers and shouted:

'Our Motherland, for all or none of us!'

In those particular circumstances it meant the latter.

The cemetery caretaker complained about the hour ('We were just closing') and only allowed the mother, brother and undertaker to pass. The students tried to go in as well but the civil guards surrounded the caretaker and barred their way. So they raised their fists in the direction of Montevideo and shouted 'Murderers !' a couple of times.

Inside the precinct, the mother insisted again, 'I want to see him. I have to see him now.'

The undertaker again went on about being implicated, squeezed his childhood friend's arm and described to them with great pathos how it would ruin him. He had taken a precaution, however, and now brought it out to negotiate with: 'The coffin has a little oval window, a peephole,' he said.

Neither the mother nor the brother had noticed it.

'Take a look at him through that.'

He took off the lid with astonishing speed, and the mother and brother saw (through the glass) the forehead, the top of the nose and cheekbones. It was indeed Hernán.

The undertaker took their consent as given and speedily replaced the lid. The guards at the morgue had probably not noticed it and no one else would be any the wiser now.

'He had a scratch on his forehead and the bridge of his nose,' the mother pointed out as if her grief had increased with such details.

'Yes,' said the undertaker, 'that was when they shot him and he fell against the barbed wire.'

The hymn began again, louder now. 'Tremble tyrants!' it went, in bellicose tones. The undertaker took the coffin by the handle and, with the gravediggers' help, tilted it towards the open mouth of the vault. The brother just had time to pass his hands over the wood, yes, caress rather than push, before the coffin disappeared. The mother took a step backwards as if seeking the warmth of the singers.

'I'll come back soon with flowers, my son, I swear to God.' she cried.

And at that very moment, from the other side of the wall, the students who had heard her promise, again took up the chant: 'Murderers!'

AURELIO RON. When a group of subversives dynamited Carrasco's Bowling on September 29th, 1970, a woman was burned to death and a man (eventually also a fatality) was trapped in the debris. However, these two victims did not prevent talk, quavering with piety, of other things as well. A cleaning lady who had refused to leave and was knocked over by the blast was the main talking point. She had children, she worked in order to feed them. What if she had died? What if she had been injured? Of course they knew perfectly well she was not going to die or be an invalid, but she was a worker and not a subversive, she was there out of necessity, not out of revolutionary snobbishness. The woman cleaned there because she was employed to clean, she worked there to feed her children. She was a victim among the victimizers, and the newspapers, radio and television gave her top priority. They had to make the most of her because she would be out of hospital the next day, and the lemon of sentimentality and piety would have been squeezed dry.

The assailants had moved a newspaper vendor and a girl away, but one of their own people was blown to bits in the explosion. Another was alive but trapped by the fallen timbers. What should the gathering crowd do about him? He's on center stage. At first they can hear him, then they no longer can: he must be dead, they say with relief, since he is a terrorist. Two witnesses tell the story: 'We were the first on the scene and we heard shouting, not very loud, but shouts nonetheless. We went in and saw a woman lying in the debris, she was hurt, and we gave her first aid outside. Then we went in again and shouted to see if anyone was left in there. Someone answered and said he was trapped, his arm was stuck and he asked us to get him out. It was a young man's voice, he sounded very near though we couldn't see him. He asked for help quite calmly. So we consulted the manager of the place, and he said we mustn't touch him or do anything, because all his staff were safe and the guy calling for help must surely be a subversive. We moved away and the police came; we told them what we'd heard. They told us to keep away. I know that a fireman also talked to the guy in there and he told him his legs were trapped. Various other people talked to him too. A special patrol group officer heard him. He told him to identify himself and the guy answered, ''What does it matter what my name is, you bastard? Just get me out of here and take me to the University Hospital.'' After that, the police cordoned the place off and prohibited

253

access...'

The fire brigade declined to carry out a salvage operation. There was no one to rescue, they say. And this being the case, there was no urgency. Let the owners contract a demolition company. The firemen's hoses pumped water into every crack, and through one of the crevices the man's voice could be heard insulting them and calling for help. 'The subversive trapped under the beams might drown with all that water,' said the imperturbable experts who sprouted like mushrooms in every newspaper and radio station after the explosion. 'Drowned or suffocated by carbon monoxide. There was also the danger that the youth was clutching a grenade and the firemen would have been blown up with him if they'd gone to help. Is it human to expect a fireman to risk his life for a man who has brought this on himself and endangered other people's lives into the bargain?'

Journalist: Couldn't you get him out now, by going in just a bit?

Fireman: No, we don't want to get close. It's pretty delicate. What if he has an unexploded bomb in his hand and we touch it with our picks by mistake? We'd all go up...

But in which hand? One you can see clearly, the other is trapped under the girder.

Fireman: Let the demolition company do it. That's what they're paid for.

The demolition company arrived but was in no hurry. It was Friday the 2nd, they would start on Monday the 5th.

Manager: My company was hired by the owners of the bowling alley. We began work yesterday, but we have

254

no special instructions, so we won't be working over the weekend. Demolition will continue on Monday, but we probably won't get to where the body is trapped until the following day...

Interviewer: Is there so much damage?

Manager: We have to underpin as we go along because of the danger of cave-ins. There are two girders pinning the body down. We have to proceed step by step.

El País apparently had a photo of the first corpse, the one which burned to death, but it was so horrific that the paper refused to publish it even though it might serve as an example for misdirected young people. It preferred to pontificate on the evils of violence, on the faces of drug addicts in the U.S. They both have the same root cause, it suggested.

Demolition proceeded slowly. But the byword 'let him rot', carelessly applied to the young man under the girders, turned out not to be apt. Dauntless chemists explained the phenomenon: gases generated by the water and the explosion acting on a corpse in a confined space.

Tuesday the 6th, one week after the event, *El País* trumpeted: 'It is known who the dead man in the bowling alley is. The information was provided by the subversive organization itself in a menacing pamphlet distributed in universities and colleges, particularly the Faculty of Medicine, where the conspirator, whose body is still under the building he destroyed, was a student. As well as distributing the pamphlet, student leaders in the said Faculty called a one-day strike yesterday to mourn the death of the misdirected youth.'

That was how they introduced the still-to-be-exhumed

(the demolition company is in no hurry) Aurelio Ron.

A day later, October the 7th, demolition workers reached the body and advised Section 26a of the police. Television cameras filmed the episode. Officers of Section 26a arrived at the bowling alley, carrying a simple pinewood coffin. Firemen, now sufficiently convinced that there were no grenades in the dead man's hand, approached the body, barely touched it, and placed it in the coffin. The examining magistrate was present and gave it a desultory glance. He was informed that there were no fractures, not even in the wrist pinned under the girder.

The journal, *Idea* publishes a poem entitled 'The Island':

A circle of useless hate
surrounds the island where
once more in you the man dies
whole and pure
alone
and watches and lets and makes you die
let it be lost
let it end
the short sweet life which escapes
the cool life which drinks the earth
and watches and makes your pain more alone
and the anguish and the throes
the arch of death.
A poor dirty sad river of hate
isolates and surrounds you
encircles you and makes you die
alone.
But no.

But no.
If the others, he, you,
do not go alone
if we carry them inside us
if wrapped in love and grief

                             they die in us forever.

Not many dead men have better valedictories. We all coexist with him in that city where he, all twenty-one years of him, died. We go to sleep in our beds at the same time in a city where he, uninjured, was left to die. We haven't even been able to find out exactly when he died. It does not appear in the demolition 'report'. The 'poor dirty sad river of hate' existed before then, perhaps it had always existed. But from then on, it advanced against us, in an increasingly overwhelming torrent, to destroy us. *Idea* did not know the man's name when it dedicated the poem to him. Doesn't that make this grotesque story even more wildly insane, more misdirectedly tragic and beautiful?

ENRIQUE. Enrique's end is as simple as Enrique, as sincere, true and as noble as he was.

In mid-1972, people were being arrested daily. Being arrested and talking every day. Enrique, however, showed no signs of despair for all that. He seems to have taken a clear decision never to show in his face or his gestures any doubt as to his fate, nor about the fate and duties of anyone else. Each time he made a routine 'contact' (contacts which were getting harder by the hour) Enrique always said the same thing. When told, 'There are fewer and fewer of us left, *compañero*,' he would reply, 'Yes,

257

but the best are left.'

In retrospect we can deduce that he chose to compliment his contact by assuming they were the best so that, when the time came, they would behave as such. What he told them as a truth was, in fact, an exhortation, a request, a prayer, a confidence, a faith. Enrique was like that. If he talked when he was arrested, he would drag a lot of people down with him, give a lot of places away, destroy work and sacrifice; *and he couldn't do that*. He'd say it as if was not important, barely worth mentioning, a throw-away phrase; no, *not that*. Blood banks, hideouts, safe houses, friends, *compañeros,* would be discovered. No. *Not that*. Enrique could see no way, absolutely no way in which it could possibly be otherwise. No. *Not that*.

Then one day, in June 1972, betrayed no doubt by someone who had talked, Enrique was captured. He must have known it would happen long ago, ever since he chose this particular path. He might have thought that the merit of being one of the best lay in not getting caught and that was it, unless one found a way of saving oneself. A single, harsh way of saving oneself. No preaching, no boasting and, in the end, no involving others. He must have thought about it, he must have known. In custody, they told him he was going to be interrogated. All he must have wanted was a situation which would give him a chance. Being a good revolutionary meant first and foremost not being caught. But when you were, you had no alternative; you had no alternative; you had to know how to keep quiet. All he must have wanted was a situation which would offer him the way out. On one side, as he walked along, there was a ventilator shaft in the flat roof, four storeys high.

All he must have wanted at this stage was not to be tied up. He was not tied up. He did not consider whether he had to go on being one of the best; it was obvious, everyone knew. He wanted to be true to himself, he had no pretentions as a moralist. He was not tied up, all he had to do was take a running jump. He jumped.

ALVARIZA. July 26th is already winter and that particular July 26th of 1972 was a freezing cold night. The sea roared against the windows of my house, as if we were in a ship out sailing in it. At about three in the morning, I heard a car stop outside the door. Someone called. I thought it was the police and hesitated; in those days you could expect a visit from the police or, even worse, the Army at any time. My friend knew the climate of the times. He put his mouth to the keyhole and shouted his name. He did not visit me often, it had to be something serious. It was. Once inside, he told me in a few words; the woman with him was the wife of a doctor friend of his called Alvariza. Alvariza had been arrested during the day, in the midst of the total rage the Army felt (or expressed) at the death of Colonel Artigas Alvarez, who had been murdered that same morning. Alvariza was a doctor, taken prisoner at the university—the kind of prisoner the Army hated most. They interrogated him, forced him to walk hooded along the top section of the military stadium, then pushed him down thirty or forty feet. He was dead. All my two visitors wanted was to retrieve his body. They gave me the name of the military judge responsible for the case.

She had brought the dawn and the wind into the room with her. Her pallor and the traces of tension in her face

259

told me it was all true. I offered her a glass of whisky. She said yes with perfect naturalness; my more conventional friend (I cannot believe he did not need it) said no. The three of us stood facing one another. I brought the glasses and the bottle; we sat down.

Alvariza was dead and there was no point feeling sorry for him. But for her yes; so pale, so deserving, so dignified, with a glass of whisky in her hand. You had to pity her. She was one of the victims Uruguay produced in those days. They took her husband away in the morning and hours later, at dawn, she had to try to get his body back. An inhospitable dawn, I repeat, and there she was, battered by the sound of the sea in our silent pauses, taking small, very small, sips from her whisky, far from the body of the man she had loved. But without his body she had clearly not yet been able to mourn. She wanted to see him, be near him, before she felt she had the right to cry.

I thought that his death had not made a particular impression on me, in that world of ghastly absurdities we lived in then. But I was wrong. I realized it later when the image of that hooded man pushed from the top of the military stadium began to flash onto my retina night after night, as if engraved on it. I thought I recognized the asphalt path or the edge of a flagstone or a corner of grass which from that height had caused his death. In a sort of surreal double-exposure I also saw a woman drinking a glass of whisky in the early hours of the morning, in the house of a stranger, only because the stranger was a lawyer and another lawyer had brought her to see him, with the assumption that law school and legal codes teach you to claim the bodies of people murdered for no reason. On

260

any other day of the year, Alvariza would simply have been beaten, injured, not murdered. The coincidence of a colonel having died the morning of the same day, cost him his life. And that was the reason for this scene in which no one hurried to the phone because for picking up the phone and speaking to the judge and asking him for the body, for that, but not for dying, it was an inconvenient hour, and they had to observe the niceties of etiquette and wait.

My friend lives in exile now, as I do. But we have never devoted a single minute of the apparent joy with which we meet now and again to remembering that early morning, that night with the clamour of the waves at two hundred yards from the sea, that woman, that drink. If we did, that man (for him a friend, for me a stranger) might start falling again in the imagination of our retinas. And obviously we don't want that to happen; the animal of sensations and memory in each of us shrinks from it.

About the same time, I was also a friend of the father of a young man (we learned all this with time) who had helped murder Colonel Alvarez, riddling him with bullets as he drove away from his house in Otelo Street. The father was an old colleague of mine, practically forgotten when I came across him again (the kind of person who for years we don't know whether they are dead or alive). He painted a picture of his son as a totally self-absorbed young man, sad and silent, whom he would see playing the guitar and often found crying (but did not dare ask anything) in the days between the murder and the discovery of who did it. Gradually over the years, my friend's son's sadness, and the desperation with which he told me, through his

261

father, that at all costs I must prevent a girlfriend of his obtaining a certificate of concubinage from the Army and with it the right to visit him (it seemed to be the only thing he was terrified of, the only thing he begged of anyone taking on his defence)—all this began to obscure the image of Alvariza falling hooded from the top of the stadium and his wife battling like Antigone for his body. And when my friend, the subversive's father, totally eaten away by grief, died of a heart attack at fifty, I realized that there was a strange balance to the whole story. One day I met my friend the journalist's widow (I forgot to say that's what he was, a journalist), and because her husband had talked about me so much while her son was in prison, she assumed I could vouch for his former professional activities and would be an ideal witness in her battle with the Pension Fund (my friend had never paid his contributions). This is a truly Uruguayan story, I thought. A melancholy story of Uruguay today, I should add. It began with two intertwined murders (even near each other in the telephone directory, Alvarez/Alvariza) and ended with a typically Latin American favour for a problem with an unpaid pension.

Perhaps that is why I buried the tale so deep inside me. There are bits of it which don't concern my friend in exile, nor would he be interested. And who else could I tell it to?

CECILIA. Cecilia, trying to imagine your death differently is absurd. Would it have happened later some other way, or would you still be alive now? No one can tell. And the stupidity of even discussing it (with dates, details of other countries, journeys) absolves your father. And your father should never be absolved, not even if we assume he was not strictly to blame. Parents' attitudes have to be judged in terms other than guilt or innocence.

Your father, Cecilia, was a man of order. He was a soldier in his youth but deserted (I don't know in what discreet way exactly). He married the woman who was to be your mother, then abandoned her for some romantic liaison or other. This all happened when you were a child, it wasn't particularly painful for you because he left home before you began to feel any affection for him.

This man, with an interrupted career and a broken marriage, was nonetheless a man of order. Under the military, he had been made a headmaster. He had some high-ranking cousins in the Army and had used their influence to persuade the parents of some of his pupils and local businessmen to put up the money for a physical training complex in the school's grounds. He imagined the System would be grateful. 'There are no strikes in my school,' he said, 'and I'll hand the decrepit place I took over back to you vastly improved.'

That was how things stood when you became active in one of the Tupamaro support cells at school, and were arrested with four other kids. You were not living with him and he was quick to point that out. You had *never* lived with him, *always* with your mother. You were not actually his responsibility, but he was going to deal with it anyway.

From the start he said he knew what had to be done for you. Talk to his Army pals, remind them courteously of the favours he had done for them, and ask for, suggest, you be released in return. It was still the period of civilian

263

judges, however, so his influence was less effective.

He offered himself as moral sponsor when you came out of prison; he was an educator after all... When your release and that of the four other *compañeros* was authorized, speedy decisions about your safety had to be taken. The other parents agreed to let their children go into exile, finance the journeys, pay the fines, do everything in their power to prevent their being arrested again. Not *your* father. He had clearer ideas (don't forget he was a headmaster) about what was best for an adolescent. Go abroad, get mixed up in a mess like Chile in 1972, not on your life! He arranged for you to go and live with his mother in Soriano. The wise tutelage of an old woman in the placid environment of a small country town would sort everything out, and bring you naturally back into line. He knew. Pity that the Army did not understand that too. While your *compañeros* went off abroad, you stayed in Carlos Nery prison, seeing and hearing the injustices that made you more and more radical. You spent several months in Carlos Nery with older, more hardened, and more politicized prisoners. They adopted you as their mascot, looked after you, and passed on to you their dreams.

When one day the jailer finally opened the door to your freedom, you saw the street as a mere stepping stone to going underground. There is no sense in debating whether or not you cared for your mother, or if the strength of your decision was greater than your love for her.

Did he pursue you again with his ideas of order, to drum his own ideals (as an ex-soldier, ex-father, educator) into you if he could? I don't know, I don't think you had the chance, and certainly not the interest, to find out either. Maybe your militancy became the affirmation of your life against his, your ideals against his, you against him. You lost.

I don't know if he really tried and you probably never knew. It was not *for* him or *against* him that you dyed your hair blond, above features too young to cope with the change. It was for your graduation to clandestinity, to become a guerrilla.

As for the rest, Cecilia, I only know what they say: that they saw you on a corner, ordered you to stop, you put your hand in a bag, they thought you were going to shoot and pre-empted you. The bag was full of guns, they said, but the guns were not loaded. Why would you put your hand in, why give them a pretext to shoot? Where would you have got that arsenal of Army pistols from anyway?

Afterwards, people told me they had seen you lying as if you were asleep at your mother's house; she was crying, but your father, at least at the time they were talking about, was not there.

It is possible to feel nostalgia. It is. Not only for the country, but mainly because of the people. People to talk to, a son who (anyway) is not there. The house is abandoned now, the stream which ran past the door is muddy and overgrown, the mice on the bank devoured and drowned. The stream had a poetic name, the Old Mill Stream. But the people who lived in those rooms have 'disappeared' or are scattered round the world, perhaps never to be reunited. We sometimes find it comforting to refer to a place (especially if the street bears the name of a King of Troy), to the memory of some trees, the outline of a shadow, or the dampness of bare feet on the lawn. But, if we really think about it, all that is anecdotal, unreliable, false. Where is your house now, where is your country?

Latin American Titles from Readers International

Sergio Ramírez

TO BURY OUR FATHERS   £5.95/US$8.95 paperback

A panoramic novel of Nicaragua in the Somoza era, dramatically recreated by the country's leading prose artist—now also its Vice President. Cabaret singers, exiles, National Guardsmen, guerrillas, itinerant traders, beauty queens, prostitutes and would-be presidents are the characters who people this sophisticated, lyrical and timeless epic of resistance and retribution.
"Very funny, very human, a must for any student of Latin America." *Punch*
"Read slowly and carefully in order to appreciate and absorb all its nuances ...Dr Ramírez is as important as the substantial literary merits of his book." *New York Times Book Review*
"The only contemporary Nicaraguan novel available in English." *Library Journal*

STORIES   £3.95/US$7.95 paperback

In these sardonic and moving tales, Sergio Ramírez explores the comic yet painful condition of Latin America, locked into the pursuit of a cruelly elusive and banal "yanqui" culture. In "Charles Atlas Also Dies" a young Nicaraguan becomes a devoted follower of the American bodybuilder, only to discover that age and infirmity have consumed his cult hero. In "To Jackie with All Our Heart" the pretensions of Managua's tiny country club set lead them into a monstrous hoax. In "Saint Nikolaus" a failed Venezuelan student, scratching a living in Berlin, hires himself out as Santa Claus to a rich West German family—only to find himself the target of tensions and jealousies beyond his control.
"Biting and satirical." *The New York Times*
"Masterfully told ... should reach readers' hearts."
Publishers Weekly
"The freshness, force and sheer bite of *Stories* is a complete delight." *Punch*

"Exquisite ... hilarious." *The Guardian*

Antonio Skármeta

I DREAMT THE SNOW WAS BURNING
£4.95/US$7.95 paperback   £8.95/US$14.95 hardback

The lodgers at a seedy Santiago boarding house mirror all the warmth and doomed enthusiasm of the last days of Allende, before the fall of democratic Chile brought tanks into the streets, enthroned the generals and turned the national football stadium into a torture centre. The growing political tension fuses with the dreams and evasions of a fleabitten entertainer, the drive of a cynical young country boy to win at football and lose his virginity, and the humbler lives and loves of the other boarders.

"Compelling and entertaining...the most ambitious and accomplished piece of literature to come out of Chile since Pinochet took power." Ariel Dorfman, *Village Voice*

"Imaginative, energetic, and possessed of its own odd charm."
New York Times

"It's easy to see why Latin American and European critics regard this as a Latin American classic of 'committed literature'." *San Francisco Chronicle*

Antônio Torres

THE LAND
£3.95/US$7.95 paperback   £8.95/US$14.95 hardback

In this modern Brazilian classic, Torres brings alive the primitive, lyrical world of Brazil's rural *Sertão* (the Backlands of the Northeast). The death of Nelo, a favourite son whom everyone believed had made good in São Paulo, is reflected in the thoughts, dreams and fantasies of his family and neighbours—an interior voyage that takes us to the heart of Brazil's conflict between rural and urban values.

"A sad, simple, lyrical novel...uplifted by Torres' melodic prose and intimate knowledge of rural Brazil." *Kirkus Reviews*

"Full of the unanswered questions of a third-world country in transition." *Publishers Weekly*

"I very much admire the warmth, the irony, the style of *The Land* which so brilliantly describes the lives of poor people in a village whose life is leaving it." Doris Lessing

Latin American Titles from Readers International

Marta Traba

MOTHERS AND SHADOWS
£3.95/US$7.95 paperback   £8.95/US$14.95 hardback

An encounter between two women evokes a decade of tragedy and terror in Latin America's Southern Cone. Irene, a middle-aged actress accustomed to the role of seductress, fears for her son in Chile's newly installed military repression. Dolores has lost her lover and their unborn child to the torturers. Thrown together in a dispirited and cowering Montevideo, the women lead us on, with an unerring sense of place. Out of the horror comes warmth, attachment and the strength to refuse all lies. Now a BBC radio play.

"A well-paced and tense story, building up to the final climactic moment. The translation is superb." *Choice*

"Impressive and very readable, exciting, and Jo Labanyi's fluent translation makes it all imaginable." *Financial Times*

Osvaldo Soriano

A FUNNY DIRTY LITTLE WAR
£3.95/US$6.95 paperback   £7.95/US$12.50 hardback

"*A Funny Dirty Little War* is an absolute of its kind: the attempt of one petty official to oust another farcically, inexorably, horribly sweeps a small Argentine town into a local holocaust of violence and murder...it is as if the amiable village world of Don Camillo were blackened by the laconic ugliness of Hemingway's war writing." John Updike, *The New Yorker*

"The black humour, dizzying action, crisp, sparkling dialogue, the rapid unemotional style...make this novel gripping reading."
Italo Calvino

"A gripping fable of power and revolution...its message is universal." *ALA Booklist*

"Masterful juxtaposition of farce and tragedy...a worthy addition to collections of modern Latin American fiction."
Library Journal

Caribbean Title from Readers International

Pierre Clitandre

CATHEDRAL OF THE AUGUST HEAT
£4.95/US$8.95 paperback   £8.95/US$16.95 hardback

On 15 August 1791, the Day of the Assumption of the Virgin, a great uprising commenced which was to make Haiti the world's first independent black republic and the first society to abolish slavery after the French Revolution. This key date lies behind Pierre Clitandre's sweeping story of contemporary Haiti. Through the eyes of the poorest people of the Americas— the higglers,the washerwomen, the tap-tap drivers of the shantytowns crowding around Port-au-Prince—we experience the dynamic current of history that has brought Haiti once again to rebellion.

"Exciting...makes this story part of our shared experience."
                                    Edward Kamau Braithwaite
"Encapsulates what the 'Third World' is all about."
                                                    The Guardian
"A marvelous apotheosis."   *World Literature Today*

READ THE WORLD—Books from Readers International

Nicaragua	**To Bury Our Fathers**	Sergio Ramírez	£5.95/US$8.95
Nicaragua	**Stories**	Sergio Ramírez	£3.95/US$7.95
Chile	**I Dreamt the Snow Was Burning**	Antonio Skármeta	£4.95/US$7.95
Brazil	**The Land**	Antônio Torres	£3.95/US$7.95
Argentina	**Mothers and Shadows**	Marta Traba	£3.95/US$7.95
Argentina	**A Funny Dirty Little War**	Osvaldo Soriano	£3.95/US$6.95
Uruguay	**El Infierno**	C. Martínez Moreno	£4.95/US$8.95
Haiti	**Cathedral of the August Heat**	Pierre Clitandre	£4.95/US$8.95
Congo	**The Laughing Cry**	Henri Lopes	£4.95/US$8.95
Angola	**The World of 'Mestre' Tamoda**	Uanhenga Xitu	£4.95/US$8.95
S. Africa	**Fools and Other Stories**	Njabulo Ndebele	USA only $8.95
S. Africa	**Renewal Time**	Es'kia Mphahlele	£4.95/US$8.95
S. Africa	**Hajji Musa and the Hindu Fire-Walker**	Ahmed Essop	£4.95/US$8.95
Iran	**The Ayatollah and I**	Hadi Khorsandi	£3.95/US$7.95
Philippines	**Awaiting Trespass**	Linda Ty-Casper	£3.95/US$7.95
Philippines	**Wings of Stone**	Linda Ty-Casper	£4.95/US$8.95
Japan	**Fire from the Ashes**	ed. Kenzaburō Ōe	£3.50 UK only
China	**The Gourmet**	Lu Wenfu	£4.95/US$8.95
India	**The World Elsewhere**	Nirmal Verma	hbk only £9.95/US$16.95
Poland	**Poland Under Black Light**	Janusz Anderman	£3.95/US$6.95
Poland	**The Edge of the World**	Janusz Anderman	£3.95/US$7.95
Czech.	**My Merry Mornings**	Ivan Klíma	£4.95/US$7.95
Czech.	**A Cup of Coffee with My Interrogator**	Ludvík Vaculík	£3.95/US$7.95
E. Germany	**Flight of Ashes**	Monika Maron	£4.95/US$8.95
E. Germany	**The Defector**	Monika Maron	£4.95/US$8.95
USSR	**The Queue**	Vladimir Sorokin	£4.95/US$8.95

Order through your local bookshop, or direct from the publisher. Most titles also available in hardcover. *How to order:* Send your name, address, order and payment to

RI, 8 Strathray Gardens, London NW3 4NY, UK

or **RI**, P.O. Box 959, Columbia, LA 71418, USA

Please enclose payment to the value of the cover price plus 10% of the total amount for postage and packing. (Canadians add 20% to US prices.)